Linking Verbs

Be a & Wee.

Linking Verbs

*In the lilt of Irish laughter
you can hear the angels
sing.*

John J. O'Boyle

John a Nowong

Writer's Showcase presented by *Writer's Digest*
San Jose New York Lincoln Shanghai

Linking Verbs

Published by Writer's Showcase presented by *Writer's Digest*
an imprint of iUniverse.com, Inc.

For information address:
iUniverse.com, Inc.
620 North 48th Street
Suite 201
Lincoln, NE 68504-3467
www.iuniverse.com

ISBN: 0-595-00170-X

Printed in the United States of America

To my Mother and Father
To Nancy for all the years
To John, Jim, Cathy, and Karen

Prologue

Sheila's Story

Frog looked like St. Christopher as he guided the pontoon boat along the Waccamaw River in the Lowcountry of South Carolina. It had taken a bit more than an hour to find the agency's boat in a hidden tidal creek.

In the setting September sun the golden fields of reeds lifted their flat tops to the Carolina blue. The soft current speckled amongst the trunks of lonesome tupelo and cypress trees.

Joanie and Sumter were alone in their thoughts in the front of the boat.

Peggy and Mary, and Bridie and I leaned back on the railings near Frog.

"All the ghosts will be gone tomorrow," he started, speaking almost as softly as the current.

"Jesus", shot back Bridie!"We are up to our panty girdles in the CIA, and the Italians, and the FBI, Frog. Not ghosts!

We have all our trust in you and Sumter!

Who are you anyway, Frog?"

He never took his eye from the river. A few speckles of gray weaved above his brow. His hardened hands hardly touched the wheel.

"Sumter's home boy", he started, "just as you guys have always been Miss Joanie's gumbahs."

The four of us would hardly have made two of him, but it wasn't his size that we trusted.

He was from a different world than ours. We had never placed this much faith in even our own kin.

"Look at Miss Joanie and Sumter", he continued, never lifting his eye from the river. "I've known you two weeks in twenty years, but I know what you all mean to her.

Sumter tells me that she was a sister for a long time. That must have been tough for her when she came back to the world. But you were her cushion, her friends, like the golden reeds welcome and shelter the birds in the evening."

"It wasn't anything," said Peggy. "We were always there with Joanie, her paisans, even when she was in the convent."

"I know, Peggy. But it's different when somebody leaves a home that has been her life for a long time. Miss Joanie was lucky to have all of you.

Sumter, he wasn't so lucky. He only got me.

He had his daddy, and the fields, and me."

He spoke slowly, a soft voice for a big man.

"You girls remember the Sumter of twenty years ago. One of you asked him why he had to go back to Nam."

"It was me," I said. "And he said he heard voices, he was being called."

"And Miss Joanie was called," continued Frog. "I was there when Sumter came home from his second tour. I asked him the same question. He had a box full of medals that he put in my bottom drawer. He said he was going back.

I told him to stay. He gave me the same answer. He still heard the voices. I told him he was crazy. He just looked at me.

I was still his home boy. All I could do was squeeze his shoulder. And then he came home in '72. Took up the land with his daddy. You all know the story.

We are as close as brothers ever could be. But he still has his ghosts. Miss Joanie has her ghosts.

Tomorrow we are going to bury them all. That's what this is all about."

I looked at Joanie and Sumter, shadows in the setting sun. And I looked at Frog who was carrying us across the river.

Chapter 1

Appear

I always had feelings. My father said that an Italian girl without feelings was like a bird without feathers and I was his little sparrow.

That's the way I grew up.

I was afraid when we moved from Murray Hill to East Cleveland when I was about seven. The Hill was an old Italian neighborhood. All my friends went to Holy Rosary School.

We lived on the third floor above my two uncles. There was a house full of aunts and cousins.

I was never lonely. I was afraid of lonesomeness. I needed to belong.

"A bigger house, more room, your own bedroom," said Frankie. Everybody called him Frankie.

"I like it here."

"You'll like it there," he answered with a soft squeeze of my shoulder. "You will make new friends, Joanie sweetheart. I'm telling you.

I came from Italy when I was barely sixteen. A long way across the ocean. Now everybody knows Frankie Cipolla.

I couldn't drive a car. Now I sing La Traviotta from the window of my cement truck. And people yell 'pipe down.'

My little chickadee will do all right."

But the feeling of being alone, being scared, didn't leave me. I was scared.

Johnny Flaherty came home from delivering his mail route at about a quarter to four each afternoon.

He'd come whistling up the street, a pipe between his teeth, talking softly to himself.

"Mother will have the dinner on the table." He always called my mother 'mother.' He had the kindest of voices.

It was 'your mother' when he spoke to me and my brothers. It was 'mother' when he spoke to her. It was 'Missus Flaherty' when he spoke about her to anyone else.

He caught me reading on the porch.

"Sheila, I've noticed a little girl about your age. She must have moved into Scullin's old house. She's been riding a scooter by herself whenever I see her.

Why don't you and your friend Bridie get to know her?"

"Bridie's brother says she's an Italian, daddy."

I didn't know what an Italian was, but the way Bridie's brother said it, it seemed like the big bad wolf in Red Riding Hood or a goblin or something.

"And there's loud music coming from her house that we hear when we go by after supper, in words nobody knows what they're singing. And Bridie's brother saw her father cutting the grass with his shoes off, no stockings or nothing, singing in the same words."

"Puccini, opera, Italian folk songs, Sheila. That's what the music is. Just like your mother plays Take me Home Again Kathleen on the victrola. Music is what separates the poet from the peasant.

After your mother has the supper done, why don't you and Bridie go down and get to know her.

Everybody is different, Sheila. We all come from different places. But everyone needs someone once in awhile. We are all linked together.

Its part of the ballgame.

I had a lady in an apartment on my mail route once. She was from France. Her husband was a soldier in the war. She always used to give me a dollar for Christmas.

One year she had not received a letter from him in about two months. She would meet me in the lobby looking for a letter.

When Christmas came, I didn't ring her bell, for there was no letter. And she caught me going down the steps, and said, 'come up, Mr. Flaherty, it wouldn't be Christmas if I couldn't spend a few moments with you.'

And I said, 'sweetheart put a flower in your hair, pour us each a glass of anisette, and we'll put our faith in the letter that's on its way.'

Less than a week later, she got the letter that she was waiting for. Her husband was fine.

That's Puccini, and opera, and romance by candlelight, Sheila. Its what makes the world go around. Its part of the ballgame."

Within a week I wasn't lonely anymore. I belonged. I had two new friends, Bridie and Sheila.

Mister Flaherty even taught us to play chess.

He had an old cigar box, with the top swinging off with big wooden pieces painted black and white. He'd set them up on a checker board on the porch and show us the moves for each knight and pawn.

When he was at work we'd sometimes play with the pieces scattering them all over. Frankie said Mr. Flaherty was a character. I didn't know what he meant.

On Friday nights he would serve us tea on the porch. We could hear the steam whistling in the kitchen.

Sheila's and Bridie's mothers would be off to say a novena at the church, swinging their purses as chipper as birds. Then they would go visiting.

"They're off to the gold coast," Mr. Flaherty would say.

He would get the finest cups and saucers from the very top shelf.

"Now, not a word to Missus Flaherty, any of you. She would give me the switch if she knew we were using these cups."

After tea, he would wash the dishes in the sink. He would let me dry them. Sheila never did the drying. And the cups and the saucers were put back on the shelf like they had never left their places.

We would sit on the porch and tell stories, looking at the moon and the stars through the boughs of the trees. Sheila had a story for every star.

Mister Flaherty said if she had been born a thousand years before she would have been a bard or a soothsayer.

I wasn't real good at stories.

Mister Flaherty would puff on the pipe between his lips, smiling.

"There's a star out there for you, little Joanie. Someday you'll tell us the story."

"Memorize them," said Sister Alphonse, our seventh grade teacher. "They are the linking verbs; appear, become, continue, remain, feel, seem, smell, sound, and taste.

Once you commit them to memory, you will never forget them. I have boys and girls whom I had in school thirty years ago that can still recite them. They come up to me and can still remember them.

Now, let's all recite them together, 'appear, become, continue, remain…'"

We girls recited them on the way home for lunch, on the way back to school after lunch, and on the walk to school the next morning. In two days there wasn't a girl in our room that couldn't recite the nine magical words. Only two boys out of twenty were our equals.

"Sister must have been lying," said Bridie Quinn. "No boys can remember anything for thirty years."

"Not the ones in our class," I answered. "But there are some smart ones. Look at the priests. They were boys. And the doctors. They write in Latin. We girls can't do that."

"Maybe boys get smarter later", quipped Bridie. "With what I can see of them, I don't see how."

There were five of us who walked to and from St. Philomena together; Bridie and me, Mary O'Brien, Peggy Masterson, and Sheila Flaherty. None of us thought that any boy could remember anything for thirty years, or for thirty seconds for that matter.

"Sister Alphonse must have been lying," said Mary.

"You ask her if she was fibbing," I answered.

"Sure," they all said.

"Who cares," laughed Sheila," my brothers can't even remember the people on their paper routes."

"They're not the linking verbs," answered Peggy. "People only remember important things."

"Sure."

"The Monsignor can't remember the Latin at the Mass," Said Bridie. "He races through in twenty minutes and skips half the prayers."

"That's because he doesn't have to look at the missal," Sheila answered.

"No, Sheila," quipped Mary. "It's because he races through to drink the wine. Don't you see his red face?"

"Let's check that out with Sister Alphonse," said Bridie.

"Sure."

"Have any of you ever been to the priest house," I asked?

"No," they all answered.

"Well, my father has. They don't answer the door. A housekeeper does that. Then she asks if you have an appointment. Frankie said 'no.' then, the housekeeper said they were all busy."

"All four of them," asked Peggy?

"She said they were saying their office."

"What's an office," asked Sheila?

"A room with a desk," shot back Bridie.

"No, you dweeb," I continued. "It's prayers the priests have to say every day, in the morning and after supper."

"What did your father want anyway," asked Peggy?

"He wanted to have a scapular blessed that grandma had sent from Italy."

"So, what did he do," asked Sheila?

"He said 'el fungula' and pinned it on his underwear."

"What's that mean," they all asked?

"It's something he learned in Italy and never forgot."

"Like the linking verbs," said Mary.

We were always talking, the five of us. Oh, we had families, mothers and fathers, sisters and brothers. Who didn't in East Cleveland? They talked at us, asked us about things, tried to lift the lids off our inner minds. We didn't need to chisel at each other.

We were linked to each other, penny loafers and poodle skirts. Was Johnny Ray really crying in the chapel? Had Elvis really lost his blue suede shoes? Could Pat Boone really sing about April love while he was wearing those crazy white buck shoes?

We harmonized with the little doggy in the window.

All of our houses had big front porches. Every house in East Cleveland had a big front porch. There were slatted wooden swings that could sit three, four in a squeeze. There were spindled railings that we could sit on, while twisting our penny loafers through the slats.

After school or after supper we'd gather on somebody's porch. It was like a rule that wasn't written down. We just gathered.

We never met at Peggy Masterson's after supper. Her father was some kind of religious fanatic. If he caught someone straddling the rail or dreaming on the swing at a quarter past seven, he would make her come in and say the family rosary over the radio with Father Payton.

Peggy said he once dragged in the newspaper boy who was collecting on a Friday night. The kid was a Protestant who went to public school. He didn't even know how to kneel down.

His father came knocking on the side door early Saturday morning. Mrs. Masterson explained that it was only a friendly mistake. When she told Peggy's father about the man's complaint, all he could say was, "Jesus, it couldn't hurt the bloke, not one bit."

We played a lot of games, jacks on the porch, hopscotch on the driveway, roller skating on the slate walks. Our brothers and their friends would be off playing kick the can or football in the street, causing all kinds of ruckus. There was always a man or a woman yelling, "get off my lawn," or sometimes a lot worse. Once in awhile a police car would come down the street and chase the boys.

We girls could only smile. We were assured we were made of sugar and spice and everything nice. We had no reason to question the jingle.

We were cooling in May's shivering breeze, on Mary's front porch, when the first faint wisp of trouble blew through the trees.

"I think Sister Alphonse was exaggerating when she said people would remember the linking verbs," said Peggy.

"What," we asked?

"Who cares," whiffed Bridie?

"I care," answered Peggy. "We should all care. Next year we are going to be eighth graders. Then we go to Sacred Heart. Don't you want to know if we will remember what we should remember?"

"I can't remember how to multiply or divide fractions and we've been doing that for two years," hyped in Mary.

"Was John a Baptist or the beloved," asked Sheila?

"What does adultery mean," I asked?

"Or covet," chipped in Bridie?

"What's a prepositional phrase," asked Peggy?

"What's a phrase," asked Sheila?

It was like a game of can you top this, so much memorized, so much forgotten.

"Maybe we should try the priest house," said Mary. She always came up with ideas that were yesterday's news.

"Sure," I answered. "We'd look like twerps."

"Teresa Mulvanity goes to Sacred Heart," piped in Peggy. "She's a sophomore. We could ask her."

"She'd tell everybody at school," smarted Sheila. "We'd really look like dweebs. She was always carrying the sisters' books to the convent. She never heard the secret she wouldn't spill."

"We'll go where nobody knows us," said Bridie. She was a whiz with ideas. "How about the Lakeside Tavern next Saturday afternoon? My mother says there are more Catholics in that saloon than at the afternoon confessions."

"Like when we sold raffle tickets," I said. "I always sold more tickets there than anywhere else. They always said, 'sure, St. Phils I used to go there.' I even sold two subscriptions to the Catholic Universe, and you know you can hardly sell them to your aunts and uncles."

"What if somebody sees us," asked Peggy?

"Everybody there is anonymous," answered Bridie. "My mother said Mr. O'Roarke used to go to the Lakeside every single day and now he's in some anonymous club."

It was raining Saturday afternoon as we gathered on Joanie's porch. It was one of those cold April drizzles that always come in May.

"Let's skip it," I said.

"Just walking in the rain," sang Bridie.

"Volare," chided Joanie. "Let's do it. Who wants to just sit on the porch?"

Joanie was a leader. Maybe it was because she was Italian. She was sure of herself. She could speak two languages, ours and Italian to her mother and father.

He smoked big black cigars and grew beautiful peppers and tomatoes in their backyard. Her mother made sauce from the tomatoes that filled their table with spaghetti for the rest of the year.

The rest of us were all Irish. Our fathers could hardly grow grass in the yard. Our mothers bought their vegetables at the grocery. We got our spaghetti from Chef Boyardee cans.

Sometimes we thought that Joanie was so independent because her parents didn't know what was going on with America, the funny language and flowers on the table and everything. Her father and mother used to hug and kiss her and her brother right in front of other people. Most of us got the leery eye or the wag of the tongue.

Joanie led the way into the Lakeside. It was like walking into Ala Baba's tomb. There were lights and smoke and mirrors and glass. There was polished wood and the beat of the jukebox. There were clanging pinballs and hanging chains of gold. There seemed a thousand eyes peering at us.

"What do you want," scowled a burly man in a stained wrinkled apron?

"We want to talk to someone who went to St. Phils," Joanie charged. She was the only one who hadn't lost her tongue. It seemed a thousand ears stretched forward to catch her voice above the din.

"Benny," called the aproned man.

Then voices came out of everywhere, glancing between the smoke and the bangles.

"Monsignor Maloney."

"He knows the church, but he never goes."

"Recite the Suscipiat."

"St. Phils grandest graduate."

"Corporal Maloney."

He appeared out of the mist, dancing off a turning stool beside the mahogany. He was fair, like our own. His eyes twinkled. He looked at us and winked. He turned again and placed his handled mug on the bar.

With a wave of his hand he guided us to a booth away from the voices. It was but a few paces, but we could see the kindness of his eyes.

"Did you go to St. Phils," asked Bridie bravely?

"I did."

"How long ago," intoned Peggy?

"Is this an inquisition? Are you from the police?"

"No, we go to St. Phils," answered Joanie. "All we want to know is what you remember."

"Do you want some pogey bait?"

"What's that," squirted back Mary?

"Candy, chips, a coke," he smiled back.

Magically, with a wave of his hand, five cokes and a few bags of chips appeared on the table.

"Do you know the linking verbs," I asked?

"You must have Sister Alphonse, the seventh grade. Sure, I know the linking verbs. How about the various forms of is; is, am, be, are, was, were, been? Did you get that far?"

"Are you sure you remember," quizzed Bridie?

"Why would I lie? You are the ones who don't trust the nuns. Hey, do you know anything about horses? Take a look at his list."

"Tommy Lee, he's a boy in our room," we all answered.

He wrote Tommy Lee on a small slip of paper, put a few dollars in it, and slid it easily to a man at the bar.

Just then the door flew open and Barney Rooney raced in. He was almost at every Mass, passed the collection basket, sold tickets at every bazaar. He seemed startled when he saw us, but went directly to the man Benny had passed the slip to.

"A ten spot from Father Donnello." We could all hear his voice.

"On who," asked the man?

"Sword Dancer...no, who's the hot choice?"

"Tomy Lee," answered the man with a spread of his hands. "Tell Father its Tomy Lee."

"Father can have Tomy Lee," smirked Barney. "I'll take the chalk, Sword Dancer. Shoemaker can't lose on that horse. I'll go for a fiver myself."

It was still raining when we left the tavern. It seemed an afternoon we'd always remember.

Joanie yelled, "see you later, alligator," as we slid out the door.

Benny opened it as we walked away. "After awhile, crocodile."

The weekend went swiftly, as weekends were want to go. We knew we were in trouble when we walked into the classroom on Monday morning. Sister Alphonse always started the day by writing J.M.J. in the upper left-hand corner of her sparkling clean blackboard.

Someone had printed all across the board:

WHO WON THE KENTUCKY DERBY

TOMY LEE

I could see Sister was flustered when she entered the room. When she saw the board, she walked to the right hand corner and wrote J.M.J. I could see the smirks on the faces of the boys around me, but didn't have the courage to look up at my friends.

The morning was like drivel, all out of sorts. Sister Alphonse was normally the most organized of nuns, from the first J.M.J. to the last ringing of the bell.

This day Sister left the printing on the blackboard. She was in and out of the room like a hare. It was;"study your spelling, read ahead in your history book, and go over your fractions."

Near the end of the morning, Sister Immaculata, the principal, came into the room. She only came to classrooms on special occasions. She glanced harshly all over the room, and then turned and looked at the blackboard.

Sister Immaculata always held court in her office during the lunch break. This day was special. Sister Alphonse was surprised to see Monsignor O'Donnell sitting in the corner when she entered the room.

"Good afternoon, Sister," he said as he rose.

"It's been quite a morning, Monsignor," she answered.

"What's the problem?"

"Five of my girls, five of the best, no one would have thought,…Jesus, Mary, and Joseph. ., were seen in an occasion of sin."

"A what?"

"The Lakeside Tavern down on Hayden Avenue. They were seen with one of the Maloney boys, Benjamin, I heard. I had the whole family a dozen or fifteen years ago. I can hardly remember this morning."

"Easy, Sister," he answered as he reached out and steadied her shoulder. The Monsignor always spoke easily and slowly, like water trickling down a brook.

"You know, sister," he was speaking to Sister Alphonse as if they were the only ones in the room, "for a long time I have served on the diocesan tribunal that makes rulings on decrees of divorce. It wasn't my choice. The Bishop asked me."

Sister Immaculata sat silently at her desk. They said in the convent that she always played her cards close to the habit.

"Once a woman from St. Timothy's, I dare not tell her name, came before the tribunal petitioning for the sanction for divorce. She said her husband was a bus driver on the Miles Avenue line. He parked his car at the end of the line, an isolated area, where he would take over the driving.

Well, the woman had been finding cigarette butts in his ashtray, colored by lipstick. I checked with the man, a stable man of sorts. He told me that sometimes there were women on his line, who seemed overcome by one problem or another. He would let them sit in his car, a bit of privacy, and sometimes he would console or counsel them. It was a plausible story.

His wife would not believe it. I asked her how many cigarettes she had found. She answered fifteen or twenty over a period of years. So I asked her if they were all the same shade of red. Could some of them have been scarlet or rose? Could some have been cherry or magenta? Could a few have even been pink?

She had no answer. The woman never did divorce her husband. I did talk to him. I told him to leave the counseling to others. It all worked out for the best.

What I am saying, Sister, is that not everything is as it appears to be."

"So the girls may have had a reason to be in the tavern," answered the nun?

"They may," he answered slowly. "Maybe it was not the best of reasons. But there is safety in numbers. They went as a group. They come to school as a group."

"Then I will punish them as a group."

"In your own kind manner, Sister. I am sure you will find a way....By the way, do you have a boy named Tommy Lee in your class?"

"Yes, Monsignor. He is a quiet boy...He never says a word. Nobody would know he was there."

"Do you understand it," Sister Alphonse asked Sister Immaculata after the Monsignor had left? "I've heard the story six different ways. I can't understand it for the wonder of me. Who is Father Donnello with the ten spot?"

"I'll tell you a secret," said the older nun. "You must promise you won't tell a soul. When the Monsignor was a young priest he was assigned to Our Lady of the Faith. It was an Italian parish. All of its priests had been of Italian ancestry. He was resented.

So he stood in the pulpit one Sunday morning, I was there myself. He told the old crones that if he put the O at the end of his name, it would be Donnello instead of O'Donnell.

He was young. He had a way about him. They gathered him in as if he were one of their own."

The boys at St. Phils had always done the steel wooling of the floors. It was a form of punishment. The girls had done the dusting, the cleaning of the blackboards, the carrying of sisters' books. It was a form of becoming more ladylike.

It seemed that whenever the classroom floors needed to be steel wooled, there was always a boy or two or three in trouble. They were usually the same ones. Steel wool took the scuffs off the floor, mostly from feet shifting under our desks. It added a gloss and a shine that was part of Catholicism.

The church had only old Mister Finneran for a custodian. He lived in a house on the corner of the schoolyard. He was forever shoveling snow in the winter or sweeping the walks. He was cutting the lawn in front of the church or directing traffic for a funeral.

He had no time for the classroom floors. There was always a boy in trouble, or a group of boys, to put the glisten on the oak.

We were surprised when Sister Alphonse called the five of us to her desk on the last day of school.

"Girls, I have a project for you the first few days of vacation."

"What's that, Sister," asked Bridie?

"You are going to work in the classrooms. It should only take three or four days. It will help get the rooms ready for next year. It will also help you reflect on your adventure of last month."

Sister had never spoken to us about that Saturday afternoon. We knew she had known. It was all over the school. It had even been spun off on the Mayo news.

The Mayo news was named after a county in Ireland where most of our parents or grandparents had come from. It traveled by phone, or on the sidewalks, or on buses to work. It told of relatives still in the old country that we'd never known. It told of births and deaths on both sides of the ocean. It told of happiness and it told of misfortune.

"You can wear blue jeans or peddle pushers," continued the nun, "but don't wear skirts. Wear a good pair of tennis shoes. Clean off the bottoms before you come into the school."

We didn't know what was up when we went to St. Phils on Wednesday morning. Sister Alphonse was waiting for us. There seemed to be a twinkle in her eye.

"You are going to work in the fourth grade room, girls, Room 8. You are going to steel wool the floors."

We could hardly believe our ears.

Sister led us to the room and began to show us. She lifted the skirt of her habit, placing two large pieces of steel wool beneath two of the tiniest feet we had ever seen. We couldn't tell if her feet were moving because of the width of her habit.

Surprise seemed to cross her face for a moment, just before she toppled straight to the floor.

"Not a word of this," she stammered as she dusted herself off. "I have confidence you will get the hang of it. Move the desks from one side of the room to the other and put them in place when you are finished."

The whole thing took us by surprise.

We had often seen the boys do the work, huffing and puffing, and leaning their hands on the desks. It wasn't for us. Call it women's ingenuity or feminine intuition, we did it our way.

We slid the desks to one side of the room. Then forming a line on the other and holding hands, we went a slippin and a slidin from the front to the rear of the room. Then we went back again, and again, and again.

We sang as we glided along. The boys sometimes swore. They would spend forever in one spot, spitting against the wind. We floated through the room as easily as sitting on the spindled rails.

Sometimes, one after another, we would break away from the line, doing a particularly weathered spot like a Ginger Rogers.

We sang particular songs for particular tasks. We always sang Mule Train while sliding the desks. We were really a jumpin and a jivin.

By two in the afternoon we had finished the room. On Thursday we finished the other fourth grade room. On Friday we did one of the third grade rooms.

Sister Immaculata came in a few times while we were working. Sister Alphonse brought us iced tea from the convent. They would always leave shaking their heads.

On Saturday Monsignor O'Donnell came into the room while we were in the line move.

"I've heard you have done an excellent job, girls. The sisters are proud of you. I am proud of you. Has it been too hard on you?"

"No, Monsignor," answered Peggy. "It's almost as if we are dancing."

That afternoon Barney Rooney walked into the Lakeside Tavern. "Father Donnello wants a ten spot on Sword Dancer. He's so sure of it, he was almost going to go for a twenty."

Chapter 2

Become

Steel wooling made the summer. We were famous in a nice sort of way. We had paid our dues. Even our brothers and the boys in the neighborhood showed us a bit of respect.

The nuns took us to an Indians game. Sisters love baseball. It must come with the habit. None of our mothers understood baseball. The women on our streets were always yelling at the boys for hitting balls into their yards. Usually they played with tennis balls, which would bounce everywhere like moonbeams out of control.

When spring came to the schoolyard the sisters took their turn at bat.

"Let me up," they would say to the boys as they walked from the convent after lunch. They would launch a ball into the girl's yard or sometimes off Mister Finneran's house. Then they would continue their walk.

Rules were made to be broken in the spring. All year long the sisters would be shushing in the schoolyard. When a sister hit a good one she would shout and dance with glee. Mister Finneran put his screens up early to protect his windows from the flying balls.

The boys were never allowed in the girl's yard. There was an imaginary line across the concrete that was never to be crossed. We learned that rule in the first grade. But during the month of May, boys were chasing balls all over our yard.

They scurried through swinging ropes. They scattered our jacks. They kicked over book bags. The sisters would never say a word.

Only Mister Finneran seemed to care. He would stand and stare. We could sometimes hear him mutter as he leaned on his rake or broom.

"If only I ran this church. I'll be glad when this damn year is over."

Frankie Cipolla was totally freaked out about the Indians. Joanie told us her father had sworn he would never go to another Indians game. It was something about them trading Rocky Colovito to the Detroit Tigers.

Joanie's family had lived on the Hill before moving to East Cleveland. It was an old Italian neighborhood. All of the people on the Hill loved Rocky.

"What did your father say," asked Peggy?

"He said, 'el fungula.' He is totally pissed off. It's been since before Easter and he's still mad."

We went downtown on the bus. It stopped right in front of the church. The five of us went. Six sisters went with us. Sister Alphonse and Sister Vincentia, Sister Marian and Sister Therese, Sister Catherine and Sister Immaculata. Sister Immaculata was in charge.

Buses from all over the city let passengers off at the Square. They were like yellow bees in a hive, circling and departing. People were everywhere. We moved step in step with the crowd, down towards the stadium.

I thought the sisters would trip on their rosaries, but they moved faster than anybody. We could hardly keep up.

It was a great sunny afternoon. The Tigers were in town. Rocky Colovito was in right field. We had the best of seats, upper deck in right field, right along the railing. I had never seen anything like it. The field sparkled like an emerald. The foul lines were the purest of white. We could see the freighters on Lake Erie, bobbing above the low seats of the bleachers.

The stadium was packed. All of the lower seats were full. There were only a few empty seats in the upper deck. There were a thousand signs: WELCOME HOME ROCKY and DON'T KNOCK THE ROCK.

The crowd roared when the Tigers took the field. The people loved Rocky. The roar didn't stop until the fielder below us took off his cap and waved to the crowd. His hair was wavy and glistening, coal black against the green of the field.

It was his crowd. All of Cleveland loved him, not just the people on the Hill. When he came to bat the crowd banged their seats. Each of us waited for the crack of the bat.

Each sister had a scorecard, putting slashes and numbers all over the place. None of us knew what they were doing. When Rocky came to bat, they banged their seats louder than anybody. The crowd around us shouted with glee.

We all stood and sang, Take Me Out to the Ballgame, during the seventh inning. We were shoulder to shoulder, holding hands with the sisters, swaying back and forth.

"What are ye doing, sisters," came a voice from the crowd.

"The steel wool shuffle," yelled back Sister Immaculata in a voice only a principal could have.

When we looked back there were thirty rows swaying with us.

It all had to come to an end. We thought it would end in sadness, but Rocky had one last chance in the tenth inning. The seats had ceased to clamor. The crowd had lost its energy. Rocky seemed tired as he came to the plate.

Then we heard the crack of the bat. The ball seemed to be in a perfect arch from the time it left the plate. It was moving away from us, towards the stands in left field. It was like slow motion.

By the time I looked down, Rocky was rounding second base. The crowd was roaring. And then he was home.

It was quick. It was fatal. It was the moment the people had come to see.

We were all spent as we walked slowly up the hill from the stadium. The sisters angled off toward the library, away from the Square.

"Aren't we going to catch the bus," asked Peggy?

"In a few minutes," answered Sister Vincentia, "we always stop at the War Memorial Fountain when we are downtown. It's the least we could do. We knew many of the soldiers. Two of the sisters lost brothers."

The statue stood in a large fountain. Shoots of water spiraled over the youths outstretched arm. He seemed to rise from the water.

"There is a statue like this at Normandy." said Sister Catherine. "It is called The Spirit of American Youth. A young man rising from the waves, his arm outstretched to the heavens.

It seemed she had a tear in her eye as she continued.

"I visited there with my father and my mother after the cemetery was dedicated. There are rows of white crosses as far as the eye can see. That's where my brother Timmy is buried, in a row of white crossed on a field of green."

No one said a word as we looked at the cooling figure. He was alone, rising from the sea. His eyes looked to the heavens.

"Requiescat in pace," prayed Sister Immaculata. "May his soul, and the souls of all our departed soldiers, rest in peace."

Catholic schools had a strange way of dealing with the differences between boys and girls. Just when we were getting to know one another, sometimes developing crushes, Catholic education would send us in differing directions. It was more mysterious than the mysteries of the rosary.

Much of the eighth grade year was spent preparing us for that division. The boys would be off on the bus to Latin or St. Joseph. We girls would wander one block down the street to Sacred Heart.

It seemed we were getting the worst of the deal. We girls could be born and die, be educated, be married and give birth, all within the few blocks around St. Phils. There was only a Post Office and a medical building on the block between St. Phils and Sacred Heart. Both schools had the Ursuline nuns.

Huron Road Hospital was just up the street. There was a theater across the street from the Post Office, with a hall for weddings above it.

Our brothers and the other boys had a world we did not know. They would be off caddying in the summer at the Country Club or Oakwood. They would be taking buses all over town. They had a pocket full of money and an early worldliness.

The five of us were still swinging on the porch on summer days. Our parents knew that we were preparing for different roles in life. So did the sisters.

Sister spent a lot of time during our eighth grade year talking about vocations. They were something God called you to do.

"How do you know when He is calling," someone would ask?

The holy pictures and statues were symbols. We couldn't see our guardian angels. The Pope was God's vicar on earth. The priests were His representatives. No one told us what the sisters were.

"You will know when He calls you. You will feel His love. Priests and sisters have special vocations."

"How about the brothers that teach at Latin," someone would ask?

"They have vocations."

By her tone, we knew they were less than priests.

"Others are called to the married life, to be mothers and fathers. Many of you will be called to that life. But we hope we have some vocations, some future priests and sisters, here at St. Philomenas."

"How about my father, he works at the Post Office," I asked.

"My aunt is a waitress. She brings us pizza," said a voice from the rear.

"My father works at Fisher Body," said another.

"Those are not vocations. Those are jobs. There is a difference."

"Jobs," said Bridie on the way home from school. "Jobs are more important than vocations. My father and uncle are pipe fitters. There is hell to pay when work is slow. My mother goes nuts."

"Why, isn't she happy in her vocation," asked Peggy? "My father should have been a priest with all the praying he makes us do."

"Maybe he didn't hear God's call," smiled Bridie.

Maybe he heard my mother's louder."

"Girls don't propose," said Mary. "Do they?"

"Maybe I'll become a sister," said Joanie.

"Why?"

We all looked at her. None of us had ever thought of the idea.

"They belong to each other," she continued almost flustered.

"So you could make some goofs steel wool the floors," quipped Bridie.

Joanie didn't answer. But as I looked at her I could see a deepness in her eye that I had never noticed before.

We were getting older, getting on with the ways of the world.

"Do you think any boys in our room will be called to the priesthood," I asked? "Some go to the seminary in the ninth grade."

"And come right back," shot back Bridie. "They can't take the praying, and the no swearing, and baths every night. Can't you smell some of them?"

"Who would marry them if they stayed out," quizzed Mary?

"Catherine Mulcahey's son Michael went three years ago," chipped in Bridie. "He's back already. She was so broken hearted she wouldn't send him to Catholic high school. He's up at Shaw with the Protestants now.

She's wearing mourner's black like when her husband died. My mother says it's so sad."

"Some stay because they are afraid of their mothers," said Peggy. "Not all, I hope. Our priests are meant to be priests."

"Why do boys go after grade school and girls go after high school," asked Joanie?

"It's romance," answered Peggy. "My father says he would have been a Franciscan Monk if he hadn't met my mother."

"How old was he when he met her," I asked?

"Seventeen. He was only seventeen."

My father always said that we would grow up with the same characteristics as our ancestors, at least one or two of them. No one could predict which ones they might be.

He always had time to talk to me and my two older brothers. Half the time we did not know what he was talking about. He was forever reading. His two most valuable possessions were his library card and the rosary he always carried in his pocket.

His favorite book was The Complete Works of O Henry. He would say that a letter carrier must do his work with 'celerity and dispatch.' He told us stories about the kindness of everyday life that distinguished the 'poet from the peasant.' Both phrases were from O Henry.

He had met my mother on his mail route. She was a housemaid. She was walking the children of her employer. He was almost thirty-five and living at home. She had come over from Ireland a half dozen years before.

"Where are your bankbooks," she asked him soon after?

"Me and my brother were living at home, supporting my mother and father. They had lost their house during the Depression. I had no bankbook, just the few coins in my pocket.

Well your mother takes me up to her room and shows me a chest filled with linen and silverware. Beneath her pillow she had two savings books, with $600 in one and $200 in another. I could tell she meant business."

My favorite relative was his sister, Aunt Frasia. She had married even later in life than my father, marrying a man who looked like a grandfather.

It didn't last long. After a few years he died. I could hear my father and my uncle laughing in the living room long after he died.

"Poor Emmett froze to death."

"Frasia would never turn up the heat. She kept the house just warm enough so the pipes wouldn't freeze."

Frasia was my favorite aunt, the only aunt I knew. All of my mother's brothers and sisters were still in Ireland. She would come over on a

Sunday afternoon and sit with me on the back porch, sometimes only holding my hand. She had the softest of hands.

"When you die," she once said, "you will be led into heaven by people that you never have known, souls you have prayed for, poor people you have helped when you sent a few dollars to the missions. They may be another color, or be from another continent. They will be waiting for you."

I asked her once about what Joanie had said, about becoming a sister.

"Sheila, who knows," she answered, "the good Lord works in mysterious ways."

My father was from the same school as Aunt Frasia. He had a small checkbook. He was always sending a few dollars to the Maryknolls or to the Indian Missions.

So, somewhere deep in my heart, I knew that a vocation wasn't any more important than a job. I knew that those who were called were no closer to God than those who knelt in the pews.

And I knew that whatever any of us did in life, Joanie or any of us, was what my father had called 'part of the ball game.'

The sisters at Sacred Heart were waiting for us when we made the journey down the block. They were planning to save quite a bit of money during the next four years.

We had done the same four classrooms after graduating from St. Phils. Sister Alphonse had asked us. We hadn't planned on it, but it was summer, and we found a certain pleasure in our work.

The sisters even brought us a victrola so we could play records. Sister Vincentia brought a large pile of records from the convent.

"These are my favorites. Your feet will hardly keep still."

"Jesus, Mary, and Joseph," mimicked Bridie as she sorted through the pile, "these are my mother's favorites. We have to wind the victrola and change the needle every five minutes."

They were the favorites of the Irish biddies; Galway Bay and Danny Boy, My Wild Irish Rose and Paddy McGinty's Goat. Gene Kelly couldn't have cleaned the floors to the tunes.

The ballads were too slow. The reels were too fast. The jigs and the fiddles were from nowhere.

Mary went home for some records. She lived the closest. She came back with Sh-Boom and Tammy, Rag Mop and Catch a Falling Star. She brought Sixteen Tons for the sliding of the desks. She brought Fats Domino on Blueberry Hill and Chubby Checkers doing the Twist.

It was like it wasn't even work.

Freshmen were supposed to be like dweebs at Sacred Heart. We didn't feel like dweebs. The sisters treated the five of us with a little bit of respect.

They had looked over our work. They had been into the third and fourth grade rooms at St. Phils, giving them the squinty eye. One old sister even got down on her hands and knees, rubbing the oak with the palm of her hand.

"It will never work," she stated. "These floors are as smooth as silk, but Harrigan Brothers Painting has the ear of the bishop. They have been doing our building for as long as I've been around. That's been a few years."

"Harrigan only paints the windows and the sills," said another nun. "They peel in four years and his crews are back again laying canvas all over the bushes. He never touches the floors."

"He has given an estimate to do the floors," said another nun. "They are getting as black as the devil's heart. He won't give a dime less on his estimate."

"He says he needs sanding machines and dust collectors, and who knows what," said the older nun. "He would ruin the whole building. He'd ruin the microscopes in the lab. He'd have dust all over the building."

"Could these girls do it," asked a sister? "Would they be willing to do it?"

"Could they do it," asked Monsignor O'Donnell as he entered the room? "Look at this floor. Could they do it!

Sisters you are like Doubting Thomas. Oh, ye of little faith! Would they do it? That is the question."

"Would they, Monsignor, without being compelled?"

"Sisters, you can take the finest painter or sculptor in the world. He won't do his best work unless the environment is right. These girls need the right environment.

They have made...I mean saved...St. Philomenas a great deal of money during the past two years."

"How could we add to their environment," asked a sister? "There are only the floors."

"They like rock and roll music, Hubby Checker and Shrimp Boats are Coming. Is Sacred Heart ready? Are you ready, sisters?"

Three boys from our class were called by God after the eighth grade. Eddie Burke and Sean Curry were called to the diocesan seminary. Tommy Lee went off with the Trappist Monks to somewhere in Kentucky. The monks took a vow of perpetual silence.

We were surprised that Eddie and Sean were called to the priesthood. They had been two of the biggest goofs in the school. Neither seemed particularly bright or handed in his homework on time. But we had been always told that God works in mysterious ways.

Tommy Lee was a different story. He never said a word.

"Maybe God has been calling him since the second grade," laughed Bridie.

The sisters at Sacred Heart were eager to begin their experiment. Sister Marcetta, our homeroom teacher, told us about it the first week of school.

"We've seen the floors at St. Phils. Would you take a look at this floor."

"Ugh."

"We have prayed for years to have the floors cleaned, but the cost was too great. We never considered that girls could do the work."

"Don't you have any bad girls," asked Bridie?

"We don't deal with troubles like that. We hoped, all of the sisters hoped, that the five of you would see what you could do with one of our floors. Then maybe you could teach the other girls."

We were floored. There was only one answer we could give.

"Sure."

"There's not much to teach," I said.

"There is more than we know. I will give you free time during some of our less important assemblies. You can bring blue jeans to school. Keep them in your lockers. You may bring records of your choice, but no Elvis or Jerry Lee Lewis."

"Sounds like a Teamsters contract," sparked Joanie, "my father, Frankie, drives a cement truck."

"My father is a Teamster, too," answered the nun. "He gave me the clauses. He told me, 'give them all they want. Those girls are doing Sacred Heart a big favor.' You could have gotten more."

"What else," asked Joanie?

"Elvis," the sister smiled.

We were all excited the third Monday of the school year. Sunday's Plain Dealer had announced that the Democratic nominee for President, Senator Kennedy, was going to parade past Sacred Heart on Wednesday afternoon.

The parade was traveling from Painesville to Public Square, where he would speak.

We knew we would see him. He was like family. He was Catholic. He was Irish. His mother was always smiling on television, serving tea to ladies, and asking them to vote for her Jack.

His family was larger than most. They had more fun than all others. They were always playing touch football on beautiful lawns by the ocean, while our brothers skimmed their knees on the cobbled streets.

Jackie was so beautiful. Everybody loved Carolyn.

"We will all assemble on the lawn," announced the principal over the loud speaker. "Be sure to have your skirts and blouses freshly pressed. There is a chance, only a slight chance, that Senator Kennedy will stop here for a moment."

We were excited.

Sister Marcetta broke the bad news. Near the end of the day she called us to her desk.

"Wednesday afternoon will be a perfect opportunity to start with the floors. There will be no classes for a few hours."

"What about senator Kennedy," asked Peggy hotly? "Are we amahdons?"

"What's that," asked the sister? She looked only a few years older than many of the seniors.

"Fools, Sister, fools! My father often calls us that when we foul up."

"No, you are not fools. I am sorry if you got that impression. But we are not sure if Senator Kennedy will stop here.

It will be a perfect opportunity to see what you can do with the floors. You can start in this classroom."

There was no way we could say 'No.'

"Upstairs, in the front of the school," shot back Joanie. Her face was almost as flushed as Peggy's.

"We want the room overlooking the lawn so we can watch through the windows."

There were no classes after the lunch period on Wednesday. Girls were all over the washrooms, primping and combing their hair. We were there, changing into our jeans

Their looks were snotty. Their remarks were as catty.

"Picnic, girls?"

"Doesn't your mother have an iron?"

"They are only freshmen."

The music revived our spirits, that and the scene on the lawn. The sisters had brought the girls out early. They were practicing their welcomes. It was hot and humid. Droplets of sweat were mapping the blouses.

The nuns were like drill sergeants, moving the girls from place to place.

"Play Tony Bennett," smiled Joanie. "We're Going From Rags to Riches."

Then we did Rag Mop, Earth Angel, and slowed to The Song From Moulin Rouge.

We opened the windows to catch the slight breeze. We could see the girls a fidgetin and a fussin down on the lawn.

We learned that we had to turn the steel wool over more often, change pieces after a time, but the grime came off the floor. It was like polishing silver that had been left down in the basement.

We could see the people coming up the side streets to Euclid Avenue. There were young mothers with strollers, old men with their pipes, people of every description. They lined the front of the theater and the steps of the Methodist Church across the street.

They were on the lawn of the library a few blocks down. No one was ever allowed on that lawn but it was a very special day.

The police were out in their three wheeled cycles keeping the crowd on the walks and away from the street.

One of us kept her face at the window, lest we would miss the parade.

Mary saw them coming first. The crowd was waving from the library lawn. The waves continued as the convertibles came the few blocks down the avenue. They stopped in front of the school.

We were all at the wide windows. We raised them a bit more. We could feel the breeze on our faces as it waved through the sycamores.

It was like magic. Each girl was in place on the lawn. Each head was freshly brushed. Each blouse was freshly ironed. We had the best seats in the house.

The Senator was up the steps to the lawn like a leaf from a tree. His head was above the girls. His smile was among them. He had a hand for each sister within his reach. He was lithe. He was strong.

Two seniors stepped forward to present a bouquet of roses. Then he turned on the steps just below us to speak to the crowd.

He spoke with the clipped Bostonian accent we had heard so often on TV.

"I have just a moment to spend some time with you. I wish my mother could be here. She went to convent school. If she pours enough tea, someday I will be the President of these United States.

A gracious lady, Francis Payne Bolton, is your Congressman in this district. I have known her since I entered the House. It seems a long time ago. She is a Republican, a fair Republican. She has always carried the hod for the common man and woman."

"Turn off the music", I said to Mary. "We can hardly hear him."

I should have done it myself. Mary turned the wrong knob. The Naughty Lady of Shady Lane came blasting over our shoulders, over Senator Kennedy's shoulders, almost to the street.

"Who are those girls," he asked looking up?

"Four freshman," answered the flustered principal peering up with a scowl.

"No, five," she continued as she saw Mary's face appear in the window.

"For a moment I thought they were the Ames Brothers," he chuckled.

"They have volunteered to clean our floors," explained the principal, while trying to regain her composure.

"Wonderful!"

Then he turned his head on high, lifted his arm, and waved us down to the steps.

In the stillness of the moment, he appeared as the young man in the fountain, the Spirit of American Youth.

In a moment we were down the steps and out the door. He took our hands in his.

"These girls," he spoke to the crowd, "have volunteered to clean the classroom floors for the sisters. It is wonderful of them. When I am elected President, I am going to ask for volunteers from people not much older than yourselves, to help and assist the people of the poorer nations of the world."

Then he was gone.

I could see his head as he descended to the street. His arm was uplifted. Again, I was reminded of the spirit, the young man in the waters.

It had been a long time since I had the feeling of loneliness. But so much was happening. It was no longer just springtime and Volare.

Sometimes I just daydreamed in class, wondering where the path would lead.

Sister Marcetta seemed to take a special interest in me.

"Gumbahs," kidded Bridie. "You guys are thicker than Micks."

But it was more than that. Sister Marcetta said she was a lot like me when she was a girl.

"Then how did you become a sister?"

"Why do you ask, Joanie?"

"Because the nuns are special, chosen by God."

She could only laugh. She had a beautiful smile.

"I wish I could play some of those rock and roll records for you and the girls in the classroom some day. What do they call them, teenage folly? But the sisters would throw me out.

I'd be shaking and rolling with the rest of you."

"You are kidding, Sister. Aren't you?"

"Not kidding, Joanie. Sisters are special, but we are only people. It's a crazy job.

We all come from someplace, families like yours. We all have brothers and sisters, those we love and that love us.

What we really do is that we try to grow closer to God."

"You mean you are not all close to God?"

"We still go to Confession," smiled the nun. "There are no saints in the convent. Although, sometimes, I think there are those who think they are."

"Sister!"

"Just jesting, Joanie. But anytime you want to talk about anything, the convent or anything, give me a nod."

Frequently during the next few years I would talk to Sister Marcetta, always leaving with a new bounce in my step. I kept our conversations close to my heart, close to where I kept my inner most feelings.

The sisters said we would be changed young women when we came to Sacred Heart. Change must come slowly. We were still walking the same streets. But our books were bigger. We were learning of Chaucer and Poe.

Only Joanie seemed to be changing. She was pert and vivacious. Her hair was the darkest coal. She had a natural curl and a natural smile. She had curves where we were narrow.

The rest of us were the children of the Micks, a mixture of freckles and pale skin, and hair that curlers were made for.

Boys from Latin and St. Joe's, from neighborhoods we had never known, were always cruising the streets around Sacred Heart. There would be three or four to a car.

There would be whistles and waves for Joanie. There would be polite conversation for the rest of us. She never seemed to notice. We were as close as we had been on the swing.

Senator Kennedy became President Kennedy. He developed the Peace Corps, sending men and women, not much older than ourselves, to help the people of the poorer nations.

He sent the common man. He sent weavers and spinners, and carpenters to build houses. He sent cattlemen and farmers, those who knew the secrets of the soil.

He asked, "Not what our country could do for us, but what we could do for our country."

The sisters were quick to take notice. They filled the steel wool detail with volunteers. Before our freshman year was over there were no scars left on the floors.

After the floors were finished, the principal asked Harrigan himself for an estimate. He came in to do the numbers. They were true to the dime to the estimate he had been giving for years.

She took it over to Sister Immaculata at St. Phils. Sister Immaculata passed it on to Monsignor O'Donnell. He looked at it, chuckled, and folded it in his missal.

We gradually outgrew some of the rules. It was part of growing up. We became riders in the cars. It would be a ride to the corner of our street, or to Ripples, the most popular spot on Hayden.

Ripples became our after school hangout. Large vinyl booths and nickel tunes went a long way. The cheeseburgers were layered with tomatoes and onions. The tabletops were layered with ketchup.

We only accepted rides from boys we knew. We never accepted a ride from Smoky Corrigan. That would have been gross.

"No thank you, Joey," we would holler. "We'll walk."

We said it in the rain. We said it in the snow. We would have said it in a monsoon.

"See you at Ripples," he would holler, gunning his engine. Smoke would emerge from the back of the old Plymouth. The trees would shake in fear as he roared away.

"My brother says Smoky would screw up a T Bird," said Peggy.

"Ford will never sell him one," answered Bridie. "He'll have that crate until the day he dies."

We formed friendships with other kids from other neighborhoods. We even went to the Slovenian Picnic at Euclid Beach. We had been going to the Irish Picnic since we had been in buggys.

The Beach's rides were the grooviest. There was a great roller coaster, whose spindled wooden skeleton danced in the breeze. There were racing coasters, tandems side by side. No one knew which coaster would win, as they flew through the boughs of the trees. There were racing horses, and Laugh in the Dark, where a boy might squeeze your shoulder, and try to steal a kiss.

Our mother's would sit in front of the stage at the Irish Picnic, gossiping like they were girls in Mayo. There were fiddlers and pipers, step dancers and storytellers.

The Slovenians were different. They had the accordion. They had Frankie Yankovic and Johnny Vadnal, and a host of other magicians on the great squeeze box.

We picked up the polka like we were polishing the floors. It was just a hop, and a skip, and a slide.

"You know," said Mary, "there is not much difference between nationalities. Each just jumps to a different beat."

"Are you going to marry a Slovenian," asked Bridie? "Your mother would kill you."

"What if I married a Protestant? Wouldn't she be happier if I married a Slovenian?"

"She would be happy if you married Smoky Corrigan. You might not be happy, but she would be."

We were ever talking about what we would be, like wanderers in the wind. No one said, "I will be this...I will be that." We were wanderers.

During our junior year we had the Spring Social in the gym. A few girls had dates. Most of us went together, much to the glory of the sisters. They thought we were too young to date, but that we must get along with the social functions of life.

The parking lot behind the medical building was loaded with cars. The cruisers had come out in droves.

We were dressed in hoop skirts and penny loafers, with flowers for our blouses.

The boys had spades on their feet and pegs in their pants.

Bill Randle had even given it a plug on the radio.

"The juniors at Sacred Heart are going to have their 32nd annual Spring Fling. Boy, that is a long time. They were Depression kids back then, doing the Lindy.

This note says they now do the Steel Wool Bazoo. That is what it says, the Steel Wool Bazoo!"

It was frigid. The boys had one wall. We had the other. A few girls danced with each other.

Then Joey Corrigan came over and asked, "want to dance?" It was said in the same plaintive tone in which had always asked, "wanna ride."

Before any of us could answer, Mary took his hand and they were out twirling to The Tennessee Waltz. Joey was as nimble on his feet as he was heavy on the gas. In a moment each of us had a partner.

We did a polka and an Irish reel. The sisters came out in a line and taught us the Siege of Ennis, an old rockabilly fling around the floor. It left us winded and laughing and in tune with one another.

We rode in the smokemobile that night. Mary sat in the middle, next to Joey. The rest of us were scattered in the seats of the chariot

"You know," said Mary the next day, "Joey's not such a bad guy. He wants to become an accountant. He's good with the numbers."

By our senior year we were almost ladies of the world. We didn't have an idea of what we would become. Jobs were more plentiful for boys.

If a boy's father or uncle was in the building trades he might gain an apprenticeship with the carpenters or the pipe fitters. The boy's choices had names. Ford was hiring. Fisher Body was hiring. National Acme, Tapco, and the New York Central were hiring.

Oh, Nela Park and all the factories hired girls for office work, but the jobs were not as numerous as for boys.

We studied typing and filing. We took home economics and sewing. By the time we were seniors none of us could darn a sock or stitch a zipper. Only Joanie could cook.

Peggy's mother could run an ironing mangle, cook a roast, and bake a few pies, all in her leisure on a Sunday afternoon. She had come over from County Cork. If she had passed six grades would never tell.

"When ye are married, ye will be able to do it," she would laugh. "Ye will be able to do it, or ye will all have to marry millionaires."

We had no millionaires in our circle of friends, only boys who would be carrying the lunch pail for the rest of their lives.

Joanie amazed us. She could make lasagna. She could bake ravioli. She could throw together salads with olives and onions that were out of this world.

Our mothers made roasts, with carrots and green beans, and mashed potatoes and gravy. That was the Gaelic staple.

One Saturday Joanie had a picnic in her yard. She made every dish, starting with the sauce on Thursday night. Each boy had an eye for her.

Joey Corrigan had spaghetti sauce all over his trousers. Joey and Mary were a ticket. He was taking night classes at John Carroll. He was working the extra board at the railroad to pay for his tuition.

Frankie came out, laughing and smoking the biggest of cigars. He brought two gallons of the purest wine.

"Made it in the basement, myself," he explained as he poured each of us a glass. "When you girls get married I will make the wine for each of your weddings. It will tear the heart out of the Micks."

It was a wonderful Friday morning. The leaves were piled on the lawns. Autumns sparkle was in the air. We all had dates for a Latin football game that night. All was well with the world.

It was half past the noon hour when the principal's shaken voice came over the loudspeaker.

"President Kennedy has been shot in Dallas."

There was the pure silence of shock. The prayers were silent. Bells did not ring. Girls leaned broken hearted on their desks.

Within a half hour the voice came again.

"President Kennedy is dead…May his soul and the souls of all the faithful departed rest in peace."

Without words we left for home, walking the silent streets. We walked slowly along the same paths we had ever walked.

We were alone with each other. Our hearts talked to each other.

Saturday afternoon we went to St. Phils. The church was crowded. No priests were hearing Confession.

Monsignor O'Donnell sat alone on the altar. He wore a plain white surplice over the black of his cassock. He looked older. His face was pale.

We met the Monsignor as we left by the side door. He could see the red of our eyes. Evening was almost upon us.

"It's a sad day," he said.

"It's a sad day, girls. I saw you in church, always the five of you together. I have watched the five of you, it seems forever.

I went to St. Thomas Aquinas School years ago with your father, Sheila."

I had not known that. I did not know the Monsignor even knew my name.

Then the story came from my tears. I told him about the baseball game, and about the sisters at the fountain. I told him of the day at Sacred Heart. I told him how Senator Kennedy had stretched his hand high, like the Spirit in the fountain.

"Come with me, girls" he said.

He took us in his car. He took us to the fountain.

It was almost dark. A lone policeman was walking the mall.

"What are you doing here, Monsignor O'Donnell?"

The Monsignor told him the story of the baseball game, about the President's resemblance to the youth in the fountain.

"Are any of the pipers on duty," he asked?

"Sure they are. I can find them. I'll even call the firehouse in the Flats."

Within minutes cars began to arrive. First came the black and whites of the Cleveland Police. Next came the reds of the Fire Department.

There were four bagpipers.

They played the ancient songs. Music drifted over the shoulders of the bronzed youth, over the water that cooled him.

They played Danny Boy. Then they played the Gaelic of hope and rebirth.

> Morning has broken, like the first day
> Blackbird has spoken, like the first bird
> Sweet the rain's new fall, Sun lit from heaven
> Like the first dew fall on the first grass...

"So long, Jack," prayed the Monsignor.

> May the road rise to meet you
> May the wind be ever at your back
> May the Good Lord hold you in the hollow of His hand.

Chapter 3

Continue

I saw a lot of Benny Maloney the tear after graduation. I got a job in the office at White Motor. Benny drove a towmotor in the shop.

"Want a ride, paisan," he would holler when he saw me at the bus stop.

He was ever smiling and friendly. I could talk to him.

"Why didn't you ever marry, Benny," I asked one morning on the way to work?

"Is this a proposal?"

"No, just curious. You're a pretty good looking guy."

He was about a dozen years older than me. He was sandy haired and fair.

"No one ever asked me."

"Were you ever in love?"

"You ask too many questions, paisan. I remember when you were a squirt, you and your four compadres. I remember the day you all got in so much trouble, eating pogey bait in the Lakeside."

"How did you know about the trouble?"

"Father Donnello told me. He goes to Confession to me."

He was laughing. He was sacrilegious.

"Who the hell is Father Donnello? We still don't know who put the money on Tomy Lee."

"Someday I'll tell you, paisan. You are still too much of a squirt to tell anything to. Someday when you have whiskers I'll let you in on the scoop."

He was a lark. He was unpredictable. Sometimes he had a sadness in his eye that I could not fathom.

President Kennedy had brought men of talent and discipline to occupy the thrones of power. They were the best and the brightest. He brought the best minds from Harvard and Yale and the universities along the eastern coast. He brought the best talent from Ford and Rockefeller and the great foundations. He brought his brother Bobby to be Attorney General.

They were the sons of the elite. They were schooled and honed for government position, just as the pipe fitter looked out for his sons, or the farmer's boy would inherit the earth.

By intellect and ancestry they were brothers. They understood history, and diplomacy, and the uses of power. They were capable of managing the wheat and the chaff. They knew the ways of the world.

They gave the hard eye to Khruschev during the Cuban missile crisis.

They sent a few hundred soldiers to be advisors in a country called Vietnam. Then they sent three thousand more.

A reporter stopped by the Justice Department one day to talk to Bobby. He asked about the buildup in Vietnam.

"Vietnam, Vietnam," answered the President's brother, "we have thirty Vietnams a day here."

Khruschev told the American Ambassador to Russia that the President was making a mistake.

"The United States has stumbled into a bog. It will be mired there for a long time."

By the day that he died, President Kennedy had placed twenty thousand soldiers in the bog.

The Irish knew what a bog was. In 1771, four score years before the great famine, English Parliament had offered to lease fifty acres of bog to each family.

An Irish historian wrote, "…you may not understand the word bog…'It means a marsh; it is almost irreclaimable; it means a marsh which you will be draining until doomsday, still it will remain the original marsh."

The buildup was supported by those who knew best. It was supported by the State Department, and the Joint Chiefs of Staff, and the Central Intelligence Agency.

The boys in the marsh were from neighborhoods like ours. They were from Plano, Texas; and Quincy Illinois, and Georgetown, South Carolina.

One group had been called to sit on the altar. The other just knelt in the pews.

"I was in love once," started Benny. I had not asked the question. I had been riding with him for over a year.

"I was in love once, paisan. She was a girl who went to Sacred Heart. We went together for two years during high school. We did everything together. When we graduated she said it was over. She was my one love. She was my joy.

I was a goofus. I drank maybe too much. I never thought it would be over. I thought our day would last forever."

"Where is she now?"

"In a suburb with three children," he smiled. "I only had one heart."

"Benny, Benny, Benny, get on with yourself. This is a big world. You are a good looking guy."

"And you, paisan? I don't hear much about your amorous flings. Maybe you're looking for an older guy like me."

I had to laugh. Benny always made me smile. Ever the kind word.

"I'm looking."

"The story of my life," he moaned. "The ballad of Benny Maloney! When you find the right one kid, hang his picture up next to mine. Then you'll know what you missed."

I learned a lot about Benny, a lot that I liked.

He had been in the Marines for six years, Korea he said. He was going to make it his career. He even sang From the Halls of Montezuma to me one morning on the way to work.

"My mother took ill. She was sick with cancer for a long time. My brothers and sisters had their own families to care for. So I took the stripes off my sleeve, came home to care for her until she died.

I wanted to be a pogey bait Marine, not the best, just one of the troops. We were like the sisters and the priests. Semper Fidelis!"

"What's that?"

"Always faithful, paisan, always faithful."

"I thought about becoming a nun once."

"You've got to be kidding."

"Why?"

"You have too much spirit. You are the leader of that rat pack with all your Irish gumbahs."

"Sisters have spirit."

"I guess they do all right, paisan. I had a few at St. Phils that could do justice with any drill sergeant.

But you, Joanie! Wow! Jesus would lock the gates."

Benny invited me to his Browns party in December of '65. The Browns were playing the Packers for the championship.

"Can you cook, paisan?"

"Is the Pope a Catholic?"

"Then come over on Sunday afternoon. Bring some spaghetti and whatever else you can dash together."

"What if I don't bring anything?"

"Bring those four also ran friends of yours. Tell them bake to some Irish bread or potatoes or something."

"What if they won't bake anything?"

"Just come with your sweet little asses and sit on the couch. There will be plenty of beer, and pretzels and chips. I was only hoping to add a touch of class to the occasion."

The house was wall to wall. Peggy's two older brothers, Bullet and Shoe were there. The man with the betting slips was there. Sean Curry was there, back from the seminary.

We came in with the biggest of pots. I had dashed together some spaghetti with meatballs, with sausage and mushrooms, and added a sprinkle of Frankie's wine. The girls had cooked two pot roasts, and thrown in some potatoes and carrots.

"What's the Deigo got," Bullet asked Peggy? "If it isn't as good as ma's leg of lamb, we'll throw you all out."

Smoky put a big ladle to the sauce and spilled it all over the floor.

"Don't worry about a thing," winked Benny. "These girls will clean the house before I let them go home."

The living room was filled with chatter. The guys were talking as fast as they could drink beer. Only the picture of the Blessed Virgin was silent.

"Why did that fucker, Modell, fire Paul Brown?"

"Wanted to show he was the boss."

"Asshole!"

"Mickey McBride should never have sold the team to that shyster."

"Words out that he gambles like a goof. Calls it all into New York so the local guys don't get a piece of his losses."

"That Lombardi, he's like Paul Brown. Modell would fire him too. Not room for two at the top."

The Packers were waltzing all over the Browns in the mud of Green Bay. Taylor and Hornung ran sweeps like they owned the field. They took the heart out of the Browns.

I knew that Frankie would still be talking when I got home. He loved Vince Lombardi like he was the patron saint of Italy. He hated Art Modell. Firing Paul Brown was almost as bad as when the Indians traded Rocky Colovito.

It was a great afternoon. There were all kinds of complements about the food.

"Best chow you ever served, Benny."

"Only food he ever served."

Bullet asked me, "Do you think you could come over and teach my mother how to cook the spaghetti?"

We were at the door when Benny waved us back.

"Thanks, gators."

"It was nothing," I answered. "It was a great day."

"I owe you all one. See you down the road."

We had been planning a trip for our twentieth year. The farthest we had ever been together was Deerfield Village on a school trip. We had become bored within an hour.

Our mothers weren't crazy about the five of us going off together.

"Isn't there enough to do around here?"

Our brothers and their friends were off to South Bend to see Notre Dame play. They would have cases of beer on the bus, flasks of the sauce in their jackets. No mother seemed to worry about them.

"Boys will be boys," Peggy's mother would say. "They can take care of themselves."

The boys would run around, be drafted by the army, go off to Germany or California. They would come home at four on a Saturday morning, all whiskied and pluthered.

"Did you have a good time," our mothers would ask the next day.

None of us knew where to go on the trip. Each of us had an objection to the other's idea.

"Miami."

"The Cubans are all over."

New York, Chicago.

"Like sitting downtown in a hotel room."

"The Poconos."

"That's where me and Joey are going on our honeymoon."

"We can't decide where to go on vacation," I told Benny. "We've been planning a twentieth year trip it seems forever, and now we're lost.

It's a special trip for me, maybe the last really long time I'll have with them."

"You sound like it's the end of the world, paisan. Is the world going to stop spinning? Are you jumping off?"

"No dear Benny, you are my friend and I'm not jumping off. But I'm going to be doing something in a few months, something that I have been thinking of for a long time.

I'm going to tell you some morning on the way to work. You've been so good to me. But for now, I am holding it close to my heart."

"Wow, little Joanie. It must be real big.

I owe all of you Joanie, from the party. Maybe I have a vacation spot for you. I'll let you know in a few days.

But, paisan, you are too good a girl, too good a friend, to be worrying old Benny.

Whatever you do, Joanie, let me know when you know it's right for you. That's the way it was in the Corps."

He broke the news to me later in the week.

"I can get you a cottage on the beach at P.I., South Carolina."

"Parris Island? I thought that was only a Marine Base."

"No, Pawleys Island, paisan. I would never trust the Marines with the five of you. Me and a bunch of guys bought a cottage down there about seven, eight years ago. When I got out I kept my piece of the cottage.

We each send in a couple of hundred bucks a year, pay the mortgage, pay the taxes. I haven't been there in three years, but it is still going strong. One guy takes care of everything, rents it out once in a while."

"Where's Pawleys Island?"

"About thirty miles south of Myrtle Beach. It's a quiet spot. There's nothing but crabs in the water and sand on the beach, but you have to look out for the local boys. They scamper after young northern girls."

"We can handle that."

"Here, I have some pictures."

We were sitting on Peggy's porch, passing the pictures.

They were all of young men, boys of our age, sitting on the widest of wooden porches. All we could see were ashtrays and beer cans.

"He's got to be kidding," said Bridie." Where is the ocean?"

"In this corner," answered Sheila, pointing to a small speck of blue.

"Will we have crabs in our beds," asked Mary? "I heard they are like spiders."

"Should we take Benny up on it," I asked?

"Sure."

We looked like immigrants when we left on the train. We had two suitcases each, and four cardboard boxes full of sheets and pillow cases.

Frankie had given us a cooler with five lengths of hard salami and an equal number of sticks of pepperoni. I was carrying a shopping bag, with eight loaves of Italian bread peeping over the top. Jars of hot mustard and peppers were rolling in the bottom.

"This will keep you for a week," explained Frankie. "Them grits and black eyed peas wouldn't even feed the crows."

We went for two weeks. We stayed almost a month.

We were to take the New York Central to Washington's Union Station. Then it was the Atlantic Seaboard to Georgetown.

"Going on a picnic," quizzed a colored conductor?

"No sir, we are going to South Carolina," answered Mary. "Have you ever been there?"

"Left there thirty years ago, the whole family. We were from Florence. We were like you, just a box full of linens and a basket of food. Ain't never been back. Where all are you going?"

"Pawleys Island."

"The middle of nowhere," he smiled. "The middle of nowhere."

He talked slowly like Monsignor O'Donnell. Maybe all men talk slowly when they get older.

"Andrew Baynes and Spots Alston in the back cars are from around that area. The Lowcountry it's called. Not a bit of it is worth a damn, but they go back every so often."

The three of them came back later when night had come to the Pennsylvania hills.

"You'll have the time of your life, girls," smiled Andrew. "Kick off your shoes and walk in the pluff."

"I did that forever," said Spots.

"The what," asked Bridie?

"It's the mud in the creek, the marsh," answered Andrew. "You'll catch blue crabs, and shrimp, and gig for the flounder. Many's the day we got our supper from the creek."

"We've got some salami and pepperoni until we get settled," I said. "Would you guys like a sandwich?"

Spots took the sharpest of blades from his pocket and sliced through the meat. They loaded their sandwiches with peppers just like three gumbares at night in the yard.

"Can you dance," quizzed Andrew?

"Can a sparrow sing," answered Bridie.

"Go to the pavilion on a Friday or Saturday night. It is the only building worth two cents on the whole island. Many years ago the sisters taught the white boys to shuck and jive to almost any tune.

They had two stepped for centuries.

Now, they taught it to their sweeties. They rock the pavilion every weekend. They call it the shag."

"Can you show us," asked Mary?

Spots took out a harmonica and played a little bit of I Feel Good, quiet enough for just a few to hear.

The other two porters, men of many a summer, took to shufflin and shakin right in the aisle. Their shoulders moved away from their waists. Their hips moved away from their knees. Everything was at angles. It was James Brown in slow motion.

"Could you do it now," asked Spots as he squeezed Honeycomb from the harmonica?

We were in the aisle like cats off the roof.

Spots looked up and raised the beat.

The two other porters took to the aisle, shakin amongst us. We rolled through the Pennsylvania night, shakin and jivin and eating Frankie's salami.

"Pawleys is on a peninsula about twenty miles long and three miles wide," explained Spots. "It is called the Waccamaw Neck. It runs between the Waccamaw River and the ocean.

The white folks flock to the ocean in the summer like Baptists after salvation. For the other seasons it is the quietest place on the earth."

"Our people were brought over," said Andrew, "to work in the rice fields along the Waccamaw, on the big plantations. There was Hagley and True Blue, Caledonia, and Brookgreen.

A white lady, Miss Julia Peterkin, she wrote a book about one of the sisters who lived at Brookgreen. It was called Scarlet Sister Mary. She won the Pulitzer Prize, a really big one for writing.

None of the white folks in South Carolina would talk to her.

And then, about a half-dozen years later, a lady in Atlanta wrote one about a white girl, Scarlet O'Hara, who lived on a plantation. The preacher said she even copied the same name. That lady got over like a rabbit in the bush.

I hadn't thought about that in a long time.

Yeah, the preacher had the answer. He said there are stories no white folks wants to hear about."

'Fidelis Semper' was the name on the cottage. We arrived at noon, after an hour drive in an old cab from Georgetown. There was nothing along the road, just a forest of pine.

We crossed a few bridges but we could not see the ocean.

"There are two causeways to the island," said the driver. "The north and the south."

"Just like the Civil War," said Peggy.

"You mean the war of northern aggression," scowled the driver.

That was our welcome.

We were in the ocean as quick as we could change. We could not get enough of the beach. The waves were like wheat, waving to the shore. The sand was without a pebble or a stone.

We cold walk out twenty yards with the water only at our waists. We dove. We leaped. We felt the salted water in our eyes.

"Jesus, this is beautiful," said Bridie. She was never easily impressed.

At dusk we sat on the high wooden porch overlooking the marsh. The setting sun reddened the intertwining waters and reeds. The reeds stood as flat as a boy's crew cut. They were flat, and unfettered, and wove easily in the breeze.

We went to the porch on the front of the cottage. We could see the full moon looking down over the sea. We had never seen so many stars. In Cleveland they were hidden by the clouds and the smog.

We sat like we had always, in the old wooden railings, or on the wide rails with our feet through the spindles.

There wasn't a store on the island. It was barely three miles long, never more than four houses wide. The cottages were balanced on great brick pillars or sturdy telephone posts at least one story high,

"Where can we find a grocery store," we asked a man walking by?

"Up on the highway. Are you just in?"

"We're looking for groceries. We're from Cleveland."

"I'll get my truck. There is a stand up on the highway. You could walk it, but I'll show you where it is."

We sat in the bed of the old pick up. There were coolers, and fishing rods, nets, and canvas all over the place.

He told us what to buy.

"Two of those watermelons, cantaloupes, fresh green beans, rice, green peppers, okra,…"

"What's okra," I asked?

"It goes with everything. You can bread it, cook it in a skillet, saute it with rice and tomatoes and beans, throw a little shrimp in it. Cook it slow, cook it low. It will take the Yankee out of all of you.

Take some tea. Make pitchers of it. Chill it in the refrigerator. It's the mother's milk of the south."

We left with bags of everything, shrimp and flounder, melons and vegetables.

He only spent a few hours with us, but we remembered him for an eternity.

Pawleys was not the type of place where you divided the day. There was no ringing of the bells, do this job or that. There was no bus in the morning. There was no Confession on a Saturday afternoon. We did not know where there would be a mass on Sunday morning.

The island was governed by the moon and the tides. It was caressed by the moon and the stars. It was smiled on by the fortunes. It was teased by the fates and the muses.

The women were of any age.

We would see them at any time, walking barefooted in the creek. They had cages for crabs. They had nets for shrimp. They had baskets and buckets to carry them home.

They dressed in house dress or shorts. They wore straw flowered bonnets.

Sheila said, "They are like the women of Mayo; Sibby and Bridget, Agnes and Kathleen___aunts and cousins we know only by letters."

They showed us how to take life from the creek. They showed how to shovel for the clam, to break loose the oyster. They showed us the tricks of the casting net and how to devein the shrimp with a pinch of their neck.

But we were all thumbs, girls from the north, and we ended up trekking up to the market on the highway.

We saw him the third morning, just a shadow in the reeds. We had been watching the snowed egrets, white arched necks amidst the green shades of the grass.

"Is that someone in the marsh," asked Mary?

"Where?"

"There," she exclaimed!

We could just catch a glimpse of the shadow, a slight bend of the reeds. It wove and weaved toward the shore on the other side.

I was pouring another glass of tea when we spotted him again. He was entering the woods. He had a long staff, leaning upon it.

We watched the figure limp into the bush.

We saw him again the next morning. He was there at daybreak, a moving shadow in the bog.

On Thursday we got a letter from Benny:

> All is well in East Cleveland. The streets are quieter.
> I have checked. None of the guys are going to use the
> cottage this summer.
> Three are in Nam and the rest are scattered all over
> the globe.
> Don't spill any spaghetti sauce on the floor. Clean the
> Place up a little. There is some paint in the closet.
> Give it a little of that feminine touch.
> Jesus Christ will love you, paisans. His mother will love
> You, too.

We went to the pavilion the first Saturday night. We had checked it out during the week. It was a ramshackle wooden building, long and narrow, overlooking the marsh. Its wooden stilts stood in the winding creek.

"What should we wear," we asked two girls sitting on the porch?

"Shorts and soft shoes," they smiled. "Come as you are, summer informal."

Even the boys wore shorts and loafers. It was all cotton and canvas as we neared the wide porch. It was like the Log Cabin at Euclid Beach, only it was laid out over the water.

The beat was soft and slow. The crowd was all over, through the door and on the floor, leaning against fenders and lounging in convertibles.

It was a hot steamy night. No one seemed in a hurry. Newcomers were greeted with a beep of a horn or an informal wave of an arm.

It seemed like every boy in South Carolina could dance. There were no Catholic wall huggers.

Mary was the first on the floor. Maurice Williams and the Zodiacs were the band. Mary followed each step of her partner as if she had been shagging forever.

In moments we were all shakin and jivin. The Zodiacs hit Stay, picking up the beat. The boys would grab a beer in the brief stop between tunes, then shuffle their feet to the floor.

They were farm boys and mechanics, carpenters and roofers; boys who earned their sustenance under the hot summer sun. There was a sprinkling of college boys from Clemson and USC, Woffard and Newbury, and schools we had never heard of.

"Thank God the group from Palatine isn't here tonight," said the boy I was dancing with.

"Why's that?"

"They are twerps. They are brassy. They are the biggest troublemakers that ever come here."

I could see the creek glistening through the cracks in the floor. Couples sat on the open sills overlooking the marsh.

Sheila asked Maurice Williams if he had ever heard of Spots Alston?

"The railroad porter," he answered as he wiped the sweat from his brow. "He was the best horn player ever in Hemingway. Laid the brass down to follow the rails."

When he went back to the stand the Zodiacs struck up A Train followed by Chatanooga Choo Choo.

We walked back to the cottage as the stars gleamed from the creek. We had a song in our heart and sand in our shoes.

"Track 29," said Peggy.

"No mass tomorrow," laughed Bridie.

"I think I'll sleep in, at least till the birds wake me," I said.

"What would Joey say," chuckled Mary, "me dancing a jig with any boy who would ask."

"I think I'll rise early," said Sheila, "sit on the back porch and say my office."

"What's an office," asked Mary?

"A room with a desk," smiled Bridie. "It's what a priest says every day, so when the day comes when he is too tired to say mass, God will understand."

Sheila was on the back porch when dawn first broke. Night's dew was on the marsh. The tide was low. The creeks had drifted out to sea.

He was almost through the creek before she saw him. His boots had drifted deep into the gob. He used his staff as a walking stick. He was across the road and walking the sandy dunes to the sea before she could get to the front porch.

Perhaps the fates drew her to the sea. She was not much for following strangers, even those who walked in the bog.

It seemed he knew she was coming.

He was sitting on the first row of the dunes.

"I saw you sitting on the porch. I don't usually come across to the ocean."

"We've seen your shadow in the reeds. For most of the week we have been watching."

"Thank you for coming to say hello."

His eye never strayed from the sea.

A line of dolphins wove northward a few hundred yards from the shore. Every thirty or forty seconds one would leap hump backed from the sea.

He was no older than the boys we had danced with. He appeared frail. His clothes were wet from the marsh.

"I have only a few more weeks here. Then I must report back to Fort Bragg."

"My name is Sheila Flaherty. Do you come here often? We are all from Cleveland, the five of us."

"All of my life. I am from Maryville, on the other side of Georgetown. Look at the dolphins, at peace in the sea. Sumter Rutledge is my name, Sheila."

"Do you want to walk for a while?"

"No, Sheila Flaherty. I've done my walking for weeks. I'm going to sit here and look at the sea. It is so peaceful."

She could not leave him. She thought back to what her father had said when she was small, "everybody needs somebody sometimes, Sheila. It's part of the ball game."

He was fine boned and fair. The summer sun had not erased the paleness from his skin.

They sat for more than an hour. Few words were spoken. The first beach combers came out to search for shells. Men came to cast their rods into the sea. Small children came with their mothers to frolic in the shallows.

"Thank you, Sheila, for sitting with me. I needed someone to be close to."

She didn't say a word.

"Sheila! Sheila!"

I was upon them before they could see me.

The sun had olived my skin. I was as dark as the young boy was fair.

"Come on, Sheila. I've made breakfast, peppers and eggs. It is Frankie's favorite. He even puts it in his sandwiches for work."

"In a moment."

"We're ready to eat. No southern cooking this morning. And here you are gallivanting with some bloke out on the beach."

"Come on, gumbah," I said to the boy. "Come on and eat some Italian cuisine. It will put some meat on those bones."

He looked forlorn. I stopped him before he could say 'no.'

"This is Sumter Rutledge," said Sheila. "And this is Joanie Cipolla.

Come on, Sumter. Joanie is the best cook in Cleveland. Try out those peppers and eggs."

We had breakfast on the back porch overlooking the marsh. The herons and the marsh hens were envying us.

Sumter came out of his shell.

"What is a gumbah? Who is a bloke?"

"Words for friends," I answered. "We have been friends since the second grade. It is if God has linked us together."

"Tell us about yourself," asked Bridie? She had never been bashful.

"There's not much," he started. Then it came out like waves washing over the shore. It was like he had been alone forever, a poor lad walking in the bog.

"My daddy has farmland, has cotton land out toward Nesmith___to be a farmer___daddy added onto his land, little by little___seventeen___enlisted___101st Airborne Division___Fort Bragg___Training___Air Cav___Robert McNamara's baby___quick strike and out___big whigs from Washington___it was their baby___quick strike and out___Vietnam."

He told us the story as if no one was there. Perhaps he had never told it before, not even to himself. It was what the critics of Joyce might call the free flow of thought, and vanished dreams, all with no future, all with no hope.

He just sat, looked over the marsh, and recalled the ghosts.

"It was a beautiful day___first test of the plan___Ia Drang Valley___it was so peaceful___landed 600 men___Cong hidden on the hillsides___Fire all round us___600 men___my friends___trained together___drank beer together___went to the beach together___600 men___closer than brothers___

Support from the copters___fires of hell___five days___shrapnel in my leg___second day___five days___600 men in___250 boys dead___McNamara's baby___Ia Drang, the greenest of valleys___

Hospital___interviews___strangers___fresh shaved___clean uniforms___all bullshit___body counts___multiplied like beans in a bag___

Home___time for recovery___daddy's fishing trailer on the other side of the marsh___feel good___walk in the woods___walk in the marsh___trails through the pines___going back___report to Ft. Bragg."

There was no sweat on his brow. There was no tear in his eye.

We were all stunned.

It was as if he were alone on the porch, a farm boy on a fence post, all alone in his thoughts.

Sumter came back the first thing Monday morning. He was completely changed. It was as if he had sorted the wheat from the chaff.

We heard the horn in the front of the cottage and looked out to see him in a teal and cream 57 Ford Convertible. It was sparkling. Sumter was dressed in the casual cottons of the south. He was as clean as a maiden's heart.

"Come on blokes," he hollered! "Come on. We are going for a ride."

Sheila sat in the middle of the front seat. We others were scattered all over the car.

"Couldn't let you girls go back to Cleveland without showing you some of the real country. How would you girls like to pick some beans and cotton?"

It sounded like fun.

We hit Louie, Louie on the radio, Then Good Golly Miss Molly. We sang along with Elvis, All Shook Up and Teddy Bear.

Sumter joined in. It was if a veil had lifted. The Fairlane had wings as it skimmed down Route 17, teal and cream beneath the blue of the Carolina sky.

"We bought 200 hundred acres last year, daddy and me. Ten thousand dollars is a lot of money. Daddy is a home boy. He is a sharp one. We lease the land, this piece and that. Get paid pack with a part of the crops.

Daddy says, 'never sell the land, Sum,' that's what he calls me. I take an allotment from the army, send it back to him. We are going to buy more acres.

We have a lot of pine. The paper company cuts it, plants new seedlings. Gives us cash, helps pay the mortgage. That's the way it is."

We were through Georgetown and in Nesmith in an hour. It was just a railroad track across a country road.

Sumter took us down dirt roads we had never known, past planted fields we had never seen. Dust was all over the car.

"There's daddy," he said excitedly. The tractor was kicking dust all over a field.

"Where you been, Sum," asked the man? Then he saw us. "You been a flirtin and a frollickin, boy?"

"No, daddy. I was a bit taken, but I'm all right now."

His daddy was the same size as Sumter. He had more meat on his bones. His face was the color of the earth, all crusty and dusted.

"Who are these lasses?"

"Sheila Flaherty, and so many girls, I can't remember all of their names."

"Joanie, Peggy, Sheila, Bridie, and Mary," we spoke as he placed the dust of his palm on ours.

"You must be someone special, Sheila, if he can only remember your name," he winked.

"Mind if I plow," asked Sumter. He was off on the tractor before his daddy could answer.

The noonday sun was settling before he left the dust of the field. He was all aglow and covered with dust.

"Stop and see Miss Sarah. Her garden is in," said his daddy. "And don't forget Frog. They both are asking for you."

Miss Sarah's cabin was this turn and that turn along the dirt roads. Nobody knew where we were going. It hadn't sniffed paint in a moon's age. Inside it was as clean as a whistle.

"Sumter, boy," she greeted him as if she did not know we were there. "I have been praying for you. The whole congregation has been praying for you.

The Lord must have heard our prayers. Praise the Lord!"

Then she greeted us.

She was one age with the cabin. Its porch boards were as the drift of the river. The railings sailed in the breeze.

"Come by to see what you got, Miss Sarah. Got to feed these fine friends."

"Take what you like, boy. The Lord has always given me more than enough. After you are done, I have peach cobbler some tea for you and your friends. There are baskets by the garden."

We picked tomatoes. We picked the finest of green beans and peas.

"What's this," asked Mary, peering over a leafy row?

"Collards," answered Sumter. "Miss Sarah is famous for her collards."

We picked okra and cucumbers. Sumter threw two great watermelons in the trunk of his car.

We sat on the porch with the old colored lady and tasted the most delicious peach cobbler in creation. She sat and rocked in an old pink rocking chair.

"Take care Sumter, boy," she waved as we left. "You are always in my prayers."

It was almost evening when we got to Frogs. How Sumter got there I'll never know. All the roads were dirt. There were no signs. It was like a camp by the river.

"Frog's a river rat," Sumter explained. He is, what do you girls say, he is my gumbah. Got this place by the Black River, won't live anywhere else.

Frog was a man of great girth. His shirt couldn't quite cover his belly. His face was as broad as the moon.

"Thought you'd never come to see me, boy," he roared as he smothered Sumter in his arms.

"Been staying at Pawleys, daddy's trailer. I had things to sort out."

"You doing O. K. , boy?"

"Pretty fair for a square."

"Been rough?"

They talked as we girls had ever talked, each one step ahead of the other's thoughts.

"Be at the pavilion Saturday night," said Frog, "you and the ladies. I'm going to shake a leg."

"Can Frog dance," asked Peggy on the ride back to Pawleys?

"Like a squirrel climbs a tree," smiled Sumter.

Then he hit a button on the radio, looking for some country. He caught Eddie Arnold with Make the world Go Away.

Chapter 4

Remain

Sumter was at the cottage the next morning for breakfast. It was if he didn't want to miss a moment of the week.

"No more farming," kidded Bridie.

"We owe it to Benny to clean this place up a bit," I said.

"Semper Fidelis," said Peggy.

"I'll help," said Sumter.

We hit the windows and floors like Irish washerwomen. We swept, shook out throw rugs, and mopped.

Sumter found a quart of pink paint in the closet. He painted two of the wooden rockers.

"A touch of Miss Sarah," he smiled. "If you girls remember one thing about this trip, it will be the taste of Miss Sarah's cobbler."

Sheila broke out a Polaroid to take pictures for Benny.

"The paisan has no faith," I explained. "He only believes what he can see."

Sheila gave a picture of a pink rocker to Sumter, a pink rocker leaning against a pillar of brick.

"What can I do with this? Don't you have a picture of yourself?"

But the camera had run out of film.

The clouds burst in the afternoon, as they are want to do along the coast. The waters came in torrents, down into the marsh.

I steamed the collards. I made a salad of chopped collards and beans, okra, tomatoes, and onions. I threw three cups of fresh shrimp over the greens, with a dash of vinegar and oil.

I had always felt at home in the kitchen. Maybe it was Frankie and my mother. Everybody cooked.

I felt it was my special birds' nest.

From the fragrance I could tell that this was something special. The tang of vinegar and the fragrance of the southern fields.

We didn't leave the cottage all day.

We found a monopoly game in the closet. We played penny poker. We just sat and did girl talk like we hadn't done in years. We made plans to return to Pawleys in twenty years when we had doubled our age.

"No family, no husbands or children if we have any. Just us", laughed Peggy.

"How about Sumter," I asked?

"If he marries one of us he can come," said Bridie. "If he doesn't he can come. Sumter, you are our Pawleys paisan."

Sumter told us about Joshua Creek where he had caught his first fish with his daddy. He told us of the wide Waccamaw River where the first planters had built their rice plantations. It was now a part of the inland waterway, on which the yachts of the wealthy could travel to Florida.

He told us of the many ghosts of the islands and the plantations, how their spirits thrived in the moisture of the Lowcountry. He told us of the beach at Deb-I-do, across the creek from Pawleys, where fellows sometimes took their girls.

"Why do they call it Deb-I-do," Sheila asked?

"Because sometimes Debby do," he winked, "and sometimes Debby don't."

There was thunder and lightning in the heavens as Sumter recalled the passions of the earth. He was a good storyteller. Sheila sat next to him on the couch.

He told us of a forsaken young girl named Alice Flagg who died in her sixteenth year. Her high and mighty brother had thrown her lover's ring into the marsh, forbidding her to see one of lower birth.

"She still roams the rivers and marshes, seeking the ring. Tomorrow I'll take you to her grave. It is a large flat stone, with only the name Alice upon it. If you walk around the stone backward thirteen times, she will grant you your wish."

"Do people believe that," sniffed Bridie.

"I don't know if they do or they don't, but there is a wide path worn around the stone."

Sumter kissed Sheila when he left. She had walked down to the Fairlane with him. He turned and kissed her. She saw the stars and the moon.

We went to Alice's grave the next afternoon. The church graveyard was shaded by great oaks and crepe myrtles. There wasn't a spot of grass around the grave. They each walked the magic number around the stone, everyone but me.

"Don't you believe, Joanie," asked Mary?

"I'll tell you later, alligators," I answered.

The cemetery was God's place. I could feel it. I could feel the peace and the sense of belonging. The trip had become an adventure in itself, a sojourn before the journey. I would tell them, and Benny, and Frankie and my mother, in another moment in time.

But now, I relished this vacation.

Sumter took us to Brookgreen Garden, which was only a few miles down the road. Brookgreen was once the biggest plantation of them all. The gardens had been developed with a collection of the finest American sculpture, set amidst the ancient oaks.

The path through the row of trees was like Scarlet's pathway to Tara. The heavy boughs of the trees seemed to sooth and comfort the earth.

We wandered the lanes, meandering here and there under the shade of the oaks. Then we all saw the hand and the arm outstretched to the heavens.

It was the boy of the fountain.

It was Monsignor O'Donnell and the sister's prayers. It was the boy of Normandy, a boy on a pedestal under the oaks. It was President Kennedy. It was the boy holding Sheila's hand. It was Sumter.

"Why do you have to go back," asked Sheila?

"My friends are there," he stared. "They are calling me. They just keep calling me."

Frog could slide his feet on the pine.

We rode to the pavilion in the chariot of teal and cream. Sumter was beeping the horn and waving his arms like the rest of the home boys.

Otis Goodwin and the Knights were on the stand. They played Twilight Time and Harbor Lights, It's not For Me to Say, and Lollipop.

Frog was a wonder on his feet. His soles were as light as the porter's on the train. He danced with Mary and Peggy, and me and Bridie.

Sumter only danced with Sheila.

The same crowd was there as the previous week. Everyone was in concert with the beat and the night.

Then a group of strange acting boys came in. They hung together. They were close cropped. They were leaners on the walls and sitters on the sills.

They had taken too much refreshment from brown paper bags. Liquor and sharp retorts oozed from their lips.

"Palace boys," said Sumter. "They are all right when they don't have too much to drink. The college teaches them that they are the chosen sons. They are stupid enough to believe it."

"What palace," I asked.

"The Palatine. It's a boy's college in Charleston. Song of the south, they are taught to fight ancient wars. Someday, they will learn."

The group cast a shadow in the pavilion. Nasty words were on their lips.

Sumter's leg was bothering him, but he was on the floor for almost every dance.

The strange boys spoke loudly, so that they could be heard.

"Even the gimp has a quiff, Colonel," remarked one sitting on a window ledge.

"I see, Captain, I see," remarked another. "These ladies have a piss poor eye for men. A real bad eye."

"Fuck em all, fuck em small, fuck em tall," said one of their burly chested companions. "I'm going to dance with that dark skinned little one before the night is over. She'll call me the prince of push ups."

Frog sidled over to them between dances.

"Say couldn't you fellows be a little quieter?"

"Just watching the gimp and his girl," answered the Captain.

"He was wounded in Nam," said Frog. "I know you understand."

"When we get to Nam," smirked the Colonel, all brave with the contents of the bag, "we'll shoot more gooks than there are fat boys in the world. Now get the hell out of here."

"If you want me, I'll be around here all night," Frog scowled. "Sorry I bothered you."

We were talking and laughing between dances when the burly chested boy approached.

"Care to dance," he asked me?

"No, thank you."

"You'll shag with me."

He reached out and as I stepped back, he tore the shoulder strap from my blouse.

"El fungula," I blurted in anger.

"What's that mean," asked the jerk, still holding my blouse?

"I'll tell you," whispered Sumter.

He pivoted quickly and hit the boy with a cross handed chop over the bridge of his nose. Blood spattered all over the pine.

Then he pivoted the other way, dashed twenty feet or so, and hit the Captain and the Colonel square in the chest. He knocked them straight backward, off the sill and into the marsh.

The smile was gone from Frog's face. He grabbed two boys from the Palatine in head locks against his enormous chest. He ran straight to the open door, flipping them head over heels into the parking lot.

Their companions took their brown bags and scurried after them.

Frog picked the burly chested lout off the floor. He jammed a putrid damp bar rag over his nose.

"Get the hell out of here, boy," he roared, "until you learn some manners. If you ever come back I'll kick your ass all the way to the Georgia border, and stop in Charleston and wipe that whole bloody school off the face of the earth."

The whole thing couldn't have taken more than five minutes.

Sumter and Sheila didn't dance any more that night. We sat on the porch just listening to the beat.

Sumter put a protective arm around my shoulder.

"Are you all right, gumbah?"

I could feel the strength of the frail farm boy. I could feel the loneliness of his soul.

Many boys had put their arm around my shoulder. But I had never had this feeling.

I looked into the lonely eyes.

"No matter where you are, Sumter, remember, I'll always be praying for you.

Find your peace, Sumter boy. Find your peace. My prayers will always be there."

"You and Miss Sarah," he answered softly. "You and Miss Sarah.

I appreciate your kindness, Joanie. You invited me to breakfast when I needed food for my soul. You will always be in my thoughts, Joanie, in a special way.

I have hills to climb and pathways to walk that may not be the most pleasant. That's the way it is.

But I'll always remember you."

We sat on the pavilion's porch and listened to the music as it drifted into the night.

Sheila walked the beach with Sumter the next night. He was to leave the next morning for Fort Bragg. They just walked the beach holding hands. Sheila had feelings for him that she had never had.

The tide was out. The creek into the marsh was little more than knee deep.

"That's Deb-I-do on the other side," said Sumter. "Would you like to cross over?"

He held her hand as they crossed the waters. They stopped in the middle and embraced. They spoke to each other in unspoken words, a boy and a girl, and the beach and the sea.

They knew not what tomorrow would bring, or if they belonged to one another.

They knew not what the fates and the fortunes held for their tomorrows.

They stood in the shallow creek and embraced. There were no fears. There were no hopes. There were no dreams.

There was only a maiden and a spirit of youth.

Frog brought Sumter by in the morning. His bulging knapsack was in the bed of Frog's truck.

"Had to come by and say goodbye, gumbahs. Couldn't leave without seeing you."

He was dressed in his uniform. Starched khakis were bloused in his boots. Two rows of medals shone on his chest.

"See you in twenty years," he said as he waved goodbye.

We watched silently as the truck drove away, weaving the narrow road beneath the marsh and the sea.

We each had our thoughts.

We all knew where he was going.

It had been an ever long time, an ever long time, such I had such a feeling of loneliness.

I broke the news on the train going home. I had been quiet most of the trip. In fact, all of us were worn. It was slumber and look out the window time.

"Gumbahs," I started.

"After we get home, in the beginning of September, I am going to enter the convent. I am going to become an Ursuline nun."

I had to say it quick and straight out. I had never spoken the words to anyone.

"I have had many talks with Sister Marcetta this past year. I have seen the joy of the convent in her eyes, her special love of God. She says it continues to grow when you are in the convent. It just continues to grow."

Did God call you," asked Peggy? "Did you hear His voice?"

"No. God doesn't have a voice like us. He only opens a door, gives you an opportunity. If you go through the door, you are following His call.

When I go through the door, I will be following His call."

They were all wide awake, peering into my eye.

There was surprise. I could feel their emotion.

And then Bridie laughed. Almost a guffaw.

"I don't believe it. The four of us, daughters of Erin, our grandmothers would dance in their graves if we became sisters.

Now, our paisan friend, her father smokes cigars and looks forward to her giving him many bambinos, she is called and we are left in the aisle."

They all embraced me. We all embraced, for that was all we could do.

I told Benny on my first day back to work. Two weeks notice to wrap up the ways of the world.

He pulled the car over to the curb.

"Are you sure, gumbah?"

"I have been thinking of it for a long time."

"That doesn't mean it is right.

Jesus, excuse me, Joanie, I never would have guessed it. I send you off to Pawleys Island and you come back looking like a million bucks, sharp as a tack. Then you floor me with this.

You know I love you, kid.

And I know you are following your heart."

I looked at him. It was the first time I did not notice the slight grin on his face. All I could see were the eyes of kindness.

He reached over and squeezed my hand.

I told my mother and Frankie in the evening. It was the hardest of all.

For I did not know their thoughts and dreams for me. I was leaving their nest.

They had given me everything they possessed. Always the kind word. Ever the softness of their arms. The songs, the feeling of ancestry.

And Frankie said, "Maria, our little chickadee is leaving the nest. They all leave the nest sometime.

It must mean we are getting older.

I will open the truck's window and sing as loud as I can tomorrow morning.

Sing like Mario Lanza. And someone will yell at the light, 'hey, pipe down.'"

"And you'll sing louder," said my mother.

Then they put their arms about me and gathered me to their bosom.

Frankie had a party for me the Saturday before I was to leave home. All the girls, his friends, my aunts and uncles and cousins were there.

Frankie wouldn't let me do any of the preparation. He prided himself on his cooking. He always said that when he retired from the truck he was going to open a restaurant.

I couldn't tell if he was happy or sad.

Peggy's father would have been overjoyed. He would have figured that God had chosen his daughter, not that Peggy had chosen God.

It was the question we had pondered since the eighth grade. How does God call you? Or do you call God?

It was Sumter's quandary. Were his Gods calling him? Or was he making himself available to serve?

Benny sensed my feelings. He was my kin, my very special gumbah.

"Are you sure," he asked me again?

"I am sure."

"Just checking, sweetheart. I can't call you squirt anymore."

I could only smile.

"But I'll tell you something, paisan, something I promised to tell you a long time ago."

"What's that, Benny?"

"I'll tell you who Father Donnello is, if you promise to keep it to yourself."

"I promise. I'll take a vow."

He whispered it in my ear.

I ran over to Peggy, and we ran to Bridie, and we all went scurrying to Mary and Sheila. We had our heads together like the girls on the swing.

"All this time, bullshit," said Bridie, in mock condemnation. "All this time they played us for twerps. Sister Immaculata knew! Sister Alphonse knew!

It makes you lose faith in all of the saints."

"Hey, Joanie," Benny yelled, "can you keep a secret?"

We were all laughing.

"Do you think she'll be all right," Frankie asked Benny?

"Like a cat on a rug, Frankie. Like a two horse parlay in a two horse field. She's a good girl. You raised a good girl.

You can take the girl out of East Cleveland, but you can't take East Cleveland out of the girl."

Mary married Joey Corrigan. We had always known they would marry.

Sheila said it was written in the book of long ago. She was so much like her father. Keep the faith, but don't forsake the moon and the stars.

Joey was a planner. He had worked the railroad all the way through John Carroll. He had the stamina of a Jesuit.

"I am so happy, so fortunate," said the bride.

Joey had an army commission from the ROTC. He was to leave soon after the wedding.

Frankie brought six gallons of Deigo Red to the reception. He was true to his word.

I was there. Mother Superior gave me a break and let poor postulant Joanie go.

It was a period of change. The nuns had forsaken their habits. I was wearing a knee length skirt with the whitest of blouses.

Oh, how I loved to dance. I danced with Frankie. I danced with Peggy's brothers, Bullet and Shoe.

"You'll never stay in," said Bullet. "Those Mick nuns will throw you out. They're prejudiced against Italians."

"They didn't like you, and you're Irish," laughed Shoe.

"They never got to know me."

"They knew you too well. They knew you too well," laughed his brother.

It was a true Irish wedding. The young men jammed the bar. The girls danced with each other.

"Look at your father, Frankie," said Shoe. "What a jerk. He brings home made vino to Mary O'Brien's wedding. I'm a truck driver, same union. And he wouldn't give me a glass of water when I got married.

What's with your father, Joanie?"

I couldn't stop laughing the whole evening.

But there was the real world.

Joey Corrigan went Vietnam for a year. Mary was pregnant before he left. She had twin girls before he came home.

Joey was lucky. He came home in one piece.

It was a period of change. It was a period so quick and so instantaneous that few saw it happening or could give the reasons why.

We were all adrift in our own little globes, while the life we had known seemed to vanish forever.

The nuns had changed their habits. The altars in church were turned around.

Some blamed it on the invasion of the Beatles and the Stones.

More women were in the work place. More Blacks moved into East Cleveland. The whites moved out farther.

College students walked the streets in protest. Students were shot at Kent State, a stones throw from Cleveland.

Some blamed it on the National Guard.

Our brothers and friends came home in body bags. Others came home broken.

There was no one to blame.

Euclid Beach closed. There was no more Laugh in the Dark, a place to steal a kiss.

Sheila and Bridie and Peggy followed Mary into wedded bliss. They weren't the marriages their mothers had known.

A man's wage no longer supported a family. They bore their children, then scurried back to their jobs.

The boys came back from Nam. They were alone and forgotten. There were no parades or distinguished monuments. Many times there were no jobs.

Fewer boys were entering the priesthood.

Fewer girls were entering the convent.

"Jesus," said Bridie. "Why don't they ordain the nuns? They are as holy as the priests."

Everybody did their best.

Benny died with East Cleveland. He was one of the few whites left in the old neighborhood.

He never lost his zest for life. He always went with the flow.

The girls were raising what they called rug rats.

Benny was taking in the ill and the forgotten.

He came by to see me at St. Paul in Euclid in the spring of '77.

"Hello, paisan," he greeted me.

"Benny, how are you?"

"Still in the old house. Just thought I'd come by to see you, shoot the breeze a bit."

"Are you down in your luck? I hear you are not working much."

"I get by. I don't need much. A few of the guys come by and see me once in awhile. Two ex-marines stay with me. Guys come and go, stay a month or so.

It's a big house.

I must be on a national directory. They find me. Or I find them."

"Are you drinking much?"

"No more than I ever did, Sister Joanie.

I hear they are closing the school at St. Phils. This is its last year. The church will stay open."

"I know. It is sad, Benny. There are not enough sisters to staff all the schools anymore. There are not enough Catholics at St. Phils. It's a shame.

A lot of the sisters have left the convent. We lost twenty in Cleveland in the past year."

"Drummed out?"

"What's that, Benny? I'm only a poor sister and you've always had this crazy language."

"When you screw up in the Marine Corps, when they let you go, I mean. But I know that none of the sisters would screw up. The Marine Corps drums you out."

"You never change, paisan," I smiled. "You'll never change, Benny. You and the Marine Corps. I can still remember you singing the Marine Hymn to me.

Here I am trying to keep the second graders straight, going out of my head, and you are drumming out us poor nuns.

You bring back so many good memories."

"That's all we are, Sister Joanie," he grinned, the grin I'd always remembered. "That's all we are Sister Joanie, old tunes and memories, old tunes and memories."

Benny died one year after the school closed. Even the embalmer couldn't wipe the smile from his lips.

It was like he knew something that nobody else knew. Nobody had ever heard him say an unkind word.

God took him in his bed. He fell asleep at night. He never woke up.

The wake was wall to wall. All the old biddies were there. Peggy's older brothers were there. The crowd from the Lakeside was there.

"Benny was one age with my oldest," said Peggy's mother. "It's a shame he never did settle."

I was there with Sister Marcetta. She was the prettiest nun in the Order. You could see the love of God in her eyes.

"Sister Marcetta is going to be leaving Cleveland next year," I told the girls. "She is brushing up on her Spanish. She is going to help the diocese open a school in El Salvador."

"I hope I can learn the language," said Sister Marcetta. "I haven't studied real hard since long before I had you girls at Sacred Heart.

Now look at you. You are all doing fine.

Sister Joan tells me that some of your children are almost old enough for her to teach. Time sure has a way of moving on."

"I have twins in the first grade at Holy Cross," smiled Mary. "I wouldn't send them to Sister Joan. She'd probably have them shining the floors."

"Those were the days," I laughed.

"Benny once told me, God rest his soul, that all we were, were old tunes and memories. In his own way, he hit it pretty close to the button."

He was right. The girls were just like their mothers at the Irish picnic, or spreading what they had called the Mayo news. Our youths were the happiest of days.

Our lives had changed.

Mary had Smoky Corrigan, who drank enough to bother her and was as nervous as a cat's tail. He was forever planning for the future.

Sheila had her Tommy, who ran a gas station, and thought the sex drive was a new type of automatic transmission.

Peggy had been on the verge of leaving her Al once or twice, but her mother would have died of shock. She finally talked him into trying A. A.

Bridie had to hide the purse from her old man, or he would spend everything they made on gadgets. He had stereos he never played. He bought an upright piano he couldn't play either.

He was thinking of taking flying lessons.

"Jesus, I hope he buys enough insurance," Bridie once said. "He even wants to take me up in the air. I think he's nuts."

"Sister Joan always had Benny in her prayers," said Sister Marcetta. "Benny, and another young soldier, I think you met in South Carolina, someone named Sumter."

"They were our gumbahs," I said with fond remembrance. "They were our friends."

We all smiled. Those were the days my friends, those were the days.

Sister Marcetta was a blue eyed Italiano.

Frankie once kidded her, "I have to watch your blue eyed brothers. They'll steal your eye teeth."

She was Napolitan. Her kin were from the hills around Naples. In Roman mythology, the women of Naples were considered most fair, to be sought and cherished for their virtue and their diligence.

"Why are you going to El Salvador, Sister," asked Bridie? "Aren't there enough hooligans around here to teach?"

"I sometimes ask myself the same question, Bridie. Maybe I have a little bit of Benny Maloney in me. He was a good man, taking in the poor soldiers and all.

God knows, it's going to be a change. I love teaching.

But I hear God calling me to the missions. Maybe that's the best explanation. I think I hear His voice. He is calling me."

I thought back to the question Sheila had asked Sumter so many years ago.

"Why are you going back?"

And he answered, "They are my friends. I hear them calling me."

Sheila thought back to the girl standing in the shallow stream, holding and being held. It was only a moment in time.

She wondered, 'what if, if we had crossed over to Deb-I-do.'

"A penny for your thoughts," I asked?

"It's time to get home to Tommy," she answered. "The kids drive him nuts. He changes clutches all day, but he won't change a diaper."

Sheila was working in the office at TRW. It had been Tapco when she arrived more than a decade before.

Peggy was in a doctor's office. Bridie was working for the County Auditor, hoping the Democrats would never lose.

Mary did book keeping for Smoky in her spare time. How she found spare time I'll never know, with four scallywags under the age of seven. They never went dancing anymore. Smoky preferred drinking Buds and watching games on TV.

My father had been right. Johnny Flaherty had been right. We did pick up the attributes of our relatives, mostly our mothers.

We girls would get together three or four times a year. We would drive our kids out to Geauga Lake one Saturday each summer. We would ask Sister Joan, but the school kept her too busy.

It wasn't Euclid Beach, our land of enchantment, but it was our children's land of enchantment.

They had their days and their dreams. In many ways they were similar to ours.

The days of wide porches and spindles were gone. No longer did the boys kick the ball in the street. There was no Ripples, where you could get a dime coke and chat for an hour.

Parcheesi and checkers had gone the way of the jukebox.

We were their mothers. We drove the car, took them to McDonalds, and even had to drive them to the library.

The kids played video games which we did not understand. They had computers in the third grade, while we had been troubled with pencils and erasers.

We did not understand their music. They did not know who the Lettermen were, or Johnny Mathis, or Neil Diamond, or Patty Page. If one of us was listening to a tune in the car, they would hit the button as quick as a cat, and be shakin and jivin like apples in the wind.

"Jesus, these kids are driving me nuts," said Bridie. "If you buy them jeans, they want to cut out the knees. If a blouse isn't baggy, they won't wear it. They want to dress like bag ladies."

"We used to have hand-me-downs," laughed Peggy. "The biggest kid would get new, and then it all would be passed down."

"These blokes would crap," said Bridie.

"I remember one Christmas," said Peggy, "when my brother Shoe got Bullet's old shoes. My father had even put new cardboard in the sole.

Shoe wore them to church in the snow. And then he came home and complained to my mom, 'ma, dad didn't put enough cardboard in.'

That's how he got his name."

New York Central closed its railroad yards. National Acme vanished. Murray Ohio quit making bikes.

The Ursuline Sisters even closed Sacred Heart.

We girls were more secure in our jobs than our husbands.

"Are we still going back to Pawleys in '86," asked Mary?

"You bet your butt," answered Bridie.

"What will we do with the kids," I asked?

"Let our old men take care of them," said Mary. "I can just see the twins picking up after Joey. It will teach all of them a little bit about life."

"We'll walk in the bog," mused Peggy. "We'll get some wide brimmed straw hats like them southern biddies wear."

"We'll get some of those nets," I said. "We'll go casting for shrimp, just the four of us."

"It won't be the same without Joanie," said Bridie. "It won't be the same."

We all felt the same way. It wouldn't be the same.

But we had our world. Sister Joan had her own.

Our world was rapidly growing. We had husbands and children. Our children would have their children. That was the way of the world.

Joanie's world was quickly vanishing. There were only three or four nuns in most of the parishes.

They were overburdened with the work of the schools. The classrooms were dotted with lay teachers.

I wondered if the nuns still made a few kids steel wool the floors. I wondered if a flock of the sisters still went to baseball games.

Chapter 5

Feel

When Ronald Reagan was elected President, my father gave full credit to Pat O'Brien.

"Sheila if it wasn't for Pat O'Brien, when he was playing Knute Rockne in the movies, Ronald Reagan would never be President."

Johnny Flaherty liked to tell stories. He was other worldly. He never put my kids on his knee, but he would talk to them as if he were one age with them.

"Yes, it was Pat O'Brien who put the Gipper in the White House. When a bunch of young actors were trying out for the role of George Gipp, kicking and throwing the ball, running all over the field, O'Brien told the director to give the job to Reagan.

That bounce of the football made Reagan in politics. He was tied into Catholic mythology, the Golden Dome of Notre Dame. It was like being mentioned in the Litany of the Saints."

Ronald Reagan brought his own people to power. He was distrustful of the Ivy Leaguers who had served former Presidents. He brought his own kitchen cabinet, power brokers from California.

He was enamored by the military and the CIA. He appointed young officers from the Vietnam conflict to the National Security

Counsel. Both the agency and the counsel worked covertly with secrecy and stealth.

If anything went wrong no one could blame Reagan, for he was tied to the Litany of the Saints.

I was overwhelmed. I had to work hard to keep up my vitality. I had to pray harder to keep up my spirit.

No longer were there nuns in each room of the house. No longer was there gossip and chatter around the great table. No longer did each nun know of each child in the school.

The lay teachers took their tales home in the evening. We sisters spent our evening in quiet solitude.

There were not as many shoulders to lean on. The sense of community was going the way of the factories and the railroad yards.

The agency had been on the Waccamaw Neck for more than forty years. No one knew it was there.

It had come during the days of World War II. Few knew it was there. Few knew it had stayed.

During the early days of the century, the old rice plantations had become the pastoral getaways of the wealthy.

Bernard Baruch had gathered16,000 acres called Hobcaw Barony. Tom Yawkey of the Red Sox gathered a lesser estate. The Vanderbilts owned more than 6,000 acres. The Huntingtons acquired more than 7,000 acres.

The soldiers came during World War II, to ride the beaches on horseback, and watch the Atlantic for foreign submarines. The navy came to practice gunnery on slow flying drones.

Winston Churchill came to Hobcaw during the 30s, to shoot southern quail and mix his scotch with the beauty of the marsh.

President Roosevelt came to Hobcaw in '44, in the last gasp of his life, to reinvigorate his energies and plan for the storm at Normandy.

The agency stayed unobtrusively, buying a plot of land here, a plot of land there. It bought in hard cash. It held title under obscure names; Creek Development co. , Long Pines, etc. The companies paid their taxes by mail.

The intelligence community was well hidden beneath the boughs of the oaks. It was well hidden on the peninsula between the river and the sea.

The CIA had two cottages on Pawleys Island. They were small cottages, built in the style of the beach, standing a row or two from the ocean.

Pawleys was a perfect cover for whatever the activity might be. Most of the cottages were occupied only by summer tenants, a week or a two at a time. People could come and go with nobody knowing their name.

The year round residents had a name for the other three seasons of the year. They called them, 'after the coast has cleared', when the beach was occupied by only the gull and the lone fisherman. The island was almost devoid of human activity.

The Neck was a perfect sanctuary for the agency. It was only an hour drive from the Charleston Naval Base. Three hours to the north were the Special Forces at Fort Bragg and the Marines of Camp Lejeune.

Visitors could come as vacationers by car. Others might sail in motorized yachts from Annapolis or DC, and tie up in the harbor at Georgetown.

Others might come in by small boat from ships at sea. They could come in through Georgetown's Winyah Bay, and tie up at one of the many fishing docks in the creeks along the river.

I looked forward to the letters from El Salvador. I knew that Sister Marcetta was sometimes too busy to write. There was more to her world than writing letters. But, oh, how I looked forward to those letters.

1980____

The village of Dia Ablo is the center of the parish. Six other villages are served by our parish. Father Daniel of the Maryknolls does his best to serve each village, but if he visits each one in two months he says it is only by the grace of God.

He drives an old land rover and wears a wide brimmed straw hat, so you would take him more for an adventurer than for a priest from Chicago. He carries medicines and what supplies he can fit in the truck, but there is never enough for those he visits. He has been in El Salvador for sixteen years and says, 'if I stay a thousand it will not be enough.'

He greets each day with a smile. He smiles through the humidity. He smiles through the storm. He greets the aged like they were long lost family. He has a kind word for each child, and greatly encourage we sisters in the work of the school.

The agency had no options. They could not carry on their most discreet endeavors in official Washington. There were too many leaks. They could not go to the committees of Congress for there would be fire and furor.

So they joined the hawk, and the osprey, and the eagle; the great birds of prey that nested in the pines. They set up shop in their safe havens along the Neck, and made plans to stem the moon and the tides.

1981___

There are six of us sisters at the most, sometimes only three or four. We have an infirmary aside from the school. The people love attention. The supplies of medicine are so short, sometimes all we can offer is a smile like Father Daniel, or a squeeze of the hand, or a rub of the shoulder.

A doctor comes about every three weeks. He stays but a day or two. His truck is almost as old as Father's land rover. I don't see how they do it. Only by the grace of the Almighty.

There are railroads to serve the coffee and sugar plantations, to take crops to the sea. No transportation was laid out to serve the people of the villages.

The profit of their labor was never returned to the people. They travel rutted roads, sometimes mired in water and mud, to come to the infirmary.

They show appreciation for everything we do.

Say a prayer for them tonight.

I felt inadequate when I wrote to my friend. I felt guilty. I couldn't tell about the drugs that had invaded the school. I couldn't tell her about the police that had found two eighth graders breaking and entering. I couldn't tell her that the Catholic grade schools were becoming a haven for students whose parents were trying to dodge the busing integration of the public schools.

I couldn't tell her of my growing doubts of my own vocation.

The agency had a global plan. It was far reaching. It was well thought out. The agency had been given a special mission, to confront Communism all over the world.

The men chosen for the community along the Neck were true believers.

Some had graduated from Annapolis, had served a term or two in Vietnam. Others were recruited out of the Special Forces, veterans of the Rangers and the Air Cavalry.

All were cold warriors. All believed that that Vietnam had been lost because the United States had lacked the will to stand face to face with communism.

Their favorite movie hero was John Wayne.

All were trained in covert actions and secrecy. They were a bit amoral in their endeavors, believing that the end justifies the means. It was written in their Bible.

1982____

There are people we are afraid of. The country has come almost to civil war. Peasants have revolted in the hills. This was once such a peaceful valley. I can hear the guns in the night.

They get their arms and support from Nicaragua. A group from Nicaragua has joined the peasant forces.

The established government is fearful of a group called the Contras, (counter revolutionaries). They put fear into anyone who does not side with them.

They have symbolic tattoos on their left forearms, arrows pointed backwards. I believe it is their view of the world. They have labeled all the missionaries as leftists or communists.

They have even cut the tires on Father Daniel's land rover, shutting him away from the other villages. The people still come to us in the infirmary, but we have little to offer but hope.

The children are as they ever have been, with radiant smiles and the joy of their youth.

Remember them in your prayers tonight.

President's Reagan's kitchen cabinet were men of a different order. Their interests were more in the commerce of the nation. They were Wall Street bankers and self made men. They understood the value of the gold and the lucre.

They understood that if they allotted more wealth to the few at the top, more would trickle down to the middle class and the poor. They gained a great tax break for the wealthy. The masses waited for the lucre to trickle down.

They found the word 'deregulation' in the sacred pages of their Bible. They deregulated the trucking industry. They deregulated the railroads. They deregulated the airlines. They even deregulated the banking industry and the savings and loans, so that the flow of funds might move with their tide.

The men of the agency were not interested in domestic commerce. They sought to preserve the countries of South Americas from communist takeover.

They formed arms cartels, sending weapons to the Persian Gulf for lucre and gold.

They multiplied and expanded their booty, sending arms and assistance to the Contras in El Salvador, taking back poison and drugs from South America.

This bounty could be bartered in the ready market of the great American cities. Few would be the wiser.

1982____

Pietro and Angelica have been coming to the clinic for more than four years. She has had two operations for cancer. Pietro brings her bi-monthly for a physical check. I think they come as much to see Father Dan and we nuns as for the check up. They always bring flowers and vegetables from their garden.

They always came by donkey cart. They came in walking last week. The Contras had shot their donkey. They accused them of bringing support to the communist clinic.

What are we to do?

The Contras are more open now. They carry American rifles. They stand in the square of Dia Ablo firing them into the air.

They stand outside the clinic shouting lewd remarks at me and the other sisters.

Remember us in your prayers.

My Tommy lost his gas station. He had it for nine years. It was a Sohio station in East Cleveland. Sohio merged with British Petroleum.

The Brits wanted a station that just sold gas; and peanuts, and milk, and shampoo. Tommy was a whiz at general auto repair at reasonable prices. We weren't getting rich.

Now his black customers would have to go to Firestone or Goodyear, pay the corporate piper.

"Trickle down, shit," said Tommy. "It looks more like gobble up to me."

The funny thing was, we seemed happier after the station was gone. No more worrying over the books. No more not getting paid for this favor or that.

Tommy got a job with Harrigan Brothers. He became a painter, with a little bit of floor work thrown in.

"I did that a long time ago," I teased him, "me and Mary, and Peggy and Bridie, and Sister Joan."

"The five of you couldn't bake a cake. You and your notorious adventures."

I thought back to the times I had thought of packing the bag. I thought back to what the stranger had told us when we first bought groceries at Pawleys.

"Cook it low, cook it slow," maybe that was what life was all about.

Bud Sweeney was in charge of the beach houses for the agency. He was a graduate of the School of Hotel Management at Cornell University. He couldn't tell his wife how he was using his degree.

The agency was set up in small groups or cells. All knew a little bit about their specific area. Group leaders knew a little more. By the time you got to senior officers and directors, all the information had been assimilated. Strategies could be formulated. Decisions could be made.

Bud Sweeney was known as Mike Taggart on the Neck. For as far back as locals could remember, the Taggarts had owned the cottages.

The Taggarts had developed a mythology of their own. Mike's grand daddy had built the cottages years ago. He had made his money in Camden, in the hardware and farm equipment field.

Mike's daddy had looked over the cottages for years. Then his brother took over. Then Mike's older brother had taken charge. Mike took charge of the property in the late '70s.

The islanders mourned when Mike's grand daddy passed. They even sent cards of condolence to the Taggart's post office box in Camden. They received sweet thank you notes from the Taggart family.

The Taggart's used the beach cottages as part of the family business. Salesmen and suppliers would come and go. They could study new products. They could plan for new markets.

1983____

There is a blood bath in the country. Churches are being pillaged in some villages. People are being chosen, here and there, and executed.

A Jesuit priest was shot in his car. Father Daniel has told us not to leave the area around the clinic. The men with the arrows are drunk with their power.

The Jesuits and the Maryknolls have been here since the turn of the century. The country is 80% Catholic.

Father Dan says the storm will pass. It has never passed for these forgotten people. I feel so sorry for them.

Personally, I feel safe, held as the Irish say, held in the palm of God's hand.

Remember us in your prayers.

Sister Marcetta came home to Cleveland in the spring of 1984. She came home in a special evacuation plane supplied by the American Red Cross.

She had been walking in the plaza on a peaceful and beautiful day, when the Contras chose to put the fear of the Lord into the peasants of Dia Ablo.

There were about a dozen of them. They came to the plaza in American made jeeps. They sprayed the plaza with bullets. Two men were hit.

When Sister Marcetta went to give aide to one of the men, her skull was cracked with the butt of a rifle.

Sister came home to the Cleveland Clinic.

Stories of the tragedy were all over the papers.

Words from her letters appeared in the papers.

Appeals were made to Congressmen and Senators. The Council of Catholic Bishops asked questions of authorities.

They received no concrete explanations.

"If there was trouble in El Salvador, it was because of native unrest."

"It was inspired by communist agitators."

In the National Security Council they knew what was going on. Down on the Neck they knew what was going on.

Bud Sweeney was up to his pockets in the thicket. He was counting the bodies, just as he had done for McNamara two score years before.

He had a feel for the job.

Chapter 6

Seem

I waited until Sister Marcetta was on her way to recovery before I told her I was leaving the convent. We were sitting in the visitor's lounge of the Cleveland Clinic, overlooking Euclid Avenue. We could see the first winter snow through the panes.

"I'm leaving the convent," I said to my friend.

"Why? Why, Sister Joan?"

She was regaining the olive tone of her skin. The first speckles of white were beginning to show in her hair.

"Why are you going, Joanie. You have done so much. You have so much to offer."

"Maybe I can't offer enough. Maybe I don't have enough to offer.

I have loved the convent. You know that. I have prayed for years that I could love it more.

Maybe it's just the changing of the seasons, the winter doldrums of my passions.

Maybe I'm just burned out with carrying the load at the school. You are the one who should be burned out, but you love God more than ever. I can see it in those blue eyes of yours.

Yours are shining. Mine have dulled.

That's all there is to it, Sister. That's all there is."

I told Frankie and my mother the next evening.

They wrapped their arms around me.

"Everything is going to be all right, Joanie," he whispered. "Everything is going to be fine."

We all went to the Dobama Theater one snowy night in February. It was the first time the five of us had a chance to be together since I had left the convent.

The Dobama was in the Heights, only a stones throw from the Hill and East Cleveland. It was in a cosmopolitan area, populated by nurses and interns from University Hospital, and students from Western Reserve University.

Cleveland had a great reputation for community theater. The Dobama was among its finest. It was located in a nondescript block of older buildings, only a small sign at the door, leading down the stairs to the basement stage.

The Plain Dealer had given rave reviews to the performance, Eugene O'Neill's, The Iceman Cometh.

".... Only the second time it has been performed in Cleveland in the more than fifty years since O'Neill first penned it....among the playwright's greatest works....only other local performance was at the Jewish Community Theater in the late '40s....length has detracted from its performance....four hour performance begins at 6:30."

The darkened basement was a perfect setting for the O'Neill drama. Fifteen or so rows of seats surrounded the stage. The lighting was subdued for O'Neill's masterpiece of forlorn hopes and dreams.

It was set in the Bowery of the '20s, only the drinking room of a flophouse. The characters sat around stain-covered tables, talking or sleeping, as they went on with stories of their yesterdays.

There was Jimmy Yesterday and Tommy Tomorrow, and a youngster who had left his dreams at the door. They chanted the sweet whiskey sotted melodies of lost dreams and faded hopes.

They were waiting for Hickey, the Iceman, the flamboyant salesman, who always encouraged them to pack their belongings and seek the fresh sunlight of hope.

I could have taken a seat at the table, laid my head in the moisture, and chanted my litany without missing a beat. They were me. I was them.

Perhaps that was the genius of the playwright.

When Hickey did arrive, he had left his dreams at the door. He took his place at the table.

The four hours went by in the wink of a lifetime. We were spent as we climbed the stairs to the street.

Six inches of snow had fallen as we sat in the basement. It had grown bitter cold.

"How about a corned beef sandwich and some coffee," asked Mary? "There is a great Jewish Delicatessen in the next block."

She was right.

The thin slices of corned beef were piled an inch and a half between the rye. The coffee mugs were steaming. The only condiment was a large quarter of kosher dill.

We sat in a large vinyl booth on the wall. There were college students with their dates. There were old men kibitzing.

"You know," I said, "Eugene O'Neill's mother was in the first graduating class at Villa Angela, out next to where Euclid Beach used to be."

Maybe it was the harshness of the chilled air, maybe it was just getting away from my ghosts, but I felt better and more refreshed than I had in years.

In fact none of us looked too bad as we neared our fortieth year.

I remembered our mothers, how they had seemed so old when we were so young. They wore laced shoes and house dresses buttoned down the front. They did their own hair, with the sweep of a bun and bobby pins tucked all over their heads.

They would have never thought to color their hair. They would be scandalized. Yet, their smiles were so wide and eyes were so bright, that it belied any age we thought they might be.

I remembered my mother's blue house dress with the flowers. She must have worn it a thousand times. It had the smell of yesterday's meal, and Sunday's lasagna. It had the smell of the wringer washer and fels naptha.

Yet, when she would hold me against it, against the folds of her loins, I felt like the safest sparrow in the nest.

I had often wondered about the children I was teaching, the lost and the lonely ones from broken homes. I wondered if they felt as secure as I once had.

"Her maiden name was Dempsey, I continued." Her father had a mercantile store downtown near the mansions of the wealthy. The Rockefellers and other grand families had large mansions along Euclid Avenue.

The girl, I can't recall her first name, was a first rate pianist. She was the apple of her father's eye.

Well, O'Neill, Eugene's father, came through Cleveland playing the Count of Monte Cristo. He was a first rate Shakespearean actor, but he found he could make a more luxuriant living playing the Count.

She was a senior at Villa Angela when she met Mister O'Neill. She ran off to New York and married him right after graduation."

"Sort of like Mary O'Brien and her Smoky," interrupted Bridie.

"Not quite," I had to laugh. "But maybe there is a bit of latent genius in the Corrigan household.

Anyway, she traveled the thespian circuit with Monte Cristo even when she became pregnant. O'Neill was rumored to be so cheap that he wouldn't even take her to a family doctor.

She gave birth to Eugene, her second child, in a dingy hotel in upstate New York. It was a painful birth. The doctor who came to her gave her several doses of morphine and a prescription for more.

O'Neill continued playing the Count, forsaking the actor he might have been. She continued taking the drug as often as she could get it."

"How do you know the story," asked Peggy?

"An old nun told me. Even the Ursulines have skeletons in their closet.

Well, the father was quite penurious. He was forever buying acres along the coast in Massachusetts.

Eugene was a feverous child. He was forever sickly. But he took to the sea when he was but a lad in his teens, stoking the furnace and chipping the paint.

He was an avid reader, studying the classics of the Greeks. He probably spent a night or two with Jimmy Yesterday and Tommy Tomorrow.

He had a latent talent. When he began to write drama, he wrote in the style of Grecian tragedy. He wrote about New England farmers, and the stokers on the ships, and the men of the Bowery who had given up chasing their dreams.

Then he wrote the drama of his own family, Long Days Journey into Night.

It is full of symbolism. The family is called Tyrone. In your Irish history, the O'Neills were the great chiefs of County Tyrone, driven from the land in the reign of Elizabeth.

The Tyrones live on a bluff overlooking the sea. The father has abandoned his hopes, taken solace in the bottle.

The mother takes her comfort from a bottle of pills. One son is sickly; the other is an alcoholic.

It is the purest of tragedy."

No one interrupted me, although I began to feel I was boring them.

Two old Jewish men sitting in the next booth were bending their ears, listening.

"Am I boring you," I asked?

"Go on young lady," said one. "It sounds like a tale from the Bible. There is nothing new in the world, not in five thousand years."

"In the final scene," I continued, "the mother is standing in the living room, listening to the ship's horn across the foggy sea.

'I remember,' she implores, 'the Virgin Mother standing in the waters.' Villa Angela had a statue of the Virgin standing on the shore."

"She was remembering happier times," said Peggy, "Just as we sometimes are. Those were her days and her dreams."

"So," I continued, "the sisters struck her name from the first graduating class of Villa Angela like she was never there.

Perhaps it wasn't their fault. They couldn't let one of their own be associated with pain and suffering and morphine. It was the time and the era."

"Have the sisters crossed your name from the record," asked Bridie? She was never bashful.

"No! No," I chuckled. "The sisters are my gumbahs, almost like you guys are. They are forever on the phone to me. They only wish me the best.

I know I can depend on each one of them, just as I have always known I could depend on each one of you.

I have known that since the second grade."

Frankie took an early pension from the Teamsters. We opened a restaurant up on Mayfield Road, where half the Italians in Cleveland had moved.

"I'll do the veal, the chicken, the steaks," said Frankie.

"I have some recipes from the south I'd like to try," I answered.

"Try them, try them, I'm not your Mother Superior," he answered while chewing on his cigar. "But no praying, Joanie. Hard work is our God. It has always been my God.

But I don't know if these gumbares will go for those southern delicacies. Southern Italy, Sicily, yes! South of Cleveland, no!

I'll bet you a fin they won't."

"How about a jukebox, Frankie? Have some oldies from the fifties, Nat 'King' Cole, the Everly Brothers, Fats Domino."

"Sure, Joanie, sure, anything you want. I'm only your old man, only an old truck driver. I'll bet you a ten spot they won't go for that either. What do you want to name the restaurant, Nascar Sock Hop?"

"No. I thought we'd call it 'Cipollas'."

I gave Frankie a kiss on the cheek and a big hug around the middle, just like my mother and he had always given me.

Within two months Frankie had to give me fifteen dollars out of his wallet. He tried to take it out of the cash register, but I caught him.

"Jesus, excuse me Joanie, but you surprised the hell out of me. This is supposed to be my retirement job. Now you are working the hell out of me."

I could only smile.

"Weren't you the gumbah who said work was your God?"

Then I squeezed the great palm of his hand.

Mike Taggart didn't like having the El Salvadorian contras at Pawleys. The heat of the battle was still in their blood. They would come in two or three at a time, from freighters headed for northern ports.

The agency had a 30 foot Sting Ray anchored in the Waccamaw. It had another 22 foot fishing boat anchored nearby. It had a few small jon boats anchored in Pawleys creek.

The contras loved to go fishing. Fishing was the only entertainment Taggart offered them. They were too undisciplined to let loose on the Neck.

But the agency had to put up with them. They delivered the goods from South America. They took military plans back.

No intermediaries could be trusted.

If any questions were asked, they were farm equipment purchasing agents from South America. They were enjoying a bit of beach hospitality from the Taggart Company, which was expanding its foreign trade.

Word came from Washington to look into the purchase of vacant land in Georgetown and Williamsburg Counties. They were among the poorest counties in the state.

Land could be purchased for a nominal price. Then the Taggart Company could draw up plans for golf courses and condo developments. Mortgages at inflated values could then be obtained from the newly deregulated Savings and Loans, institutions that were eager to expand into the coastal retirement and golf communities

It was part of the trickle down economic theory; expand and prosper, and the masses will gain their fair share.

One cottage was given to the architects and the land buyers to put the plan into effect. The schekels from the banks could then be used to purchase more arms for the fighters of communism.

It was a capital plan.

'Cipollas' hit the restaurant scene on the run. Diners were looking for lighter meals. Our salads and vegetable dishes from the south hit the ticket. They were a mixture of the beach and the soul, with a little bit of Italiano thrown in for spice.

I put a little bit of okra and a dash of mustard greens in, with a touch of crab meat or a little shrimp thrown over the top. Served on a bed of rice, with a few field peas thrown here and there, it proved an exquisite dish.

But it was the old jukebox and the music that made the place. Diners had tired of soft elevator music. They wanted to relive their youth, hear the songs they once danced to.

Frankie was amazed.

The Plain dealer gave our new restaurant rave reviews. Cleveland Magazine gave the salads and vegetable dishes four stars.

The teamsters came in. Middle aged boys from Latin and St. Joseph came in with their wives. The large Jewish community gave us thumbs up.

I even had a few of our recipes printed on the napkins.

"Are you crazy," asked Frankie? "Here we have a gold mine and you are giving away our secrets."

"It's not the recipes, Frankie," I answered. "It's what they call the ambiance. It's the music and the soul. It's a happy place.

People can forget their troubles, if just for a moment."

He shook his head.

"Jesus, Joanie, I think you're right."

The girls came out to 'Cipollas' the summer after we opened, the four of them and their husbands. Peggy's brothers, Bullet and Shoe came along with their wives.

Peggy had always said the two of them weren't packaged very tight. We all had known that since we were sitting on the swing.

Shoe was one of the biggest ball busters in the Teamsters, a union full of ball busters.

Frankie and I joined them at a huge round table. It was East Cleveland night.

The first words out of Shoe's mouth were to me.

"Any of these Deigos hitting on you, Joanie?"

"No bullshit," Frankie clamored. "I shouldn't have let you two goofy Micks through the door, but your sister vouched for you."

"Thanks, Peggy," said Bullet. "I just came to check out the menu.

Do you have any leg of lamb or Irish stew on the menu, Frankie? Maybe I could have my ma come up and show you how to cook."

"El fungula," roared Frankie. "We wouldn't serve that Irish garbage. Even the crows wouldn't eat it."

They were off and running and we hadn't been seated for five minutes.

Bullet went over to check out the jukebox.

"Hey, Frankie," he yelled across the room, "these are all old songs. Are you so cheap that the mob wouldn't give you any new ones.

You shouldn't even charge for these songs."

"Play My Wild Irish Rose," hollered Shoe.

"Doesn't have it."

"Danny Boy."

"Doesn't have that either. Doesn't even have Janice Joplin or the Pointer Sisters."

"I give up," laughed Frankie. "Quit bustin my balls.

If I knew I would have to put up with all this crap, I would have told Joanie to stay with the nuns, and I would have joined the priests myself."

Johnny Seeds visited me at the restaurant late in the summer. I had always known him as Uncle Johnny, although we were not related.

His real name was John Loparo.

Once when I was about eight or nine, I had asked Frankie why they called him Johnny Seeds.

"Because he knows where all the trees are planted, Joanie, sweetheart."

"Like Johnny Appleseed?"

"Yes, Joanie, like Johnny Appleseed in a way."

Johnny was a dapper man. I knew many dapper men, but none compared to Johnny. His shoes were always the shiniest. He never had a hair out of place. He was always dressed in the best of suits. It was if he had stepped from the pages of GQ.

He had been a salesman for a jukebox and vending company for as long as I could remember.

"Everything going well, Joanie," he asked?

"Hunky dorry, Uncle Johnny."

"You know, Joanie, the boys at the company didn't think this 50s stuff would work. You've proved them wrong. That, and those salads, sweetheart, you've got it."

"Thanks. Maybe we were just lucky."

"Maybe you were. But our phone is ringing off the hook. Half the restaurants in town are requesting the golden oldies."

"I hope you are saying 'no.'"

"We are, Joanie. We are. We owe you and Frankie one. That's the way we do business.

By the way, how is Sister Marcetta doing? Half the guys on the Hill went to school or worked with her father.

He was a blue eyed Napolitan, a sweetheart of a guy"

"She is doing fine, Johnny. Everyone's prayers have been answered. She hopes to go back to teaching in another year, if it is God's will."

"A bunch of the guys," he started slowly, "have been looking into what happened to Sister Marcetta. Guys in New York, guys in Chicago, guys in Washington, all wonder why this Italian sister got almost killed.

It's not just that they are whacking their own, but they are whacking the sisters and the priests.

We pay lawyers in Washington good money, Lord knows how much, to find out things. They don't find anything. There is what you would call a conspiracy of silence.

Nobody knows nothing. Nobody in Washington seems to give a damn.

They say they are fighting communism. We fought communism in Italy for decades, but nobody whacked the holy sisters."

I could only nod as I listened.

"We know that Sister Marcetta had written to you many times. You are her paisan. Were there any clews in her letters?"

"She said the contras had new American weapons. She said that they had backward arrows tattooed on their arms. Does that mean anything?"

"Made men," he answered. "Made men and secret deals, that's what it means. I've played the game a thousand years, Joanie. I know what it means.

Everything does not appear as it seems. That's life.

Some guys are called hoodlums. They are helping people, maybe get a job, maybe make a little more money for their family.

Other guys are called patriots, solid MF citizens. They are always taking things away from people; their money, their dignity their life.

Let me tell you this, Joanie, just between you and me and the lamp post. A contract has been let on whoever set this thing up.

Some SOBs have been horsing around, trying to curry a favor or get a bigger government pension. They have shit, excuse me, Joanie, all over the little guys.

Guys chase schekels and they forget where they came from. It is like a guy chasing horses or broads. He leaves behind whatever values he once possessed."

I was still nodding.

"It's the spook agencies that are doing it. If you should happen to hear anything, sweetheart, give me a call.

If anybody that you don't know comes in and asks questions about Sister Marcetta, give me a call, too."

"I will, Uncle Johnny. You can be sure of that. Sister Marcetta has always been more than a friend to me. She has been my gumbah."

The FBI had more than twenty wiretaps on the mob in Chicago. Their main interest was the Teamster's Central States Pension Fund, which had financed many of the casinos in Las Vegas. They also picked up titillating information on who was screwing who, who was screwing up, and sometimes who was going to be taken out.

When they heard of the pay back for Sister Marcetta they didn't know what they had.

"Where's Sister Marcetta," asked one agent?

"Is it a new casino," asked another?

"Wait till Jack Foley comes in," said another. "He's been chasing the Deigos for so long he can read their minds.

He may be too old for the street shit, but he knows them Italians and Jews like a book."

When Jack Foley came into the office the transcription was on his desk.

He was tall and gaunt and disheveled. He looked like he had been riding the el for three days.

He looked quickly at the transcription and roared.

"Jesus, Mary, and Joseph! Don't any of you assholes read anything but the comics and the sports pages?

Sister Marcetta was the Ursuline nun who was almost killed last year in El Salvador. Looks like the gumbahs want to play a little get even.

I don't blame them. It was some wicked cricket.

A friend of mine, Father Daniel Healy of the Maryknolls was in the same village.

He has been in the jungle almost two decades.

Don't get out the dictionary guys. A decade is ten years. Two is twenty.

Danny Healy was Loyola's last great two handed shooting guard, 1942 I think. He was as tough as scrap iron.

Then he went in the Marines, the big one guys.

He got the Silver Star and the Purple Heart at Gualdacanal. His brother, Billy, says he should have got the big one, the Medal of Honor.

He came out and joined the Maryknolls. Father Dan we call him. He just helps people.

It's called the Corporal Works of Mercy; feed the hungry, look after the sick, comfort the afflicted.

That is what this Sister Marcetta was doing in El Salvador, helping Father Dan.

It looks like the boys from the mob think the bureaucrats at the CIA were mixed up in getting her head almost bashed in. This message seems to say that."

"What do we do with the transcription," asked a young agent?

"Wire a copy to Headquarters, 'Top Security'," answered Foley. "If the Deigos are right, some of those tight assed bastards at the agency deserve to get hit."

The message from Chicago was at the FBI Headquarters that afternoon.

It was sent to the CIA immediately.

It was discussed in the National Security Council the next morning.

Word went out to Bud Sweeney on the Waccamaw Neck that the gang in Chicago had authorized a contract for whoever had been responsible for Dia Ablo.

He shrugged it off. No one had ever discovered the Taggart family business beneath the boughs of the oaks.

In Washington it was different. There were too many leaks.

Three young officers in the enterprise were told to take some of the lucre from the sale of arms for their own protection.

They each bought a modern security system for their homes; complete with lights, and sensors, and the ringing of the bells.

Bud Sweeney ordered the same system. Then he canceled it. His cover had never been broken.

Within a week the FBI Office in Cleveland was visited by two men from the agency. They had called ahead for an appointment. They requested that the Cleveland Office gather any information they could find on a Sister Marcetta, an Ursuline nun.

Mike Blackwell, a long time legend of the Cleveland Bureau, met them in his office. He had worked the mob for many a summer. He was a good friend of Jack Foley in Chicago.

Foley had called him about Sister Marcetta.

Mike could read the agency men. They spent too much time in their cubicles he thought. They were antsy. They were as friendly as two Dobermans.

The agents of the FBI were more gregarious. A lot of them, like Mike himself, were local boys. They knew the docks and they knew the streets.

They worked with the local police, and the Postal Inspectors, and the Federal Attorney's Office.

"How can I help you fellows," asked Mike?

"Whatever is said in this room is top secret," said the spokesman.

"I understand. I've been around the block a few times."

"We are looking for background information on Sister Marcetta, the nun who was injured in El Salvador."

Bud Sweeney sat quietly and let his partner do the talking.

"There's not much we could gather," answered Mike. "Putting together dossiers on nuns has never been a major work of the Bureau.

Why do you want this information?"

"We are investigating what happened."

"All I have are two pictures and some newspaper stories from the Plain Dealer."

The first was a picture of Sister Marcetta being wheeled on a gurney into the Cleveland Clinic.

"That was last year," said Mike. "I hear she is getting better."

The second was an older picture, taken many years before.

Bud Sweeney could just look at Jack Kennedy. He looked so young.

"Why this picture of President Kennedy," he asked?

"He was running for President then," answered Mike. "The picture is as I'll always remember him.

I was new to the Bureau then, doing security duty as he drove through town. The picture was taken on the lawn of old Sacred Heart Academy. It is torn down now.

Take a good look at that picture. It is all you wanted to know.

The young nun reaching out to shake Jack Kennedy's hand is Sister Marcetta. She was twenty-six years old. She has the most beautiful smile in the picture, even purer than that of President Kennedy.

That was Sister Marcetta then. This other picture is of Sister Marcetta now. She never hurt a flea. She always tried to help people.

Tell your bosses that is her complete dossier."

Johnny Seeds received a call at the vending machine company that afternoon. He was told two agents were in town. He was told what they were asking.

"Thanks," he said on the phone. "I owe you one."

Chapter 7

Smell

I had anguished for years about leaving the convent. I had anguished for a lesser time before I entered. That's the way I had always been. I had been born an anguisher.

It wasn't the way of my mother and father. They could take life as the moon glows.

It wasn't the way of my Italian heritage. They could make a banquet out of some peppers and some eggs. They could find joy in a few flowers in a vase.

Maybe that's why I got along so famously with Peggy and Mary, and Sheila and Bridie. They were in one step with life. They always had been.

They had always accepted me as I was. I was Joanie to them.

When I was a girl on the sidewalk, I was Joanie to them. When I entered the convent, I was Joanie to them. When I came out, I was still Joanie.

They were my treasures.

Sister Marcetta was the same, but in a different way.

She offered me hope. She offered me comfort. She gave me inspiration. All the Ursulines did in a way.

But gradually over the years, the dark anguishing clouds would reappear.

Maybe it was like Benny once told me, 'we were nothing but old tunes and memories.'

I felt that life should be something more.

I felt that somewhere, out there in the green of the fields, there was something more.

Perhaps responsibility came too early to me in the convent. The Ursulines asked me to be a school principal when I was barely past thirty.

Years before, when all the cots were full, a sister might be in her fifties before she was given this task. She would have friendships and the history of the Order to fall back on. She would be part of the community.

Those days vanished forever. Perhaps I would not have left if there had not been so much change. Perhaps I might have grown gracefully in the convent I first had known.

That I'll never know.

Johnny Seeds didn't shock me when he told me of the contract on those responsible for Sister Marcetta. It was the rule of the land of long ago,

There is a certain continuity, a sense of community in we Italians that does not change with time.

Some people don't understand it. Many of our people claim no knowledge of it.

Many of our people remember the days when our parents were looked down upon because of the broken English they might speak. Our fathers were not welcome at many jobs.

We remember the help of the men of silence, who opened up work for Italian truck drivers and dock workers, laborers and lathers.

The Irish had their own unions, the plumbers and the fitters. They fought the good fight to take care of their own.

Johnny Seeds and the others had done the same.

Their work was outside the realm of religion. Sometimes it was outside the rules of civility.

But each nationality has its own gospel, advancing slowly forward according to its own lights.

I was looking forward to the trip to Pawleys Island. The remembrances of the trip were so delightful.

Bridie said, "Let's take a full month in the fall, after the coast has cleared of tourists."

The others were all for it.

I wondered how they could be so carefree.

I had only a restaurant to leave. I had a father to look after it.

If I had a husband, and children, and a house to keep clean, and a job to go to, and school work to watch over; there was no way I could pick up and leave.

"That's why we are all going," laughed Sheila. "Next year in the fall we'll be walking the marsh and the beach at Pawleys.

They can be making the peanut butter sandwiches and going to McDonalds."

"We're almost forty," said Mary. "I've had almost twenty years with Smoky.

That's like perpetual Purgatory. You get the drift?"

"Sure," we all answered.

Two men came into 'Cipollas' late that summer. They asked to speak to me.

They were strangers. It's not that I had never seen them before that caused them to be strangers. They were different than all others that normally came in.

They had neither smiles nor frowns. They were as clean as a new dollar bill. They looked like life had never beaten them, nor had they ever laughed at life.

"I'm Joe Henry," said the spokesman. "We are with PBS, the Public Broadcasting system. We are getting together a documentary on the troubles in El Salvador. It will be shown early next year during a complete series on South American nations."

I could feel the chill in the air. They were antiseptic.

I could hear Rosemary Clooney singing, "a guy is a guy, whoever he may be," in the background.

I could tell they did not hear her plaintive wail.

I remembered the Lakeside Tavern on the rainy day so many years before.

My sandy haired paisan had smiled at the five of us and asked, "Are you from the police? Is this an inquisition?"

He was right on the money. Old tunes and memories were a part of us.

"We have heard that you received many letters from Sister Marcetta before she was injured."

"How did you hear that?"

"From other Sisters, from many that knew her. We thought that we might be able to study her insights to get a better view of the troubles in El Salvador."

"They were only light correspondence," I answered. "They were only the gossip of the day that travels among friends.

Once Sister Marcetta asked about a boy named Tommy Lee who entered the Trappist Monastery. She wondered how anyone could keep a vow of silence for more than twenty years."

I called Johnny Seeds after they had left.

"Thanks, sweetheart," he said. "I owe you one."

Marty Lupo was sitting at a corner table eating some ravioli. He was often there.

That evening he was in a card shop on the Hill. He was talking to an old man with dark glasses, who was leisurely puffing a cigar.

"I took a picture," he said. "These two MFs were talking to Joanie Cipolla.

It's a good picture. One of the best I ever took.

I had the camera in my napkin as I was wiping my lips. That Joanie makes some good sauce."

The old man nodded as he looked at the picture. He slowly relit his cigar.

"Never got enough matches," he said.

Then he took a Racing Form from the pocket of his jacket and folded the picture inside.

Sumter spent many evening's at Frog's place out on the Black River.

Frog never changed. Neither did his house by the river. It could be called old south, cluttered and unkempt, but in tune with its surroundings.

River oaks and tupelo trees framed the flowing waters. Marsh reeds and the flowers of the field each came in their season.

There was no reason to change. Nature dictated what man should do; sow or reap, plant or harvest. The seasons dictated which fish would run, which bait to choose, when the geese would come to the woods.

Frog worked with Sumter, or Sumter worked with Frog, or they both worked with Sumter's daddy. They all seemed one and the same.

Sumter had spent three tours in Vietnam.

In 1971 the voices quit calling him.

The fields of Carolina beckoned him home.

Maybe it was the dust and the heat. Maybe it was the solace of the shade beneath the great oaks. Maybe it was the sweat on his handkerchief as he wiped his brow.

Maybe it was the summer afternoon storm, the singing of the field crickets, the sparkling of the evening stars, or the sacred blue of the Carolina sky.

He walked out of the barracks at Fort Bragg one spring morning and knew it was time to leave.

He looked at the young men trotting past in perfect cadence. He looked at the copters across the field. He looked at the hardness of his hands, his daddy's hands, and knew they belonged to the soil.

"I'm leaving," he told his battalion commander.

"Are you sure, Top," the Colonel asked? "You could stay ten more and come out with a pension."

"I've thought about it. Many times I have thought about it, but it's time to get on with life, see where the path might lead."

Two weeks later he threw his duffel bag and a few suitcases in the trunk of the chariot of teal and cream.

He didn't take the interstate. He drove the winding two laners, through small towns, past yellow jasmine and purple wisteria.

He stopped at an old ramshackle house a few miles out of Kingstree. The windows had been broken and open for years.

The thick purple vines were in full bloom covering the siding and roof. He walked in and looked around, feeling the looseness of the floor.

He knew the world was right.

He searched through his scuffled wallet. He took out an old faded picture, a pink rocking chair against a pillar of brick. He put it back in its place and walked slowly to the car.

'Memories,' he thought, 'all we are is memories.'

Anthony Calabria was a lesser partner in Skinner & Hoehn, a Washington law firm. Its specialties were banking and bonds.

His mother had grown up on the Hill. His father had been an organizer for the Teamsters.

He had worked his way through college doing summer trucking jobs. He had worked as a Pepsi driver. He had worked on a cement truck. He knew what a sore back and sweaty shorts were.

Once in a while he would take care of a task for the Teamsters. It was in his blood.

Johnny Seeds called his house to set up the meeting. They met for breakfast at a Holiday Inn in Arlington.

"There's a picture of two guys in the envelope," said Johnny. "See if you can find out who they are."

"Quietly?"

"Quietly. As quiet as an undertaker. I'll give you a hint. They may be tied into the CIA."

"Anybody else looking?"

"Only us gumbahs."

Sumter and his daddy continued to buy land. They bought cleared fields. They bought woodland s and pine. They bought wetlands.

They were sort of the middlemen in nature's plan. They would lease the land to a farmer who would provide the labor and the machinery. The crop would provide for the farmer and pay for the machinery. The lease payment would pay the bank.

Nobody became extremely wealthy. That wasn't nature's plan. Yet, the Rutledge family had a few dollars left each year to finance more land.

Frog was just Frog. He could take care of any job.

He could size up a field and tell what the yield would be.

He had tractors, and back hoes, and well drilling equipment. He bought and leased the equipment like the Rutledges did the land.

He wasn't afraid of work. He could clear a forest of brush or hoe the straight line for tobacco or cotton.

If no work was on the horizon, he could be as happy as a jay bird fishing by the river.

"You still got that picture in your wallet," he asked Sumter one day?

"What picture is that?"

"The rocking chair, boy, the rocking chair. What other picture would you have in there."

"Sure I have it. It's like an old silver penny. You put it in a drawer and its there forever.

You never have to think about it. Its there."

"I was telling Alison Follett about it," said Frog. "She's sort of sweet on me."

"Sure, Frog. Alison has been sweet on a lot of guys. What's she married, three of them?"

"You got that right, boy. She leads them to the altar like calves to the pond. She's got a way."

"So, what's her interest in the picture, Frog. You trying to entice her with an old rocking chair?"

They could sit and talk by the hour. Sumter's daddy marveled at it. Their words were like warm spit on the fire, slow and sparkling, and quickly dissolved.

"You're like two wrens in a nest," he would say, "two wrens in a nest."

"Alison's between mates," said the big man. "She's got ants in her pants. She's going to open a shop down at Pawleys, down where they sell the hammocks.

Well, she's looking for a name to put over the door, something down home, like a joggling board or a casting net.

So inspiration hits me, like it does every so often. I say to her, 'how about the Pink Rocking Chair?'

I hold her in my arms and tell her the story of requisitioned love. It's like moonlight and roses."

"Its unrequited love, Frog. It is love that has never been answered."

"Well, Alison is almost in tears. She couldn't understand why anyone in love couldn't express it.

That's the way of southern Baptist women, they'll open their heart to even a stranger, let you know how they feel

She says if I can get the picture from your wallet, she'll do it in oil. Alison's quite a painter. She did portraits of all three of her husbands before she showed them the door"

"Maybe she'll paint you someday," laughed Sumter.

"And maybe my friend will fall in love again," answered the big man.

Tony Calabria had the patience of Job. That's why he was such a good attorney. Banking and bonds took patience. Deals had to be made and researched long before the paper came to market. Lawyers had to be close lipped.

The men in the photo were in their young to middle forties. They were trim, close cropped, and well groomed.

Either military or Ivy League he thought.

He began to research old college yearbooks. Mug shots the police would call them.

Once in a while Johnny Seeds would call.

"You doing any good?"

"Not yet."

"Keep looking," Johnny would say.

It was like looking for a needle in a haystack. Washington was full of trim fortyish guys.

He kept looking. Anywhere there was a picture, he looked.

He looked at photos of political gatherings. He looked at photos taken at the White House. He looked at photos of military and college reunions.

The Taggart Company's first land purchase was for almost two thousand acres between Andrews and Kingstree. The Taggart Company paid $100 an acre for the land.

It had been on the market for years. It was mostly pine scrub and wetlands. The Taggart Company paid hard cash.

Within weeks Mike Taggart was making arrangements for a large mortgage from a Savings and Loan in Texas.

Plans had been drawn up for an 18 hole golf course, an upper scale housing development, and about 1500 condominiums.

The Kingstree Courier wrote:

Softwoods will be developed by the Creek Development Corporation of Camden. It is a wholly owned subsidary of the Taggart Hardware company.

It will be the largest new development in Williamsburg County since before World War II.

A Taggart family spokesman said, "This is an ideal area for growth. We have been looking over this area for a lengthy period of time.

Softwoods will be a bridge between commercial center in Florence and the vast number of golfing communities in Myrtle Beach and along the Waccamaw Neck."

The Texas banking officials were totally impressed with the Taggart operation. They had a similar development near Colorado Springs, in which a totally new town was being developed.

"This whole inland area, forty to sixty miles from the ocean, is ripe for development," Mike Taggart told the bankers. "We have plans for two or three more communities. One will be south, near Moncks Corner. Another will be near Nesmith."

"No problem," said the banker. "Cotton fields to condos, these are the types of projects we have been looking for."

Within three months the Taggart Corporation had a line of credit for more than 30 million dollars.

"Deregulation is a wonderful thing," mused the banker. "Cotton fields to condos!"

Frog didn't miss much that went on in Williamsburg County. If a newspaper cost 25 cents, he would pay 35 cents for some good gossip. That was the way of small southern communities. Everything traveled by the wind.

There was nothing going on when Frog stopped by Softwoods to see what kind of work might be available.

There was only an old construction trailer with the Taggart Corporation sign on it.

"We're going to start with one building," said the man behind the desk. "It will be four row houses first. Then we plan to build two more buildings of four, then four more of four."

"Takes quite a while if you build like that," said the big man. "The paper said you were going to wheel and deal the whole thing, golf course, too."

"It's a long term project. When it gets bigger I'll give you a call. We'll need some of your equipment."

"I'll be around," smiled Frog.

Tony Calabria made one of the guys in the picture by sure chance. He had always believed in the fates and the muses.

Tony believed that if you turned enough corners, one day the sun would shine on you. He didn't mind the looking at the mug shots or doing the plodding detail work of banks and bonds.

He was a long distance runner, never quickening the pace, lest he would lose his stamina. He was not born to corporate law, like so many in the firm, but his tenaciousness and diligence had won him high marks.

His hands were those of a working man. His heart was that of a working man. He liked to stop on the street, talk to a cab driver, or a mailman, or a construction worker; shoot the bull for a few minutes.

It was his release. It was his touch with reality.

He tired easily of the daily conferences, the yellow legal pads, and the small memos that always crossed his desk. But they were the source of his house, his income, his children's welfare. They were the miles he had to run.

A smile, a quick 'hello', a nod of the head, a 'howyou doing'; they were the fresh breeze that made each day bountiful.

Johnny Seeds was that type of breeze. He didn't owe Johnny anything. He would never do anything illegal for Johnny.

Johnny was his touch with the Hill, his heritage, just as his hardened hands were his touch with his father.

Tony made the picture by talking to some construction guys. He didn't know their names.

"How's work," he asked two electricians on his way to lunch.

"Remodeling's the thing," said one. "Every doctor and lawyer is remodeling his office. It's the tax write offs."

"Thank God for us lawyers," laughed Tony. "at least we do some good."

"You a lawyer? Need any cherry paneling in your office or security around your house?"

"Do much of that?"

"Novello Alarms did three of the damnedest jobs, rush, in a hurry, about six months ago," offered one of the men.

"We couldn't figure it out," cut in the other. "They were small piss pots of houses, not the kind you would put ten thousand of security around."

"You never know," said Tony, "maybe they have the queen's jewels or are tied up in drugs."

"No," answered one of the electricians. "One guy was some sort of college professor. Said he was working on an important manuscript. Wanted to keep it secure."

"I think I know who you mean," said Tony. "In fact I have a picture of him in my wallet.

He is a friend of my brother. They were at lunch together about a year ago."

"That's him," said both men.

"Isn't it a strange world," chuckled Tony. "You never knows who knows somebody you know."

"What's with the alarm system," asked one of the men?

"He writes," said Tony. "But I don't know. Those college guys test a lot of shit. They test things at home sometimes.

You'll probably be installing one of those things in a girls dormitory some day, prevent a panty raid."

Something that Johnny Seeds told me bothered me. He told me that the guys were going to get even for Sister Marcetta. He told me there was going to be a hit.

I couldn't ask Frankie about it. There were things that he knew that we never talked about. There was a world of my own that we never discussed.

There was a wide universe that we shared, we loved, we gloried in. But each of us had our own little closets.

"Something bothering you, Joanie," he would sometimes ask?

"Nothing, Frankie," I would answer, or, "I'll tell you sometime."

We each knew we had our separate worlds.

Everybody has to find his own path. That is what life was all about.

Each of us had our own dreams, our own pains, our own sufferings, our own separate joys. We were linked together and we were separate. That's what life was all about.

In the convent, I could have my reliance on Jesus on the Cross. I could pray to His Father or to the Holy Ghost.

I could be like one of the Irish biddies in the back pew of the church, just fingering the beads, having a complete reliance on the spiritual.

But I had been around the corner enough to know that even the biddies had their woes. There were husbands who drank too much, or children that were ill, or the rent to be paid.

Yet, they had a faith in the beads that belied belief, and was always a source of strength.

I caught Johnny one day in the restaurant and took him back to the kitchen.

"Johnny, I've got to talk to you."

"Sure, sweetheart, everything okay?"

"It's been bothering me, ever since you told me about the getting even for Sister Marcetta.

She's doing fine now. She is making a good recovery. Nobody's going to get hit, are they?"

He smiled. He took my hand, squeezing it softly.

"Your conscience, Joanie?"

"Something like that."

"Maybe I shouldn't have said anything," he mused. "But I knew other guys were going to come by and ask you things about Sister Marcetta. It's how the game is played."

"Learn anything," I asked?

"We learned some things. We learned some things maybe the politicians and the bishops couldn't learn.

Don't you worry your pretty little head now, Joanie. We learned some things that had to be learned. The whole thing smells. That is part of what we learned.

Maybe we were just shaking some apples from the trees, seeing which way the wind blows. Seeing where the apples would land."

"That takes a lot of worry off my mind," I said. "Sister Marcetta is getting better. More violence doesn't help anything.

It's like the Irish say, 'let the dead bury the dead.'"

"Is there any other way I can help you," asked Johnny?

"I was thinking, me and my girl friends were going down to South Carolina in the fall. We were there 20 years ago after high school. It seems so long ago.

There was a country song I heard on that trip, Eddy Arnold with Let the World Go Away. Can you get it for our jukebox?

It would be such a great number to finish the day."

"Sure, sure, Joanie, anything you want.

For a moment I thought you were going to ask for, what did you say, 'let the dead bury the dead.'

I never did understand those Micks."

Sumter liked Alison's painting of the pink rocking chair. She had it hanging behind the desk in her office.

"Frog tells me you have been carrying that picture for more than twenty years."

"He's right. Twenty years this summer. It 's like it wouldn't go away.

I guess everything in my wallet's been turned over three, four times, lost some things, threw other things away. But the picture was like skin to me.

You know what I mean?

Now, you've done it more than justice. That's a wonderful painting, Alison.

Do I get half the profits from this store for helping you name it?"

"Sumter, boy," she charmed him, "if I had half the money you and your poor daddy got buried under the woodpile, I'd be ashamed to ask a poor girl for money."

"Just trying, Alison."

"Frog told me the story about the picture. That time must have meant a lot to you."

"I was just a lonely boy. There was a whole group of girls, you remember how the beach used to be.

They took me in, gave me a ray of hope when I needed it. Maybe it was only a teenage crush. They all helped me."

"Frog said you were partial to one in particular. I've been partial to many in particular, but only one at a time. You know the story."

"That's you, Alison.

I'm a little different. I was partial to one. She was so nice. But over the years I'd look at the pink rocker and I'd think of another.

She was the prettiest of the five. Joanie was her name. She was an Italiano.

One night she held my hands softly and said I would always be in her prayers. I needed that then.

Wherever I was, I would always know that I was in her prayers, hers and Miss Sarah's, who was over in Nesmith.

They carried me a long way. You'll never know how far."

Alison was touched.

"You know, boy, sometimes stories are written in the moon and the tides. That's how life is. The Greeks called it the fates and the muses.

I know that for sure. I've ditched three husbands waiting for my true love to come down the road.

You've kept your dreams in your pocket, close to your heart, Sumter Rutledge. Now that's an envious position to be in."

Jack Foley in the Chicago FBI Office was puzzled. No word on Sister Marcetta had been heard since it first came over the tap.

He called Mike Blackwell in Cleveland.

"Heard anything on the Sister Marcetta thing?"

"Not since those two limeheads came in from the CIA. Something is happening. I don't know what."

"You know that line we were listening on," said Jack. "The ginzos know which lines are tapped. They've been at this for a long time.

We never heard any hit business discussed on that line. It's been strictly pension plan and gossip.

Do you suppose they sent out a message as fodder for the cannon?"

"Like they're sniffing something out," answered Mike.

"Could be," said Jack. "They are wise old foxes. That's why they have lasted so long.

The agency guys sure showed up in a hurry. They got the message from Garcia."

Chapter 8

Sound

Mary took care of all of the arrangements for our trip. Managing Joey's office had been a great education for her. She was a stickler for detail. Between the office and her home, she had to be.

Mary was a bargain hunter. She loved to shop.

We all loved to shop, but Mary was passionate about it.

"Who'll make the reservations and everything," asked Bridie?

"Mary," we all answered.

"I don't have the time."

"Sure."

That's how it was. It was as we'd always been. The years had not detracted from our closeness.

Each of us had traveled different paths. Each of us had her own ventures, and joys, and sorrows. That, I was beginning to believe, was what the road was all about.

Mary called us together the first week of August. She gave us the complete itinerary.

"I got a deal. We have a five bedroom beach house starting the second week of September. The real estate agent said we can rent it for a month, for the price of a week and a half during the summer."

We were all impressed.

"Do we have to paint it," queried Bridie? "Like we did with Benny's pace."

"That was a trip," smiled Sheila.

"The rental agent says that everything shuts down on Pawleys after Labor Day. There are only a few locals and the fishermen."

"Sounds great," I said. "But won't you girls be homesick away from your families?"

"Like yesterday," answered Peggy. "Its all arranged, Joanie, like in the stars."

"We said we'd be going back twenty years ago," said Bridie. That is a lot of torn pantyhose. And we are going! We are ladies of our word."

Mary took out a thick manila folder and handed some stapled papers to each of us.

"Read them carefully."

"What's this," asked Peggy?

"Our schedule for the first week," smiled Mary. "Just read it."

The first page started:

Saturday	5 AM	Meet at Sheila's
	7 Am	Stop for breakfast in Canton.
	3PM	Stop at motel in Wytheville, VA.
	5 PM	Go out to dinner.

"This is worse than what the sisters would give us," roared Bridie. "My kids would laugh at me if I gave them a written schedule. Holy cow, Mary, it's the 80s."

"You did a great job with the reservations, girl," said Sheila. "But that's it. You've been leading Smoky around by the nose for too long."

"Gotcha," laughed Mary. "All the other pages are blank."

It was pure pleasure to be with them

We had all grown. We had all changed. Yet, in a miraculous way, we were all the same.

What had Benny said to Frankie on a happy day, ever so long ago?

"You can take the girl out of East Cleveland, but you can't take East Cleveland out of the girl."

We were bonded by friendship. We were bonded by love. We were bonded by memories.

"I'll have Frankie stuff us a big paper bag with salami, and pepperoni, and baseball bats of Italian bread," I laughed.

"We'll drive straight through," said Bridie. "The heck with a motel."

"I was only pulling your legs," said Mary. "I thought about calling Amtrak to see about taking a train."

"That would be too much," laughed Peggy. "I think we almost killed those old porters with all that dancing. I know it would kill me now.

But God, they were nice to us."

No one would think that Edward Blythe worked for the agency. He was known to the world as a scholar and a gentleman sailor. He had tenure at National University in Washington, teaching and doing research on Revolutionary History. He had a fine yacht, the Osprey, moored in the Potomac Basin.

His schedule at the University allowed him to teach only two quarters during the year. He could devote the summer and the fall to the sea and the agency.

For more than a dozen years he had been a gofer, a primary connection between the agency and the Taggart family on the Waccamaw Neck. He would sail the Osprey down the Atlantic coast, through the inland waterways, to the Carolinas.

Sometimes he would carry passengers. Sometimes he would carry messages. Sometimes he would carry packages.

He considered it the best of two worlds. He had both scholarship and adventure.

He didn't consider himself a patriot. He would have two grand pensions when he retired, one from the university and a better one from the agency.

He had the sole use of the Osprey, a motorized sailing vessel he could never afford, even in his dreams. He could use his leisure time in the Carolinas to study and research the mostly ignored southern campaigns of the Revolutionary War.

He wrote many widely accepted papers on the antagonists of the southern campaigns; the English General, Lord Cornwallis, and the Swamp Fox, Francis Marion. He was fascinated by the strategies of Marion, who held a superior force at bay for over two years in the Lowcountry of South Carolina.

His code name at the agency was Swamp Fox.

He did not curry favor with his southern contemporaries or his students. He would lecture them that the Civil War leaders, Robert E Lee and Stonewall Jackson couldn't hold Francis Marion's saber in the pages of American history.

"The Revolution was a monumental turning point in the pages of world history. It was the first chink chiseled from Mother England's dream of world domination.

The Civil War was only a quarter and dime skirmish necessary for the evolution of the country.

One was revolution. The other was evolution. One brought the birth of a nation. The other signaled the direction in which that nation would grow.

Now, tell me boys and girls, which is more important, birth or growth?"

"Softwoods is a funny deal," said Frog.

"How do you mean," asked Sumter?

They had spent the night fishing for catfish on Frog's dock. An old Coleman lantern and a cooler of Bud were all they needed for company.

They didn't talk much.

The crickets sang their nightly symphony. The sparkle from the stars danced off the ripples of the river.

All they ever needed were a few lawn chairs and a bucket of bait. Their ancestors had followed the same paths, had fished the same streams.

The crickets, and the jays, and the wrens, had always been there.

"Softwoods even sounds like a funny name," mused the big man. "Like a forest going nowhere, like a woods without trails."

"Like two home boys," answered Sumter slowly. "Like two home boys sitting on a lazy river on a Saturday night."

"No, this is different. Softwoods is like a development that wasn't meant to be. They built four units in nine months. I heard they sold one, some fool fireman out of New Jersey.

There is no advertising. Nobody but farmers travel that road.

There are no roads being built. No work is being done on a golf course. It's like a dream of a development.

If it gets going, its maybe ten, a dozen years, down the road."

"That's funny," said Sumter. "A real estate fellow from Andrews came by last week and asked daddy if he wanted to sell any pieces of land. Said he was representing the Taggart Corporation.

Said the Taggarts had great plans. The golden bowl was right around the corner."

"What did your daddy say?"

"What he always answers, you know daddy. He's like Scarlet's daddy in Gone With the Wind. He loves his land.

'It's the land, Scarlet O'Hara, it's the land. Don't you know that Tara will provide for you.'

Daddy told him he was happy with what he had. Someone else would have to search for the golden bowl."

"He's right," said Frog. "The land does provide. It buys us these worms."

"It provides real well," said Sumter. 'We Rutledges won't sell the well that gives us our water. We got cotton. We got tobacco. We got green beans and melon patches.

We've got good tenants that make a living off the land.

Daddy says we don't need any condos and golf courses. He's right. Maybe Taggart knows something that we don't know, but that's the way of the world."

"That Scarlet was a looker," said Frog slowly. "If I ever found one like her, I'd reel her right in."

"And give up this good life," answered his friend.

Edward Blythe wasn't a flamboyant soul. When the agency told him to arrange for a security system around his small bungalow, he resisted. What did he have to fear from some rum dums from Chicago?

Bud Sweeney gave him an envelope with twelve thousand dollars in large bills. He told him to contact the Novello Alarm company.

Professor Blythe considered it one of the nuisances of his government job. He didn't even know if the system worked. The only thing he found useful was the intercom system on which he could play his music.

He could hear it all over the house.

He didn't have the faintest idea that he had been identified by the mob in Chicago.

A man had broken into the office of the Novello Alarm Company. He had taken four names from the file.

One was Edward Blythe, a professor at National University. The second was Samuel Hasely, a retired naval officer, who worked somewhere in the White House. The third was William Lassiter, an official with an international bank, who spent much of his time traveling in Europe and the Far East.

A man named Bud Sweeney had ordered the same system, but canceled it.

Eddie Blythe loved sailing the wide Waccamaw as he traveled through Georgetown County. He felt at home on the rivers and streams of the Lowcountry. Happenstance and location had allowed

Georgetown County to remain one of the lasting undeveloped paradises in the eastern states.

Five great rivers flowed into Winyah Bay at Georgetown. The Great Peedee and the Little Peedee met the Waccamaw in the Bay. The Black and the Sampit also joined the merging waters.

They were tidal rivers. The ebb and flow of the Atlantic dictated their currents. They had been governed, since time immemorial, by the moon and the stars.

The rivers were treasure troves of American history. The marshes and the wetlands prevented them from being devastated by development and greed.

King George had first granted the lands to favored English settlers in the 1730s.

These settlers had developed vast rice plantations, flooding and cultivating their fields according to the flow of the tides. Slaves had been brought from the rice culture of the northern Africa coast to work in the fields.

Vast fortunes had been made in the flick of a century. The rice planters saw them vanish in the years of the Civil War.

The former fields of gold were reclaimed by the marsh and the reed. The otter, the coon, and the gator thrived in the former fields of rice. Tupelo and river oak thrived on forlorn dikes.

It was as if the song of the field had never been sung. It was as if the rice laden barge had never drifted with the fall of the tide.

Francis Marion grew up on the rivers and streams. He was at home in the marsh and the swamp.

The British thought they could march unquestioned through the Carolinas, then mass their forces for a northern triumph.

But Marion and his soldiers were will-o-the-wisps. Marion had no wish to mass his forces, to engage the British in the midst of a meadow.

His encampments were on wooded peninsulas near sheltering marshes. His forays were night time excursions along damp river banks. He was forever one stream fording ahead of the British.

He took their heart. He stole their wish to fight.

Sumter and Frog knew the rivers and the marshes. They were Lowcountry boys to the soul. They could smell the turn of the tide, hear the roar of thunder before it pierced through the skies.

They grew up under the hot hazy sun, with the mist rising over the marsh. They could watch the flight of the hawk, or listen to the song of the wren, and know if a storm was coming. That's the way Lowcountry boys were.

Sumter won the big one during his second tour in Nam. It was along a tidal river in the Mekong Delta.

It was one of those nights during the rainy season when nothing seemed to be happening in camp. A few patrols were out.

About ten in the evening, a corporal, shot in the shoulder, was brought in by a patrol.

"There are eight guys trapped in a rice paddy about two miles down the river."

Sumter volunteered to be the gunner on the rescue boat.

"You don't have to go, sarge," said the captain. "Leave it to one of the younger guys.

You're Air Cav. What do you know about air boats?"

"I was brought up on a river like this," answered Sumter, as he threw two Browning automatic rifles into the craft.

"The tides are my friends. If we don't go in a hurry, the water will drive those guys from their cover."

Sumter told the corporal to cut the engine about a mile down the river.

"Let the stream take you along, like you're tapping for flounder."

The boat and their faces were blackened with the mud of the Delta.

"We don't want the fish to know we are coming. The patrol is in a paddy on the right, about two hundred yards past a large clump of bush and trees. Probably a dike of some sort.

When we get about a hundred yards short of the trees, I'll get out. You float about a hundred yards past the trees, then click the engine.

Cut it quick. Then go to the shore. Those guys will be waiting for you."

"What about you, sarge?"

"Pick me up on the way back. I'll be in the middle of the stream."

The corporal didn't know what to make of the sergeant. His voice was soft and slow, almost like the current. He seemed to see things, know things about the river.

"I'm outta here," said Sumter, sliding chest deep into the water.

"I can't see anything," whispered the corporal.

"Count to two hundred slow," came the voice from the water. "Then hit that engine and cut it in a hurry. You'll be all right."

Sumter slid to the shore and approached within twenty yards of the trees.

All hell broke loose with the sound from the engine.

Flares and fire came the Cong, nested high in the trees.

The Cong had roped themselves to the high limbs, awaiting the kill. They couldn't move.

Sumter had an angle on the treetops from his spot in the marsh. The Cong were all facing the sound of the motor.

He stood and sprayed the tree tops like he was hunting for quail. But the birds could no fly, for they were entwined in their perch.

Within minutes the firing was finished. The night was as soundless as it had been.

Sumter met the craft in the river. He could see the relieved faces as he clamored aboard.

"Jesus," said a doe faced lieutenant, "that took a lot of balls."

"Hit the gas," said Sumter. "We can all use a cup of coffee."

Eddie Blythe first went to Vietnam in 1963. He had been with the agency for two years.

He went under the cover of an agricultural mission that was to study the distribution of land. There were half a dozen agents on the mission.

Their real purpose was to identify Cong leaders in the hamlets, to arrange for their disappearance or assassination. The agency thrived on this sort of work. It was a part of their mission.

American journals were kind to the leaders of the agency. They were often described as pure in purpose and ascetic in habit.

One journal compared them to the Catholic Order of Jesuits. But the Jesuits sought the salvation of souls, while the agency had no scruples in burying them.

After Vietnam, the CIA continued its fight against the forces of Communism, wherever they might find them. It was governed by its own legends and its own myths. It had a supreme sense of righteousness.

The agency was divided into small cells. Each had different goals and different agendas. It had information gatherers and scholars on worldly ways. It had philosophers, and soothsayers, and those who predict the future.

It had burglars and assassins. It had diplomats, and politicians, and women of the night.

It had access to the powers that govern. Sometimes it had power over those who governed.

In a city of power, the agency was a power unto itself.

It had access to spy planes and satellites. It had access to the newest and finest of weaponry. It had formed nondescript corporations of former military men, who trained foreign soldiers.

It had a budget that was unquestioned by those who governed the purse.

The agency operated in the darkness of the night. Its errors were as common as autumn leafs falling from the trees, but they were hidden in the shade of the forest.

The first wisps of the savings and loan trouble were appearing by the spring of '86. Bankers had their choice of a variety of investments that had formerly been closed to them.

They were into horse farms in Florida, desert communities in Arizona, and cotton fields in the Carolinas. Their loan officers were eating steak in five star restaurants, and sipping champagne out of cowboy boots. Some were taking a percentage off the top.

Land speculators were drawing blueprints for every sort of development, and stuffing hard currency into their jeans.

Bankers were selling stock certificates to the elderly, rather than placing them in government insured certificates.

The Taggart Corporation was new at the game. It was hidden under the boughs of the oaks.

It had no economic worries. Its cash flow was abundant. It had more than enough lucre to pay the piper.

It was receiving gold from the sale of arms to the Iranians. It was receiving hard cash and cocaine from its venture into South America. There was a steady flow of milk and honey on the rivers of the Lowcountry.

Autumn brought a brilliance to the marsh at Pawleys that could not be matched by the other seasons. The green of summer became bronzed and golden.

The fishing was the best of the year. Spots and grunts came in with each tide, to languish and banquet along the winding creeks.

The sun rose a little later in the morn, and began its descent as the dinner bell would ring.

The moon shone brighter in the chill of evening's air. The ways and the dippers gleamed off the waving sea.

Summer tourists took leave of the shore. Shouting children were back in school. Volleyballs and beach chairs were put away for another season. Rafts were put in storage.

Egrets and herons nestled in the reeds. Great flocks of birds stopped on their southern journey. The wren and the mockingbird said goodbye to their summer home.

Only about a quarter of the houses on Pawleys were occupied after the summer season. Owners might come for a weekend or two. But most of the cottages rested silently on their stilted legs, waiting for another season.

The agency contacted Eddie Blythe in early August. He was to sail the Osprey to Pawleys the last week of the month.

He was to meet a Salvadorian freighter about forty miles outside Winyah Bay. He was to take two Contra officers back to the freighter.

He was to pick up four Contras, leaving two at Pawleys, and taking two to Wilmington,NC, where they would be transported to Fort Bragg.

He was to carry whatever cargo they might have.

Eddie considered himself as part of the agency transportation department. He liked it that way.

He hadn't enjoyed the trip to Cleveland with Bud Sweeney, but that was a part of the Pawleys operation.

Years before he had qualms and doubts.

He wasn't brought up to be a spy. He had minored in French in college. His facility with the language had gained a position as an interpreter in the army. French was a major language in Vietnam, an offshoot of the years of French colonialism.

One thing led to another. Army intelligence led to his selection by the agency. It was in need of French speaking agents.

Before he could say, "This isn't for me," he was on a team in the Vietnamese hamlets, choosing who should live and who should die.

He was drawn into the agency. He was privy to false reporting and multiplied body counts. He was given top security clearance.

He had only sought to serve his country. The agency had woven and weaved his soul, until he was fully clothed in its garment.

It wasn't like joining the forces of his beloved Francis Marion, fighting the Redcoats, then returning to the farm. It wasn't like being drafted in World War II, slogging through the Bulge, then returning to hearth and home.

The agency had become a land unto itself, equal to State, equal to Defense, with its tentacles into almost every foreign policy and endeavor.

Once ensnared, it was difficult to leave.

The Osprey was well equipped for its journeys. It had a full sail, and 500 horse of inboard motor. It had major communication equipment. Its quarters could sleep eight comfortably.

One change was made when it began to carry contraband from South America. Charges of explosive were placed in the hold. Eddie was ordered, that if he was ever to be boarded, if his cover might be blown on the waters, to push the detonator.

He never thought that day would come.

Mike Taggart had been debriefing Contra intelligence officers at Pawleys for more than two years. It was the best place to debrief them.

Fewer agency men had to face the dangers of the jungle. Maps and enemy estimates could be gone over in a relaxed atmosphere, where the Contras might be more likely to deliver the truth.

Mike viewed every bit of information with a grain of salt.

He had been active in gathering information from Diem's officers in the early days of Vietnam.

He remembered the overlay maps provided by the officers. He remembered how they contrasted with the word of American officers in the field.

The Vietnamese would show great portions of provinces free of the Cong. American officers, fresh from the field, would give a contrasting view.

Because of the political reality of the time, only the most favorable view would be advanced.

The agency's policy was to present both views, but if the most favorable was accepted by the politicians and the generals, the agency would not argue the point. The agency had done its job.

Although it was moral subterfuge, and cost the lives of both peasant and soldier, it was a necessary concession in the war against Communist aggression.

Softwoods bothered Mike Taggart. Newspapers and periodicals were beginning to report on trouble in the banking industry. Soft loans were being uncovered in institutions all over the country.

A large bank in Illinois went belly up. Congressional committees were beginning hearings.

The New York Times had called the failures a Ponzi scheme. Depositors, widows and orphans, were being fleeced.

Mike had never been in favor of the land deals. But word had come down from Washington.

Development at Softwoods was dead in the water. It was a gigantic pain in the ass.

Four condo units had been built. Only two were sold.

"When are you going to start the golf course," the buyers would ask?

"The market has slowed," the real estate agent would answer. "When the economy picks up, Softwoods will take off like a rocket."

'Its like Vietnam intelligence,' Mike would think to himself. 'Always give them the most favorable report.'

Chapter 9

Taste

It was almost dusk when we arrived at Pawleys. Perhaps it was the clearness of the Carolina air, or the gentility of the farmer's fields, but we could almost sniff the ocean when we were twenty miles away.

It was the pure feeling of being away, of a long looked for trip, of a season of rest and relaxation.

We didn't say it, but we could feel it as we drove south.

We threw our sweaters off when we came out of the Virginia mountains into North Carolina.

Inviting warmth seemed to come from the earth. We viewed a land that progress had not changed.

We passed old barns and rusted tractors. We passed leaning tobacco sheds and colorful laundry hanging on the lines.

The land of the Lowcountry was fragile. Like Irish lace or fine English china, it had to be protected and cared for.

Perhaps it was the sandy soil. Perhaps it was the mixture of vine and heather, the fine woven weaves that hovered over the fields. Perhaps it was the palm reeds, the waving of the fronds, the beauty of the pines.

Like a dowager aunt, the land seemed to accept its beauty, to cherish it, and to hold it in eternal faithfulness.

There was not the feeling of creeping development, the high rise and steel girders, that we were familiar with.

We drove through small towns that looked like Rockwell paintings.

We saw a lot of pick up trucks, their beds laden with old equipment or a dog, tooling slowly along the road.

The two lane road seemed to drift beneath us at an unhurried pace.

Perhaps that was a part of the fragileness.

Jack Foley of the Chicago Bureau was asked to get involved in the savings and loan mess.

In Cleveland, Mike Blackwell was doing the same thing.

They often compared thoughts on the telephone.

They were part of the institutional memory of the Bureau, of a place and time when the pace was slower, of a time when agents depended on their instincts and their street contacts.

They had come up in a time of foot leather and patient surveillance. The newer agents placed their confidence in psychological profiles and computer banks.

"God, the world has gone screwy," said Jack.

"It's a big mess," chuckled Mike. "I remember a time when you had to sit straight on the stool to get an extra dime from the banks.

They really used to give me the evil eye."

"That's the way it was," answered Jack, "when I went to get a mortgage on my first house.

Me and the wife almost got the double whammy because we forgot to list $200 we owed Sears for a washer and dryer. I had to write two letters to explain my forgetfulness.

Now some loan officers are getting high flying commissions on some very questionable paper. You got the same problem in Cleveland."

"It's the same game. We did a comparison study at the beginning of the year; two good sized S&Ls.

One was going belly up. It used to make upscale loans in the more prosperous suburbs. It was doing very well.

Its Board of Directors wanted more. They made loans in Florida swamps, in new condo developments, in racetracks, in art and antiquity that they had no expertise in.

You get the picture. Now their ass is in the swamp.

The other was run by an old Polish family, had been around forever. It gave mortgages on old singles and doubles in the city, in old neighborhoods that other banks red lined.

They were the savior of the working man. When these guys moved out to the suburbs it gave them another mortgage.

They paid an extra quarter percent on CDs. They never changed its policy when deregulation came in.

They never lost a dime. Just followed the old time worn maxim that it first started with."

"I'm going down to South Carolina the week after Labor Day," said Jack. "The Bureau wants me to look into some squishy loans from a S&L in Texas. It has 30 million in paper on some sandy soil that wasn't worth half a million three years ago.

I asked for you to go with me.

It'll be just a few interviews and a bit of follow the money. Congress doesn't trust the bank examiners and is all over the Bureau to see what is going on.

We can play some golf and bullshit a little. Are you up to it?"

"Nothing could be finer than a week in Carolina. I'm with you, buddy. But they'll probably want to send some hotshot."

"That's why they're sending me," answered Jack. "And you are going with me. The Bureau wants some guys with whiskers, guys who have seen almost every con."

The beach house was a beauty. It was called Two View. Every house on Pawleys had a wooden sign with a name on it. It was a part of the ambiance.

The house was on a narrow spit of land, stretching southward on the end of the island. There were about fifty houses on the spit, balanced precariously between the ocean and the marsh.

We spent Sunday morning in the surf.

Bridie set the tone.

"If Jesus expected us at mass, he would have woken us earlier."

"Wakened," said Mary.

"Awokened," said Sheila.

"Got us up," laughed Peggy.

"In the convent they played reveille," I said with a smirk.

"No kidding," smiled Mary. "That's better than Smoky rolling over with last night's brew in his throat and patting you on the butt."

It was going to be that kind of month.

Friends. Moonlight and roses. A time to smell the flowers!

I walked about twenty yards into the mild surf, watched the salty water sizzle about my knees. The water was cool. The autumn sun caressed my shoulders.

It was God's earth and I was a part of it. That was the secret of Pawleys.

I dove forward and floated beneath the waves. I could taste the salt and the sea.

"Thank you, Jesus," I whispered. "I am your servant, wherever I may be."

Late in the afternoon we all jumped in the van and took a tour around the island.

"Let's check out the pavilion," said Sheila. "That was a blast."

"Looking for Sumter," mocked Bridie?

"Sumter, who," smiled Sheila coyly.

"Sure," we all laughed.

There was no pavilion at the end of the North Causeway. There was only an old scrabble parking lot that weeds had reclaimed.

A group of rotting wooden pilings angled leisurely from the marsh. A slabs of concrete clock lay barnacled in the reeds. The water of the creek nibbled at the relics.

"Jesus," said Bridie. "It is almost like nothing was ever here."

"It was right here," said Mary. "I can feel the beat."

She did a little shuffle on the scrabble parking lot. Then she and Peggy broke into the Twist.

She was right. If you had ever been there before, you could almost hear the tunes weaving off the golden grasses of the marsh. You could see the shuffling of soft sandals gliding on the pine.

We were young. We were innocent. The sun had been golden on our shoulders. The wind and the tide had guided our every step.

Perhaps that was the secret of fond memories. They were our dreams and our past. They were something we could rest safely on, a pillow on which we could safely lay our head.

Sheila took off her shoes and waded out to the farthest piling. The water was barely at her knees as her feet sucked into the muck.

"What are you doing, girl," laughed Mary? "You are too cool for a fool."

"Come on, gumbahs. Come on and touch these pillars. They are a part of us.

We're forty years old. We are on vacation.

It's a time to act crazy!"

Before you could say Jack Scat we were all in the marsh. We joined hands and made a ring around the piling.

"How about a little Steel Wool Shuffle," commanded Bridie.

It was a little crazy, but we just jived in the muck.

We sang, "sixteen tons and what do you get, another day older and deeper in debt."

Then we did a bit of Rag Mop.

We were beat.

"Too much," panted Peggy. "Too many apples in the basket. That was twenty years ago."

We leaned our hands on the sodden wood, the sun shining on our shoulders.

"Let's say a prayer for Benny," I said. "He brought us to this place. God rest his soul."

"And for Monsignor O'Donnell and for Jack Kennedy," said Bridie.

"And for our mothers and fathers and children," said Sheila.

"And for our husbands, and for sister Marcetta, and for all the nuns who are all a part of us," said Peggy.

"And for all we've known who Jesus took into His sacred bosom," said Mary.

We stood silently, our feet in the ooze of the bog, and let God know our thoughts.

The priests used to say, "keep the faith." It was a part of their litany.

When we were young, we couldn't grasp what they meant.

Now, when we were forty, we held that faith close to our hearts.

Eddie Blythe loved entering the Waccamaw. He had entered South Carolina's intercoastal waterway near its northern border. He motored about thirty miles in the man made channel, past the development and glitter of Myrtle Beach.

This was always the most boring part of his journey. When he hit the turn bridge at Socastee he knew he was nearing the tidal currents of the river.

Often he had to blow his foghorn to wake the watchman to swing the bridge. But as he glided past the aging bridge, he knew he was nearing the Lowcountry and the rice fields of the plantations.

The water ran swifter. The current cleansed both the stream and the shore. The wrens and the hawks were more abundant. The Osprey seemed to sail better on the river waters.

The Osprey was following the path of the old mail boats, the barges of rice and pine, which had floated the tides to the markets of Georgetown and Charleston.

It was passing the ancient plantations; Wachesaw, Springfield, Brookgreen and The Oaks, Litchfield, Caledonia, Hagley, Jericho, and Arcadia.

More than thirty plantations had dotted the Waccamaw Neck.

Eddie could feel the ghosts of the ancient inhabitants. He had studied the planters and the settlers. He was an acknowledged expert on the slave communities and people that had made the plantations prosperous.

His trips on the Osprey had given him opportunity to explore. It gave him time to talk and exchange thoughts with southern scholars and archaeologists, who were doing work in these fields.

Mary couldn't wait to go shopping.

A group of quaint stores had been built on the highway near the North Causeway. A large sign proclaimed the Hammock Shops.

They were built on the land of an old nursery, with winding brick paths between bush and bough.

We were wandering from shop to shop when we came upon The Pink Rocking Chair.

"It's an omen," said Bridie. "Shall we go in and see what this is all about?"

There were three rockers on the wide porch, all painted startling pink.

Mary and Peggy plopped into two of them and drawled in unison, "It's so nice to see ya. Would ya all like some tea?"

"Hi, girls, I'm Alison Follett," the friendly lady in the store greeted us. "Can I help you with anything?"

She was about our age, all agog in the flowers and prints of the south. She was close clipped, and blonde, and bronzed. Her voice was melodic and soft, like a feather in the breeze.

"We're staying on the island," offered Mary. "Just looking around."

"Looking for souvenirs," she asked?

"How did you guess," smiled Sheila? "Something reasonable. They want an arm and a leg for everything around here."

"I've got just what you girls need. My specialty is pink rockers.

I've got bird feeder rockers. I've got small planter pink rockers. I've got porch rockers and small children's rockers. I've even got an alarm clock and pencil sharpener pink rocker.

Anything for your taste and the size of your purse! I even have some table napkins that have flowers and pink rockers."

"Look at these magnets," said Mary. "'Rockin at Pawleys Island' and 'we're in the pink.'"

We each bought a little something. The shop was quaint and inexpensive.

"Do you sell much of this pink rocker stuff," I asked Alison?

"All I can get my hands on. Just look in your shopping bags.

The tourist bus crowd loves this stuff. They love small inexpensive mementos, a pot holder or a planter that they can put on a kitchen sill.

It's a quirky business. I was going nowhere. Luckily, I happened on the pink rocking chair. Its like I invented the pet rock or the mood ring."

"I run a restaurant in Cleveland," I told her. "The same thing got us over.

We play fifties rock and roll on an old jukebox. It's the nostalgia. The music reminds people of happy days.

Sheila had joined us. She had a few small pencil sharpeners in her hand.

"These are so cute. Where did you get the idea?"

"I have a friend named Frog. Actually he is my beau, but he doesn't know it yet.

Well, he has a friend who has been carrying a picture of a pink rocking chair in his wallet forever.

I do a little painting. I was looking for a name for the shop and The Pink Rocking Chair struck my fancy.

I did a painting of the old rocking chair and everyone who came in wanted to buy it. Usually I couldn't give my canvases away.

I kept this one, got it in my office.

Some suppliers said they could manufacture anything in the shape of a rocker. It all happened as if by chance."

We were amazed.

"Can we see the painting," we both asked?

We all went to the clutter of her office.

"Hey, Sheila," laughed Bridie. "That's the picture you gave Sumter when we painted the cottage for Benny."

"I know the story," Alison said softly. "You took the picture and gave it to a soldier named Sumter. Frog told me the story.

That is what I love so much about Pawleys. There are so many good stories. They seem to be a part of the sand and the beach.

They are told by one person to another. They seem to be lost or forgotten, then drift in on the tides through the marsh."

"Like legends or Grecian myths," I said.

"They are forever held in the moon and the stars," said Alison.

Samuel Hasely was a loose cannon in the National Security Council. He was a CIA agent, a consultant to the Council.

He had been personally chosen by the Director to be his liaison. He answered only to the Director.

He was as assured of himself as a lion trainer in center ring. He was fortyish, boyishly handsome, spit polished, and secretive.

In meetings of the Council he was outspoken in his affection for the Contras and all fighters of Communism. He spoke scornfully of those with different views.

In thought he was shallow, self serving, quick and abrupt. His brazenness and charm clouded his weaknesses well, making him a rising star in the firmament of secrecy and stealth.

In another era he might have been a supernumerary, a spear carrier. In the Reagan Administration he became a star.

President Reagan loved America. He saw the house on the hill. He saw the city of light. Like O Henry, he rejoiced when the shop girl married the millionaire, or when the poor lass gave her lover the gift of the Magi.

He remembered old games, and long runs, and the spirit of the team both in loss and in victory. He admired the sacrifice of men in uniform, the honing of fine minds, and the diligence of the laborer.

He rejoiced in the basic goodness of the American spirit. He ignored the baser goals of more menial men.

He had a spirit of generosity. He abhorred confrontation. He knew that America would win one for the Gipper.

He confined himself to the Oval Office. He had no curiosity about the rest of the historic mansion. He knew that Ed Meese, or James Baker, or Donald Regan had offices down the hall. That's where they came from.

He had no curiosity about what went on in the offices and cubbyholes of the other offices of the White House. If the ship was adrift, his aides would let him know.

He was passionate about his intolerance of international Communism. He looked on Communism as a neighborhood bully. He knew that bullies grew older and wiser, and eventually lose their stamina.

That might have happened if the Gipper had never been. It would have been part of the tides of change and nourishment that are common to the sea.

Sam Hasely hated Communism as much as the Gipper. He had three rows of medal from a war that had never been won.

He served as an intermediary between the Director of the agency and the NSC. He was the control officer over the sale of arms to Iran, and the Contra ventures, and the safe houses in the Lowcountry.

Older men, wiser men, men with a sense of history and the sea, might have let the tides and the stars take their course. They might have been attuned to the winds and the waves.

Sam didn't like Eddie Blythe. He controlled him as a courier, as a sort of donkey he thought, but he didn't like him.

He had gone down to National University to hear Professor Blythe speak on the Revolutionary campaigns in the Carolinas. It was during a symposium sponsored by the Daughters of the American Revolution.

Blythe's thesis was that the British were fighting the wrong war in the wrong place. Blythe stated that the Redcoats had no real chance against the forces of Francis Marion. The men of Marion had knowledge of the rivers and the marshes, and the support of the people of the fields.

The Redcoats might capture a town or a village, establish a garrison but they had no popular support from the people. Each movement of the British might be reported to Marion by local lads and lasses.

Marion's forces would attack like thunder in the night, forcing the Redcoats to scatter. This not only sapped the British armaments, but it caused its army to lose its spirit.

"They were three years in the Lowcountry," concluded Professor Blythe, "but they were like the ancient tribes of Israel, dispirited and wanderers in the desert."

A young student asked Professor Blythe if his analogy wasn't reminiscent of U. S. policy in Vietnam, "the wrong war in the wrong place, with a populace that was not on our side, ___ten years in the bog?"

"We never learned from the French," answered Eddie Blythe. "Robert McNamara was too much of a reactionary, a pleaser of power. He depended too much on graphs and computer printouts.

We would have been better served if we had more historians and poets at State and at Defense."

"Jesus," muttered Sam Hasely to himself. "He's a fucking pacifist."

Ronald Reagan couldn't hold a grudge. He saw the past as a prelude to a better future, not the cause of frigidity or chaos. He gave America hope.

On a state visit to Germany he visited a cemetery at Bittburg, the resting place of former SS soldiers. His advisors scorned the planned visit. The Jewish community was adamantly opposed.

He let the dead bury the dead. He marched to another drummer. He had a feeling for graciousness, for the spirit of America.

The gang at the National Security Council didn't believe in magnanimity. They were kick ass, hard ass, no fooling around types of guys.

They were made up of military and civilian, State, Defense, and the agency. They were true believers, cold warriors. They were still fighting Vietnam, never letting the bodies rest. They wouldn't let the dead bury the dead.

They had taken the domino theory, of one small nation falling after another, as divine doctrine. They had transferred it from Southeast Asia to the countries of South America.

They could envision millions of bronzed Commies, marching like fire ants through Mexico to the Texas border.

When Congress, reflecting the view of the American public, refused funds for the Contras, they were aghast.

They proposed that the Gipper go on national television and lend his support to the Contras.

But the President was wise in the ways of the world. He told an aide he'd put it under advisement. Then he forgot it.

The furies were free to take their course.

The NSC laid its hopes and its dreams in the hands of the agency, in the hands of Captain Hasely.

Jack Foley and Mike Blackwell were completely unimpressed with Softwoods. There was only one four unit building, with two units occupied. There was no golf course. The sign by the road was faded and bleached by the sun.

"Ten million dollars and what do you get, the country's another day older and deeper in debt," sang Jack.

"Wow," answered Mike. "this has to be one of the best scams I've ever seen. Somebody robbed the bank without using a gun."

"Want to look around," asked Jack? "Take a walk through the brush."

"I'm an old man," smiled Mike. "Besides they have snakes in them woods Brother Foley.

I've been reading about good old South Carolina. The state has every poisonous snake possible; water moccasins and copperheads and things like that."

They spent three days lazily, just looking and talking.

They talked to the real estate broker in Kingstree who had sold the land to the Taggarts.

"Darndest deal," he said slowly, "darndest deal I've seen in awhile. Never even advertised the land. Worthless to a farmer. Too wet and mucky.

Taggart comes in with hard cash. Surprised the hell out of me and the owner."

"No mortgage," asked Jack?

"Didn't even have to check his credit, by golly. But I asked around.

The family has a truck load of money, a lumber distributor from Camden. They've got a few places down by Pawleys Island. When I needed to get him, I called him at the island."

"How about Softwoods," asked Mike? "Any action?"

"A bit at first. The plans were in the paper and everything. It's a slow go.

But a guy that has money around here has got the world by the ass. Like the Taggarts do. They can sit on the land for ten, fifteen years, till the coast fills up and the Yankee retirees come inland.

I figure that's when the money will be made."

"Anything else exciting happening around here," smiled Jack?

"Only when the train goes through. South to Charleston about eleven in the morning. A lot of Black domestics take it. There is no work in Kingstree. Catch it back about seven in the evening."

"You sell a lot of real estate," asked Mike?

"I'm an old man, older by a dozen summers than you guys. Some days I just come in here and look at the train pass in the morning. Then I go home when it comes back in the evening.

I'm sort of like a domestic at the depot. Just waiting on the train."

Chapter 10

Is

Two View should have been called Great View. The cottage allowed us a wide panorama of the sea and the marsh, the green of the reeds and the blue of the Carolina sky.

It was everything we could have asked for, a great room with a wide planked floor, a marvelous kitchen, and separate rooms for privacy. The house was scented by wormy cypress paneling and the aromatic salt of the sea.

A wide planked walkway led to a cupola covered dock on the marsh. This became our favorite spot.

The creek ebbed and flowed with the tide. The golden rods of the reeds waved in the breeze. Salty scents of the sea enveloped us.

"Its like a ship," said Mary. "We can fish and crab from this thing without getting our feet wet."

"Its like an office on the stream," said Peggy.

"What's an office," we asked in unison?

"A room with a desk," we all giggled back.

We were the girls of our youth, the young scallywags of Hayden Avenue.

We were the girls who sat on the swing, who dreamed with their feet in the spindles

"Let's play 'what's missing'," smirked Sheila.

"How?"

"We go around in a circle. Say something you have at home or at work that's not here."

"An office telephone."

"A dictaphone."

"Fax machine."

"Typewriter."

"Kids."

"Bosses."

"Mother-in-laws."

"Salesmen."

"Report cards."

"A broken dishwasher."

We went round and round. Nobody missed a beat. Finally, we could only laugh and quit.

"This is a good ship," smiled Peggy. "We don't have anything but nuts on it. No captain! Only a crew of nuts!"

The marsh was part of a salt water estuary, where the fish of the sea had ever come to feed. Its streams and cord grass were drawn in the book of long ago.

Up and down the Atlantic coast, in New Jersey, and Maryland, and Florida, similar tidewater marshes had been filled. Great condominiums and hotels had been placed over them.

Tourists would sit in the midst of progress, peering for the beauty of nature.

Georgetown County was slow to develop. Progress passed her by. The good old boys who governed the county, loved the land that God had given their ancestors. They protected God's gift through good planning and restrictive zoning.

They sought to preserve the natural habitat for their children and their children's children.

I had read once that Thoreau once wrote that fishing was one of man's delights.

He must have been crazy.

Everything we did on the dock was an adventure.

We had all the goods; rods, hooks, bobbers, and weights. We had crab nets and two large screened crab traps.

We bought blood worms and blue blooded worms for the fish. We bought chicken necks and chicken backs to bait the crab traps.

The crabs just nibbled the worms off the hooks. We would feel a tug on the line, sometimes more than a tug. When we would reel the line in, Mr. Crab would release his claws as soon as the hook emerged from the water.

"I thought worms were to catch fish," said Bridie. "Those crabs just gobble them suckers."

We took to catching crabs with a vengeance. We lowered stringed nets with the chicken bait tied in the middle.

We only had to wait a few minutes, count to fifty or a hundred and fifty, and pull up the net.

It was great sport. Within a few hours we had half a five gallon pail with the hard clawed critters.

They were gray and blue, with bright orange claws. We shook the grandfathers and the other big ones into the pail. The little ones were shaken back into the stream.

"Crabs must be stupid," said Mary. "They don't give any warning to the other crabs in the creek."

"They are like kids," said Sheila. "They love that chicken. But what are we going to do with them?"

When I told them, they were aghast.

"Boil them while they are still living," said Peggy, "You've got to be kidding."

Into the boiling steamer they went.

I salted the water and threw in a little cloth bag of crab boil.

In five minutes they came out rosy and misty pink. The kitchen was as steamy and as fresh as a fisherman's cabin.

"Now what, gumbah," asked Bridie?

"It's a group project," I answered. "Everybody get a big glass of iced tea or a coke. We're going to clean these critters."

The kitchen had every utensil imaginable for living by the sea. It had nutcrackers and crab crackers, sharp bladed knives, and small silver picks for digging out the meat.

I brought a pile of old papers and some large vinyl garbage bags to put around the large round table.

"Wait a minute," said Peggy, as she and Mary disappeared into their rooms.

They came back moments later, wearing large flowered smocks with straw bonnets on their heads.

"If we are going to do this old stuff," said Peggy, "we've got to dress the part. Now you guys get ready."

Sheila put on a fifties tape, with The Wayward Wind and Que Sera Sera. We sat around the table grumbling, and cracking, and picking.

It was like steel wooling the floors at St. Phils. We each found our own method. We showed each other what to do.

There were no slackards.

We sipped iced tea and picked. We threw the meat into a large salad bowl in the center. We threw the leftovers, the shells, and the claws, and the entrails, onto quickly sogging newspapers. We threw the soggy mess into the garbage bags.

We were singing This Old House when Alison walked into the kitchen.

"I knocked on the screen door but all I could hear were you singing. I don't guess you girls could hear me.

I t looks like you guys are cooking for a revival."

"Just picking and singing," laughed Sheila. "Pull up a seat and show us how the home girls do it."

"I will in a minute, but I have some presents from two of your friends. They said you could use them on the porch."

We all scurried to the porch.

There, looking over the sea, were two large pink rocking chairs.

The two FBI agents spent the better part of a week looking over the Taggart holdings.

It was hard work. It was time consuming.

There were no four lane highways to make travel easy. The interstate system had bypassed eastern South Carolina. There were only two lane country roads, rolling lazily through fields of cotton and tobacco.

For every newer house there were a hundred older ones. There were ramshackle wooden houses living on the edge of final distress. There were house trailers in abundance. There was little sign of prosperity.

The people along the byway were poor.

"Dirt poor," commented Mike.

"Better than the tenements," answered Jack.

There were old men riding rusted bikes. There were ever present clotheslines, warming cloth in the Carolina sun.

There was space, and the blue sky, and the whiteness of the cloud. The two men had a feeling that they were caught in the midst of the past.

There was a rhythm to their wanderings.

There was little industry. Each town might have a shop or a weaving mill, but there was nothing but the field and the sky in the vast rural areas.

Johnsonville had the Wellman Company, a recycler of plastics. Hemingway had a Tupperware plant. Some towns had plants where they made pallets of pine.

Middle aged men walked the lanes heading for a thresher or a reaper. Young men walked the roads aimlessly, as if headed for nowhere.

Concrete block stores or places of conviviality appeared randomly along the wayside. Their names were spray painted; graffiti like, on their mantles.

"Thirty million dollars down here somewhere," commented Jack.

"Where do these kids get jobs," asked Mike?

They were traveling roads hidden from the interstate, weaving lines on a map wrapping poverty to despair.

The grandest buildings were the Black churches.

Some were small and neat, like Puritan meeting halls. Others would do credit to any cathedral, with brick and stone arches reaching to the heavens.

Often there was a small well cared for graveyard, with fresh colorful bouquets adorning the simplest of stones.

"It's almost like the churches of Ireland," said Jack.

"No, its not," winked Mike.

"Sure it is. Me and the wife were over there a few years ago. The greatest monuments were the churches.

Centuries ago, even in the days of Henry and Elizabeth, and the true black hearts, the English were wondering why a people so poor, would build such grand churches."

"Why, good buddy, Chicago philosopher, why?"

"It was their faith, you heathen.

Maybe we've seen too much, become a little too callous on the concrete, chasing who know who. That's life.

But our ancestors in Erin, they flocked to the church. It was their salvation. It saved the country. Gave comfort to the hopeless.

There's probably a lot of that faith down here in this hot scrabble. The churches are the bulwarks of these forgotten people. You can make book on that."

The car followed the roads almost aimlessly. Their words had little direction.

They spotted a large red brick church on the horizon, its steeple rising in the midst of nowhere.

"Let's stop here," chuckled Jack. "If anyone knows what's going on down here, it will be a minister."

"We're quite a pair of country sleuths, you and I," answered Mike. "Our bosses would give us the door if they saw how we operate."

The minister's name was on the sign on the lawn, Reverend Myles C. Croffer.

"We Catholics would never put our priest's names on the marquee," smiled Jack. "Some of our guys might be wanted."

Reverend Croffer was a small rotund black man, balding and silver haired, with the friendliest of smiles.

"Can I help you fellows?"

"We were going down the road when we came upon this beautiful church," answered Jack. "We are just a couple of old blokes from Chicago, traveling the back roads and looking around."

"Catholics, I suppose?"

"How did you guess," asked Mike?

"I could tell by your Irish kissers. I grew up near an Irish neighborhood in Buffalo. I can spot them blue eyes."

"Why did you leave," asked Jack? "Buffalo is a great town."

"Too much cold and snow. Work was slow for my father. He got up and packed the bags and we all came back here when I was fifteen. Thanks be to the Lord."

He was quite a guy, street wise and smart, with the rolling voice of an accomplished preacher.

"Worked and sweated in the fields," he continued, "until the army got me. Best thing that ever happened. Got to school under the GI Bill. Met my wife in college.

Now I do my sweating doing God's work. Thanks be to Jesus."

"Thanks be to Jesus," intoned Jack.

"How can I help you fellows? Who are you looking for?"

"What makes you think we are looking for someone," asked Mike?

"I'm a reticent man, a God fearing man. But I'm also a Black man. I can almost sniff the badges in your pockets. We Black folks have a way about us.

You fellows look like good guys. Let's be open with one another."

"Right on, Reverend," said Mike.

"We are looking for the proverbial needle in the haystack," started Jack. "We are looking for a cobra among the reeds."

"Not a Moses in the bull rushes," offered Reverend Croffer.

"We don't often look for a Moses," said Mike. "I can't tell you where we are from, but we do have badges in our pockets. You can believe that.

We are looking at land, who owns it, what's done with it, who works it, who profits from it."

"Genesis," started the Reverend. "And on the seventh day God created man, and gave him domain over the Garden of Eden, and man lost that domain because of his sin."

"That was a long time ago, Reverend," smiled Jack. "We are interested in the here and now. What is."

"Well, our people take their sustenance from these fields," started the minister.

"White folks own it. Many Blacks work it. They earn their living by the sweat of their brow."

"Do the Blacks own much land," quizzed Mike? "Not that we are looking into Black ownership, just a question of personal interest."

"The Pharaohs owned the land and the Israelites were in captivity," intoned the minister, "making bricks out of straw. That's the way it was, and still is in a way."

He was full of Biblical allusion, like the pages of the testament.

"Many of our families own plots of land. Some have clear title to it. Others hold it in time and space.

Heir land we call it. It has been in their families for generations. There is a house, and a brother adds a house, and a son adds a trailer, and a daughter marries, and there is another trailer.

That's what we call heir land. Sometimes the whole caboodle is held in just one title. Sometimes the title is old and lost, with no record even in the courthouse.

Families stay together. Some of the boys used to go to the big cities, work in the steel mills or the factories. Not so much anymore.

Many come back with a pension, come back to the fields they have never forgotten.

This is their Eden."

"Do the white folks help your people," asked Mike?

"Some do. Some don't," chuckled the minister. "Depends on the weave of their cloth.

There is a landowner around here, Tommy Rutledge and his boy Sumter; they will give you the sweat off their brow. Like father, like son. You know.

Well, Sumter was off in the service during the sixties. He was away perhaps a dozen years.

An old Black sister, Miss Sarah, was always having the congregation pray for him. He was like kin. She had looked over him after his mother passed.

Well, when Miss Sarah passed, when we all gathered to send her home, that was the time we were building this church. We had planned a smaller wooden structure, something more common, but we really prayed for a church of brick and stone.

After the burial, right there out the window, in the field of victorious souls, Mister Tommy and Sumter came up to me and handed me an envelope.

On it was written, 'In Memory of Miss Sarah.' In it was a check for fifteen thousand dollars.

There was singing and jubilation that day, the day we carried Miss Sarah home.

That was a day!"

Each of the agents pressed a twenty to the Reverend's palm as they left.

"I don't have a feeling that the Taggarts give too much to the Black churches," said Mike as they got back to the car.

"That's the spin of the globe," answered Jack. "Some people are givers. Others are takers.

You are probably right. I bet most of the Taggart money stays close to the hip.

But that's what we're here for, good buddy, to find where all the schekels are.

Let's take a ride up to Camden tomorrow, take a look at the lumber business."

Alison sat with us most of the afternoon, picking and chatting.

"Take a taste when you pick," she codgered us. "It makes the job more tolerable.

Save some of the crab shells. Wash them clean. Then stuff them with deviled crab. Bake awhile. That's the way it has been done forever."

"I could not do this for a living," said Bridie.

"Why not," asked Sheila?

"First of all, I don't throw living things in the pot. Second, there's more mess than meat. And it's too damn slow."

"Most people don't do this anymore," said Alison. "But it is a taste of years ago. My mother and my aunts used to sit around like this. Iced tea, newspaper, and all.

That's what Pawleys is, a place which time has past. That's why families come back year after year, some for more than thirty or forty years.

They experience what their mothers and grandmothers had felt, oh so many years ago.

People can tell you about the past. This is the past, just shuckin and jivin, and talking around the table.

And, I forgot to tell you, we'll all be over in the evening, me and Frog and Sumter.

Put on the porch light. We'll be here about seven."

I made a casserole called Crab Surprise and a Crab/Shrimp Pie out of a recipe book. They were as simple as snapping a twig.

"Did anyone ask if Sumter is married," quizzed Peggy? "Did you ask Alison, Sheila?"

"Why should I have asked?"

"Did you forget," smiled Mary? "He was your beach walking beau."

"When I met Tommy," Sheila smiled coyly, "I filed all my past loves in the farthest, darkest recess of my mind.

That's how true love works."

They were a pill. As wacky as Abbott and Costello.

I did all of the work in the kitchen; the casserole, the pie, a fresh garden salad. I cut some pepperoni and cheese while they played Monopoly in the other room.

"Is anyone going to help me," I hollered?

"No gumbah," shouted Bridie. "This is your month to cook. But we'll sample some of that stuff if you'll bring it out."

"Not until dinner," I answered

All I could do was shake my head.

Frog and Alison arrived a little after seven.

Frog hadn't changed a bit. He was still a behemoth of a man. His hair was a bit thinner. His voice was a bit raspier.

He was as light on his feet as a doe as he came up the steps.

"Hi, gumbahs," he greeted us, hugging each of us in his massive arms.

"I'm not great at remembering names, but I did remember gumbah."

"What's a gumbah," drawled Alison?

"Italian, for friend," we all answered.

"We say sweetheart or dear, in the south," smiled Alison. "If I called my lady friends a gumbah, it would ruffle their petticoats."

"We don't wear petticoats in Cleveland," said Bridie. "We wear woolen sweaters and tweed coats and galoshes.

But we can take this weather. Maybe we'll learn how to dress like southern belles."

Sumter arrived moments later. We knew it was him when he was a way down the road. The Ford Fairlane, teal and cream, was aglow in the moonlight.

'Déjà vu,' I thought. My heart was aflutter.

There was a happiness, a joy, that the boy for who I had prayed so often was whole. God had answered my prayers. I gripped the rail tightly, lest I should fall.

"Paisans," he greeted us, as he stretched his arms.

"What's a paisan," quizzed Alison.

"Another Italian word for friend," we all answered.

"Well, darn. I come for dinner and I learn a whole new language. What's the Italian word for enemy?"

"You don't want to hear it," laughed Bridie.

Sumter was as lithe and lean as a willow. His brow was bronzed from the field. His smile was as fresh and as soft as new fallen snow.

"Do you remember these girls," asked Frog?

"Can a squirrel sniff an acorn? My daddy always asked why five pretty ladies wide ride around the fields with me."

"I wondered myself," answered Frog.

Sumter had a kiss and a hug for each of my friends as he greeted them by name. I could see the strength of his soul as he grasped them, turning them lightly and kissing them on the cheek.

I was reminded of Frankie, in our back yard of so long ago. Oh, how he could charm my friends, with the strength of his voice and a kiss on the cheek.

"I'll dance at your weddings," he would say, and twirl them about the yard.

I was standing beside Alison, on the far side of the porch. I could hardly let go of the railing. I felt alone in the glow of the moonlight.

"You're forgetting someone, Sumter Boy," whispered Alison. "You kissed all the married ladies, but you missed the single lass."

"How do you know which is which," asked Frog?

"Rings and things," she answered.

Sumter was beside me before I knew it, lightly lifting my hands from the rail.

His strength radiated through his hands

"Joanie," he whispered, looking straight to my eye.

I felt so small. Then he held me tightly, ever so tightly in his arms.

It was just a moment in the universe, like the first songbird of spring, but a moment like none I had ever known.

I forgot everything I had been. I rested in his arms, cherishing the moment.

Only the kitchen could be my salvation.

"Where are you going," asked Bridie?

"I have a casserole warming in the oven," I lied.

"Me and Bridie are taking care of the serving," smiled Sheila. "You are so goofy, Joanie. You don't have to do everything."

I was flabbergasted.

I ended up on the sofa next to Sumter, while they served iced tea and cheese as graciously as Irish maids.

It was as fine a moment as I had ever known; the sheen of the wormy cypress, a dimly lit chandelier, the breeze skipping through the screen doors.

"Quite a place," said Frog, his deck shoes stretching forth from a great easy chair. "It's almost as grand as my own."

"You have a place like this," asked Peggy?

"Only pulling your legs. I is where I was when you last saw me."

"Frog's the last of the Black River rats," teased Alison. "I go out once a month to give his place a scrub, but he's afraid to become too domesticated."

"You're making one hell of a try," smiled the big man. "One hell of a try!"

"And you, Sumter," asked Mary. "How are you doing."

"Same car, same guy," he answered easily. "You are the guys who look great. Morning sunshine, you all look great!

And you, Joanie," he said leaning toward me, "what are you taking? You look, what do they say, simply vivacious."

I was middled. I leaned closer and kissed him on the cheek.

"Thank you, Sum."

"Jesus, Mary and Joseph," said Bridie coming in from the kitchen. "What's going on here? Poor Joanie is loose."

The dinner was great. We sat around the large round table passing the bowls and catching up on the past.

"This casserole is great," chimed Alison.

"Crab Surprise from a recipe book I picked up at your store," I explained.

"I know its Crab Surprise, honey. But what did you put in it? It is scrumptious."

"Joanie and her father have one of the hippest restaurants in Cleveland," beamed Sheila.

"This is really good. Tell her your secrets, paisan."

"A great recipe is a great recipe," I started. "I added a bit of garlic, a little oregano, a few red peppers, and a little bit of vinegar and oil.

I cook by instinct, a small dash of this and that"

"Don't be so modest," said Alison. "You can cook, girl."

"I knew you could do most anything," smiled Sumter. "I learned that a long time ago."

I hadn't changed a bit of the recipe for the Crab/Shrimp Pie. It was delicious. It had a tiny bit of sherry and a taste of Worcestershire sauce that slid on your palate.

"What's your secret, honey," asked Alison? "I've been at the beach my whole life and I've never tasted anything so good."

She was so nice. The evening was so different.

In the city it was dine and dash. Everyone was in a hurry.

Here it was slow and gracious, winding listlessly with the ebb and flow of the tide.

"Cook it slow, cook it low," I answered. "I learned that a long time ago."

"It sounds like the way, I fish," smiled Frog. "I sit sort of like leisurely on the dock, letting them come to me.

In fact, it sounds like the way me and Sum lead our lives, just little old home boys, casting and waiting."

"Don't be so modest, big guy," jested Alison. "You two guys have more irons in the fire than Satan himself."

We sat in the great room, talking and reminiscing, we girls in our flowered blouses, Sumter and Frog in the casual cottons of the south.

Mary had brought a whole slew of tapes from the fifties and the sixties. Somehow they were the great years, old tunes and fond memories.

"The pavilion," asked Peggy?

"Burned down years ago," answered Alison.

"Ever dance there?"

"Will never forget it. Met my first husband there. Forgot him a long time ago."

We sat and talked and listened to the soft melodies of Johnny Mathis and the Four Aces and Nat 'King' Cole.

We sipped evening coffee and listened to the crickets. We walked to our office on the creek, and watched the full moon and the ways and the stars.

One by one our companions drifted into the night. First Frog and Alison. Then the girls floated away.

Sumter took my hand, saying it was about time to go. We glided to the porch, but neither of had the heart to let the evening pass.

It was as if the evening was extended by the stars, held tightly in the grasp of infinity, ever extended by the fates and the muses.

We sat in the pink rockers, peering at the weaving shadows, brushing lightly from the sea.

Our souls talked to each other.

"Where have you been, Joanie?

I have often thought of you. I felt your prayers on my shoulders. Miss Sarah and Joanie Cipolla, I often said your names."

"Where is Miss Sarah?"

"She passed maybe half a dozen years ago. She was more than a mother to me.

But, you, Joanie. I never expected to see you again, although I often thought of you.

You are so beautiful. Why did you never marry?"

We sat in the pink rockers, words flowing easily in the night.

"I was in the convent. I was a sister.

I prayed for your safety every morning. I prayed for your safety every evening.

I even had the other nuns remember you in their prayers. They were great at praying. Perhaps that's what you felt."

"It was something. I felt that someone was looking out for poor dumb me. I never dreamt that you would enlist a whole regiment oh holy Catholic sisters.

That's amazing!

Why did you leave, Joanie? I bet you were a good sister. You do everything so well."

I told him of a life I had almost forgotten. I spoke of a life that had vanished forever. I told him in words I had never spoken before.

"You were a good sister," he whispered.

"That was then. This is now, Joanie. This is our now."

The mist from the sea laid a soft mist on the marsh. The wrens and the egrets slept safely in their nests. The sea had lost its energy.

"Go slow," I said softly.

"That's the way I am," whispered Sumter.

He held me closely. He kissed me on the cheek.

"What a night," I whispered.

Chapter 11

Am

It was like facing the Irish Inquisition the next morning. They were all stretched out in their pajamas and their slippers when I arose. I could hardly get a cup of coffee in my hand before they were at me.

"Midnight stroll on the beach," asked Bridie?

"A little scene from Here to Eternity, Deborah Kerr and Burt Lancaster," chirped in Mary.

"Sumter's too cool for a fool," offered Peggy. "Jesus, none of our guys look like that."

"Sweep you off your feet," smiled Sheila.

They were at me.

I sipped the coffee slowly and shook my head.

No! No! No!

"Sure," they all nodded.

"Who made the java," I smiled coyly at them?

"We were waiting for you, Joanie," whispered Bridie. "We were all up with the birds, and you were still cutting some ZZZs."

"It was a long night," I answered softly, stretching out in a chair.

"We know, Joanie, we know," answered Peggy intently. "But we are your lifelong gumbahs, your friends, your paisans from Hayden Avenue.

We knew you when you were a wimp."

"We sure did," chimed in the others.

"I was never a wimp. You guys would still be skipping rope if I wasn't there to lead you around."

Word games. Street lingo. Linking lives.

God, we were still at it. It made me feel so good.

The four of them, biddies like their mothers and grandmothers, gave me so much solace.

The memory of the evening, the strength of Sumter's hands, gave me so much joy. There was peace, but there was much more. I could hardly contain my joy.

"Are you ready," I asked in all seriousness? "I'll tell you all about what you want to know."

Bridie slid her chair closer. The others leaned forward intensely.

"Sumter is a doll," I started. "I think if any of you guys were still single, you'd fall for him.

But my friends put me in the trick bag. You guys set me up. That's the biddy in all of you Micks. I feel sorry for your daughters."

I got up and stretched, walking leisurely to the kitchen for another cup of coffee.

They were sitting on the edge of their seats.

"Anyone want more java?"

"Forget the java," piped Bridie. "Get on with the good stuff."

"Oh, the good stuff. It was so wonderful.

After all of you girls went off to dreamland, Sumter and I sat on the dock for a long time. He held my hand.

It was a foreign feeling, a most beautiful feeling to sit over the creek and hold his hand.

Then we went to the pink rockers on the porch, and sat and rocked, and looked at the ocean.

And talked."

"Wow," exclaimed Peggy. "Get to the part where you are getting it on."

"I'm getting there."

"You don't have to tell us everything," chirped in Mary. "None of us have shared our most intimate secrets."

"Who wanted to hear about you and Smoky," brandished Bridie. "Get it on, Joanie."

I loved them. They were so dear to me. We would do anything for one another.

"We sat there and we talked.

Miss Sarah died about five years ago. Sumter's daddy is fine. Sumter and his daddy are still buying land, just like years ago.

The Fairlane runs great. Sumter changes the oil every 3000 miles. Frog and Alison are a ticket. Sumter never thought he'd see the day.

I told him about my years in the convent. I told him about 'Cipollas.' We talked about recipes.

We talked about the price of fresh vegetables, and beans, and okra."

"No smooching," queried Sheila coyly?

"A girl has to have some secrets."

A girl has to keep some things close to her heart, I thought. And then it hit me. It had been ever so many years since I had thought about myself as a girl.

Eddie Blythe anchored the Osprey near a fishing dock in the Sampit River.

There was a grand marina where the wide Waccamaw flowed into Winyah Bay, but the fishing docks of the Sampit had a character that he loved.

The docks were just a step or two off Front Street, the commercial center of Georgetown since the time of first rice planters.

Georgetown was much like its brother city Charleston, sixty miles to the south. Winyah Bay was every bit as wide and as beautiful as the bay at Charleston. But the plantation owners had chosen Charleston, two an a half centuries past, to be the greater center of commerce.

Charleston was big, abundant, and bountiful.

Georgetown was small, fragile, and serene.

Eddie Blythe could walk its oak shaded streets, past homes with small wooden placards, telling their date of birth.

1740,1758,1816,1787; they were all measured by antiquity.

Georgetown's secrets were open and visible to the discerning eye. The yards were open almost rustic, not like their gated brethren in Charleston.

He could walk a cobbled path, feel an ancient cornice, wipe his brow beneath a spacious oak. He could visit the manuscript room of the historic library, studying the aspirations and the hardships of the past.

Sometimes Eddie wished, in the quiet of the night, that he were only a writer or a teacher.

But the agency had swept him from the stream so long ago, so easily, so enchantingly; that he could only dream.

The Taggart address in Camden was a concrete block building. It sold automobile supplies.

"Looking for Taggart Lumber," Jack told the young man at the counter. "This is the address I was given."

"Never heard of it. We sell auto parts. Been here a long time. There is a Lowes down the road. Take a right at Hucklebeys Barbecue."

"Phantom," said Jack when he returned to the car.

"Nothing's easy," answered Mike. "Different country. Same game."

"Let's check into a Holiday Inn and find a golf course," suggested Jack. "I'll call the Postal Inspectors in Columbia, get one of them down here. Check out the Post Office Box."

"Quarter a hole," said Mike. "No mulligans."

"Can't play without takeovers. Two mulligans," answered his partner.

"I'll buy the dinner tonight, Hucklebeys Barbecue. Well get a little grease on our kissers."

Sumter wore me out. He totally wore me out. I'd never been with a person with so much going on.

"It's not me, it's the car," he chided. "I go where it takes me."

Cleveland had its neighborhoods. It had the Hill. It had the Heights. It had Downtown.

This was different. Sumter's chariot took us down dusty roads, through fertile fields.

It took us to a tobacco auction. It took us to a field where a machine was picking cotton. It took us to a bank in Kingstree. It took us along the Black River to Frogs.

It took us to his daddy's house.

"Miss Joanie," his daddy greeted me.

"Just Joanie."

"Okay, Miss Joanie," he winked.

"The south, Joanie," Sumter squeezed my hand. "All pretty girls are called Miss in the south."

The Fairlane took us to a red brick church along the road.

"This is where Miss Sarah is buried. Do you want to stop?"

We were walking hand in hand from the grave when a small Black minister came scurrying from the parsonage.

"So this is Miss Joanie. She is even prettier than I had heard."

"Reverend Croffer," said Sumter. "This is Miss Joanie, Joanie Cipolla. Joanie, this is the Reverend Myles Croffer."

I was flustered as I extended my hand.

"How did you know my name?"

They just stood there and chuckled, man sort of chuckling, like two home boys out in the field.

"Sumter boy, has been driving that shiny old car around here for a long time," smiled the Reverend. "Everybody knows Sumter Rutledge and his daddy. They are like furniture.

Well, the only one we ever see riding with Sumter is his daddy, and sometimes old bull necked Frog.

Sumter boy is like John the Baptist, out by the river, just looking for the Lord."

"I'm not the Lord," I laughed.

"I know, Miss Joanie," he continued, just rocking and talking. His voice was melodious, scented by the freshness of the autumn air.

"You are too pretty to be the Lord. Well, Sumter has been carrying you all over for two or three days.

Sister Louise, she called me. Sister Bertha called me. Spider Maxwell, he called me, and he's been sick in bed for more than a year, and can hardly see.

The phone has been buzzing off the hook. I hardly had any time to do the work of the Lord.

They all said, 'Sumter is buzzing around with this pretty young lady, Miss Joanie.'

That's the way this old minister, in the middle of the Lord's lush fields, came to know your name."

When we got back to the car, I squeezed Sumter's hand as tight as I could. I wrapped my arms around him and kissed him mightily.

"What are you doing to me?"

"About the same thing you are doing to me, Joanie."

"Are you just showing me off, gallivanting whoever knows where? Showing me off to all the sister Berthas and the spider whatever man?"

"That's the way I am," he answered, returning my kisses. "I'm always out here, doing this or that. That's my way.

Nobody gives a big damn most of the week. But Joanie, Miss Joanie, you've got most of South Carolina talking."

I couldn't hide my feelings from the girls. They had read too many romance novels.

"Out there by yourself," said Bridie.

"Just looking around."

"You are doing more than looking," laughed Peggy.

"Maybe so. What have you guys been up to?"

"The beach," said Sheila. "Collecting shells. Doing a little shopping. We all called home this afternoon. All the kids are doing great."

"Smoky's a McDonalds freak," said Mary. "Notre Dames on TV tomorrow and the Browns on Sunday. He's all set."

"Frog and Sumter are coming by tomorrow morning. They are going to show us how to catch shrimp."

"Sumter who," they all smiled?

There was no way I could explain.

"He's taking me to dinner in Georgetown tomorrow night. Down by the river on Front Street.

Do my paisans want to go along as chaperones?"

"Not a bad idea," said Bridie. "But we bought a big pot roast up at the store. We are going to be Irish biddies tomorrow night; cook the roast, make some highballs, and gossip on the porch.

We are all getting old, damn it. Our days of romance and adventure are behind us."

Frog was a magician on the water. He was like a giant leprechaun on the dock.

"Let Frog show you everything," counseled Sumter. "He went to grade school on the water."

"Not exactly, Sumter boy, but there are things I can show these girls. What have you ladies been trying to catch?"

"Shrimp, with this casting net," answered Peggy. "We throw it but it never opens up."

"Not for ladies," answered Frog. "Too hard.

I'll show you how grandmother used to do it. The way the Indians used to do it. It's an easy way, but you won't be able to sit on the dock. You'll have to get in the water and get mud on your feet."

He unwrapped a small screen net. It had short handles on either end. It had small weights along its bottom.

"This is a seine net. Not much different than the nets you see hanging from the shrimp boats. Except they're bigger and stronger.

In fact, I have an arm from a shrimper at my place now, fixing it for the captain."

"Frog does everything," explained Sumter. "If something's broken, he can fix it. If something is in the water, he can catch it."

"I used to dance a little," chuckled the big man, doing a little shuffle across the deck.

"Now I'm just an old handyman. Well, the shrimp, they swim along with the tide, going nowhere in a hurry like me and Sumter, sort of.

You have to get down in the water, take your shoes off, stretch out the net a person on either handle, and walk against the tide.

Then close the net, handle to handle, and pour the shrimp into a pail."

First Frog and Mary did it. Then Sheila and Bridie. Then me and Peggy gave it a turn.

They were squiggly wiggly beepy boppers. They had long whiskers and tiny staring eyes.

"You have to pull off the heads," said Frog.

"You have to be kidding," we pleaded.

"We don't eat if you don't clean them."

"Yuck," said Mary.

"The shrimp has a long vein," Frog explained

He held up a spindly critter. Then he squeezed its back, and pulled off the head and the vein.

"The vein pops right out when they are fresh from the creek. Throw the shrimp into this other pail and the heads into the grass. The birds and the raccoons will feast on them."

We spent the afternoon feasting on fresh shrimp and a salad out on the dock.

A few fishermen waved as they went by on flat bottomed boats. Blue herons and snowy white egrets nested among the reeds. A raccoon came by and made fast work of the heads.

I held Sumter's hand. The world was at peace.

Postal Inspector Bob Santo arrived at the Holiday Inn as the two FBI agents were finishing breakfast.

"Had to get up early. Long drive. How can I help you fellows?"

"Looking for a Post Office Box record, an application, an address, anything you can find," answered Jack.

"Here is the number. Name is Taggart, maybe a lumber company, when it was first rented, years ago, I suppose. Who picks up the mail. All the who, when, and hows.

Take long?"

"Sometimes. Depends. These offices keep their records on 3x5 cards. Sometimes they are up to date, sometimes not.

I'll see what I can see. Meet you back here about four."

"What do we do today," winked Jack?

"What else," answered Mike? "Nine holes of golf. Try to shoot our age, break fifty-five."

Bob Santo was back a little after four.

"Covered the whole route for you guys today."

"The whole route," smiled Mike. "You must have been a mailman."

"I was. But now I'm making a special delivery to you."

He handed Jack a manila envelope.

"What have you got," asked Jack?

"A miracle! They had an old time box clerk named Notes Baldwin who took care of the boxes for more than thirty years. He kept notes on everything. His boxes were his domain, if you get what I mean.

Then his niece, Miss Emily Baldwin, a real spinster eccentric inherited the job. She is almost as crazy as her uncle was.

She keeps meticulous records. I had to show her my badge three times and get the Postmaster to talk to her before she would let me look at the records.

I told her it was a general check up. She said she would like to call her uncle, Notes, to see if it had ever been done before. But he had died. I was afraid she could still contact him.

Well, I got the current file card, and file cards from long ago, and got you copies."

"Good job, brother," laughed Mike. "She go for you?"

"She almost called Washington. Said the box files were not a public record," roared the Inspector. "I told her this was going to be an annual thing, but I wouldn't go back, not on my craziest day.

The records show that the box was first rented by the Taggart Lumber Company in 1948. That's a long time ago. If it wasn't for Notes and Miss Emily you'd never have that record."

"Who picks up the mail," asked Mike? "Did you find that out?"

"A courier service, Camden Delivery. It was duly authorized in 1974. Camden Delivery also pays the box rent every year.

So I went over to Camden Delivery and looked at their records. They didn't give me a hard time. These courier services will always let us look at their records. We could put them out of business.

They pick up mail from over forty boxes. Taggart is only one of them. They have no idea which record I was looking for.

All their records are on computer. I got a printout of the whole shebang. Taggart Lumber is on the list. They forward the mail to an address in Arlington, VA. Care of a Bud Sweeney.

There is another name on their file, Mike Taggart, Pawleys Island, and a telephone number."

"All in the envelope," asked Jack?

" All in the envelope," answered Inspector Santo.

"Keep this under your hat," said Jack. "Nothing, even to your boss."

"Like a cat in a bag," answered Bob Santo.

The girls were on the porch when we left for dinner. They were like house mothers.

It was a beautiful evening. The stars were showing their first sparkle. A full moon was rising over the Atlantic.

I chose a faint pink flowery cotton, which seemed to be caressed by the scent of the pines.

It was the first time I had seen Sumter wearing a suit. He wore a light tan gabardine, which took my heart away.

"You're beautiful," he said, as we drove the road to Georgetown.

"You're not so bad, yourself," I whispered, laying my head close on his shoulder.

"First formal date. Had to put on my best for the occasion."

"Sumter, Sum," I answered. "My Sum."

We parked near an ancient clock tower. Front Street was lit by small globed street lamps. The walks were of weathered brick.

He guided me through a small formal garden, stopping to cut a rose.

"You are a thief."

"A cheap rascal," he answered. "But you, Joanie, you are the one who is stealing my heart.

Now, how can we pin this on?"

"A girl always has a pin in her purse," I smiled, kissing him softly on the cheek.

We walked a long wooden promenade by the river. It was like a picture off a post card, iron railed, stretching along the river. Large wooden barrels of impatiens and lantana were everywhere.

Globe lit lamps gave it illumination. Wooden park benches cast their shadows on the river.

Shrimp boats, their nets uplifted, bobbed in the water. A lonely sailing vessel, shiny and crimson, looked askance at its brothers.

"Osprey," I said to Sumter, "a lonely ship on a lonely river. What is an Osprey?"

"A hawk of the river. Its wing spread is almost that of an eagle. It swoops down and lifts fish from the water with its talons. A lonely bird of the sea."

It was a wonderful night. We dined leisurely, like it could go on forever.

The restaurant was oak tabled and wooden chaired. Ancient ship's lanterns provided dim light. It had the décor and aroma of the sea.

The walls were of ancient brick. The beams were splintered and chiseled by the seasons. Slowly turning ceiling fans wafted each aroma.

"Like it," smiled Sumter?

"I love it. I'm a restaurant person."

"Among other things, Joanie. Among other things. I bet your place, 'Cipollas', is fancier than this."

"In a different way. I would give my eyeteeth to have this ambiance; the walkway, the river, the comfort of the brick.

I feel like a Miss Joanie."

We had an appetizer of Clams Casino, with a small glass of wine.

We ordered broiled grouper, seasoned in the most delicate of sauces, and laid exquisitely over a bed of the purest rice.

We looked into each other's eyes, into each other's souls, into each other's hearts.

We had another glass of wine, and tiny tea cakes for desert.

I was in love with the evening. I was feeling I was falling in love with Sumter.

It was a feeling that I had never had before.

It was as if the present was perfect, and it would be the present forever, and ever.

My slippers were hardly on the floor, my hand lightly on Sumter's arm, as we left the restaurant.

As I glanced into the restaurant bar, I was startled. My feet became leaden. A chill appeared in the warm evening air.

"What's wrong, Joanie?"

"Let me sit for a minute," I pleaded.

"Is it the food?"

We wandered to a bench on the walkway.

I told him the story of Sister Marcetta.

"She is my friend, the closest friend I had in the convent. She is my Italian gumbah. She is the first one I told when I decided to leave.

She was my teacher, all of ours teacher, when we were only in the ninth grade. It seems like a lifetime ago.

She went to El Salvador to work in the missions___to aid the forgotten.

She wrote me so many beautiful letters, full of God, and goodness, and grace.

She wrote me of the Contras, the soldiers, who were pillaging the villages.

She said they had tattoos on their arms, arrows going backward, symbols of an evil brotherhood.

She said they had the best of American arms.

They killed two peasants in her village___bashed in Sister Marcetta's head___almost killed her.

That was almost three years ago. She has recovered now, by the grace of God. She is teaching this year.

No authority in this country could find out anything___not news-papers___politicians___Not the Bishops.

My uncle, Johnny Seeds, really his name is John Loparo, said some Italian guys, maybe like La Cosa Nostra if it really exists, were looking into what really happened.

Somehow, I think, they started to learn something___more than any other could learn. They are very close mouthed.

Uncle Johnny asked me to call him if any strangers came asking about Sister Marcetta.

Two strangers came to the restaurant soon after. They came to 'Cipollas.'

I saw the two strangers again tonight. They were sitting in the bar as we left the restaurant.

Johnny Seeds, Uncle Johnny, told me they were mixed up with a secretive government agency, like the CIA.

He said his guys had a way of finding out things. It was part of their business."

Sumter held me tightly. His strong arms were around me.

"I'm here. I'm here, Joanie."

"So am I, Sumter. But a few moments ago, I was in another place and another time with you.

I had no thought at all of what I just told you."

"Are you sure they were the same two men? It might have been your imagination."

"I am sure. When they came to 'Cipollas', it was as if a dark cloud hovered over their table. I could sense the same cloud when I saw them tonight.

I am sorry, Sum, to spoil the evening. I loved every moment of it."

"You didn't spoil anything, Joanie. You could never spoil anything for me.

I love you, Joanie."

Chapter 12

Be

I couldn't hide my feelings from the girls the next morning.

"What's up, Joanie," asked Mary?

"Just thinking," I lied.

"Want to talk," asked Sheila?

"Later, gumbahs," I answered halfheartedly.

I knew I had to tell them something, but I didn't want to drag them into anything. There was so much on my mind.

Sumter and me, and the two strangers popping up from nowhere, and Johnny Seeds.

"Let's go to church in Georgetown," I said. "We've sort of let the spiritual thing slide when we're on vacation."

"Great idea," seconded Bridie, "like the priests would say, keep the faith."

I looked for a sign during mass, something to give me direction. But God just stared back at me, as if I was one of the multitude.

I felt alone.

After mass we walked silently, wandering down to the boardwalk beside the river.

"All right, Joanie," started Bridie. "What's with the funk? You were in great spirits yesterday."

"Is it about Sumter," asked Mary?

"Partly. He told me he loved me. I think I love him."

"Then what's wrong, Joanie," Sheila's voice befriended me. "Don't be afraid of love."

"I'm not afraid of love. I'm not afraid of Sumter. But I don't want to hurt him. I don't want to hurt you guys.

I don't want to involve you in things which I know only a little bit about."

"You are talking in riddles," offered Bridie. "Come on, Joanie. We've been together since the second grade. We have all had our problems. We have always stood by each other."

Bridie was strong. She had always been outspoken. She would have made a great Mother Superior.

She was dark Irish. She was blunt. She wasn't a philosopher like many of her brethren. She was a doer.

"It goes way back. It goes back to when Sister Marcetta almost got killed in El Salvador.

You guys remember all the stories that were in the paper and everything. Nobody could get a straight answer about what was going on."

"It was a cover up, like Nixon and Watergate," answered Bridie.

"My uncle, John Loparo, they call him Johnny Seeds, he came to the restaurant and said some Italian guys were looking into what happened to Sister Marcetta.

Uncle Johnny is tied in with a lot of guys on the Hill, a lot of stuff that is kept under the table. But he is a good guy.

Sister Marcetta was my closest friend in the convent. You guys know that. She wrote me many letters about what was going on in El Salvador.

Uncle Johnny told me that if any strangers came by asking about Sister Marcetta to call him.

Well two strangers came by, well dressed men in their early forties, asking about Sister Marcetta."

"And you called Johnny Apples," said Mary anxiously.

"I owed it to Sister Marcetta. She is my gumbah."

"She is a gumbah to all of us," said Sheila. "She is the salt of the earth. I think she passed us all through the ninth grade just for steel wooling the floors.

But what does this have to do with your droopsy today?"

"We were leaving the restaurant last night, right here on the river, me and Sumter, all romantic kind of. I looked over and saw the same two men sitting in the bar."

"Are you sure," asked Bridie? "Maybe you were only getting the romantic fidgets.

We all got those things when we first met our old men, something about taking the next step in life. Once I thought I saw Jesus waving a finger at me."

"Yeah, like warm hands on unwilling flesh," piped in Peggy. "We all got them.

Danielle Steele puts them in all of her romances, in one form or another. But of course, you never read many of her books in the convent."

"No, I'm sure it was the same two men. They were dressed in casual clothes, but I'm sure it was them."

"Did you tell Sumter," asked Sheila?

"We sat out here for maybe an hour. The night had taken on a chill. The stars had disappeared from the sky.

I told him about Sister Marcetta and Johnny Seeds. He held me in his arms and told me that he loved me.

I can't involve you guys and Sumter in all this. You all are too dear to me."

We sat quietly looking over the water. Each of us had her own thoughts.

When we were young, the girls of East Cleveland, we would have skipped off the spindled rails, seeking adventure down the street.

But time and the passing of the years had taken some shimmer from the cloth. Each of us had her own life to lead, her own personal problems to sort out.

I wondered if I did have the fidgets. I wondered if I had the right to get them involved in how I felt for Sumter.

Maybe the merry-go-round was spinning too fast.

We wandered aimlessly, listlessly, down the boardwalk. We wandered toward a group of shrimp boats, their nets hanging loosely in the autumn air. I glanced offhandedly at the sailing ship I had seen the night before.

"El fungula!"

The words leapt across my lips before I could catch myself.

"Jesus, Mary, and Joseph," exclaimed Bridie. "The broken hearted paisan has come back to us."

"Quiet," I said.

"What's up," asked Sheila?

"See that large sailboat. It was there last night. The man in the white T shirt, up on the deck, is one of the strangers."

"Who are the others, the two darker men," asked Mary?

"I have an idea who they might be. Two of you go up closer, sort of touristy like. Get a good look at their arms. Look for tattoos."

The day was sparkling again. The sun was dancing off the waters. The fog had lifted.

Bridie and Peggy skipped along the boardwalk like a pair of southern belles. They went far down the walk, picked a few flowers from the baskets, threw petals on the water, and stopped to tweak the chin of a baby in a stroller.

God, they could play games. I thought they would never get back.

"Get anything," I asked when they returned?

"The boat is named the Osprey," said Bridie. "It has a Virginia registration number on the hull. Your stranger isn't bad looking."

"The other two could be of Spanish descent," chipped in Peggy. "They have long hair like sixties flower children. They have black arrows tattooed on their left arms."

"Fidgets," I said. "My friends accuse me of having some sort of fidgets."

"We're all in the dark," exclaimed Sheila.

"Lets get back to Pawleys," I answered. "I'll let you all in on what's going down."

"How did you know about the tattoos," asked Mary after we were settled back at the beach?

The others were all listening with serious looks on their faces.

"Sister Marcetta mentioned it in her letters. Johnny Seeds told me that the marks were a symbol of solidarity, of a secret brotherhood, like made men."

"What are you going to do," asked Sheila?

"Whatever you do is A-okay with all of us," said Peggy.

"Right," they all nodded.

"What would you do? What would each of you do?"

"Call Johnny Seeds," they all answered.

I called Johnny that afternoon.

"Ya mean they got a sailboat and two of the tattooed guys on it?"

"I saw it this morning."

"Wait a minute, Joanie. Let me check some papers."

"Is the boat named the Osprey," he asked when he returned?

"How did you know?"

"How do you get to that place you are?"

"Fourteen hour drive, or take a plane to Charlotte, then transfer to Myrtle Beach."

"Too slow. We want some pictures of them SOBs on the boat. I'm flying down tomorrow morning on a trucking company's plane. Marty Lupo, you know the photographer, will be with me.

I'm going to see if I can dig up a guy called Danny Moriarity, who's the best surveillance guy around. He's a nice guy. We call him Bus Stop, because he's always sitting looking at something. Nobody ever sees him."

"There won't be any heavy stuff, will there, Uncle Johnny. I'm down here with four of my friends from forever. They all have kids and families, just plain people."

"No, Joanie, sweetheart. I can assure you that. I'm just an old man. Marty Lupo takes pictures. Bus Stop looks at people. That's all we'll do. Get us three rooms at the Mariott."

"There's no Mariott at Pawleys."

"Holiday Inn, then."

"No Holiday Inn, either."

"What's in this Pawleys burg," he stammered.

"A Ramada Inn up on a golf course."

"I hate golf. Get us three rooms, all in my name. We'll be there tomorrow. And, Joanie. You listen, sweetheart.

This is our business. Stuff you don't know nothing about. You don't know nothing about it. Frankie don't know nothing about it. Your friends don't know nothing about it.

You all go on with whatever you girls do on vacation. It sounds nice. Go on with the whole thing. Stay away from the boat, what you told me about."

"We will, Uncle Johnny."

"And, Joanie, one other thing, an important thing, for your peace of mind and your friends. The outfit that these guys are with depends on secrecy.

We've cracked them and they don't know they are cracked. That's the way it's going to be until the time is right.

You got my word. You can take it to the bank. No heavy stuff. Just don't worry."

"I won't, Uncle Johnny. I won't."

"Thanks, Joanie. I owe you one."

Jack Foley and Mike Blackwell arrived at Pawleys on Sunday afternoon. They checked into a Ramada Inn. It was on a golf course.

They had stopped at a small Catholic Mission in Kingstree in the morning. There was no priest. There was no mass.

Two graying sisters ran the show. They read from scripture. One gave a sermon on the gospel of the day. They read announcements on when the food bank and the clinic would be open.

The congregation was small, both white and black.

One sister spoke with a brogue.

After the service Mike asked her if she'd been born in Ireland.

"Where else would I be born?"

"What town, sister," asked Jack?

"Swineford, in County Mayo."

"Never heard of it," said Jack

"A lot of her kin in Cleveland," said Mike. "A lot of people from Mayo."

"A lot of my kin everywhere," she smiled. "We packed our bags and headed for England or the States."

"That's the story of the Irish," said Jack. "Ever sorry that you left, Sister?"

"I was barefoot there. I'm sort of barefoot here.

Jesus called and I answered. These people need all the help that God can give. It's not much of a story."

"It's a story that's been going on forever," smiled Jack. "Thank you, Sister. You made our day."

"I feel like we have been going in circles," said Jack after they were settled in the motel.

"It's been that kind of a week," answered Mike. "I'm beat. We have a nice room on a beautiful golf course and I don't give a damn if I ever play again."

"Me either, Michael. Golf is a diversion, a relaxation to me.

This Taggart thing is a puzzle. Sometimes I am thinking we are looking for someone or something that isn't there. A sham."

"I've got the same feeling," said Mike. "Who is what is who?

This fellow Taggart borrowed thirty million bucks on three pieces of land that are almost scrabble. Nothing is being developed or sold.

The mortgage payments are up to date. The bank is going under from all kinds of loans like Taggarts. Where is the pile of schekels?

Taggart, whoever he is, could be about to fold the whole caboodle and take a walk. And we can't figure it out."

"We have a telephone number here at Pawleys," said Jack. "And only a fool would call it. Not you or I, buddy boy.

We have to work in circles on this thing. Find Mike Taggart without him spotting us first, Bureau Primer 101, the old slow way."

We were sitting on the porch when Sumter drove up.

"Checking if you were all right, Joanie," he said as he grasped my hand.

"Better than last night."

"That's good. I was worried. It might have been something you ate."

"No, Sumter," I answered, holding his arm tightly. "It wasn't the food. I was right last night about the strangers.

We went to mass this morning in Georgetown. I spotted one of the men again. He was on that sloop in the river, the Osprey."

"Are you sure?"

"A-one positive. There were two dark skinned men with him. The girls got a good look at them. They had arrows on their arms, like Sister Marcetta described in her letters."

Sumter looked over at Bridie.

"She's telling you like it is," nodded Bridie. "We all thought she had a case of nerves when we saw her this morning and heard about last night, but everything Joanie said is gospel."

"You will all have to go back to Cleveland," started Sumter. "There is something going on here that is bigger than all of you, bigger than all of us."

We all looked at him. I loved him. He was so damn serious.

"I'm not going," I answered, squeezing his arm a little tighter.

"Neither are we," said my paisans.

"Are you all crazy," he half stammered?

"You all have lives to lead, families, children.

I love Joanie. I love all of you. But this isn't your business!

You know that, Sheila! You know that, Mary! You know that, Peggy! You know that, Bridie!

Even if everything you said is true, and I believe you, I know that you girls can't do anything about it."

"Wait a minute, Sumter," said Mary. "We've all thought a long time about this."

"Just listen," said Bridie.

We all sat around on the porch, leaning close to each other, like the girls we used to be.

There was no sound from the sea. We had no eye for the flight of the gull, no ear for the song of the wren.

"I called Johnny Seeds," I said as I looked into Sumter's eyes. "I didn't know what to do until I saw the strangers on the boat. They were like Sister Marcetta described them.

I was going to let the whole thing slide, let the dead bury the dead. But I got totally pissed off when I saw those men."

"Joanie swore," exclaimed Mary.

"I did more than that. I made up my mind. We Italian women have minds too.

A long time ago we had a friend named Benny Maloney. He was a friend to each of us. He's dead now, God rest his soul.

He used to say, 'all we are is old tunes and memories.' He would go with the flow. Benny was wrong. I hate to say it, but Benny was wrong.

Each day is a new day. This day is a new day.

Sumter, you know how I feel about you. But I can't just walk away like when I left the convent. I was right to leave, but leaving left a few scars in my heart.

The wounds are healing; time and the joys of my new life have helped heal them. My friends have helped heal them. The work in the restaurant helped heal them. You, Sumter, have helped heal them.

But if I don't help Sister Marcetta, even if I can't, there is just another wound."

"She hears a voice calling her, Sumter," pleaded Sheila.

"A long time ago, it seems so long ago, I asked you why you had to go back to Nam. Remember?"

"I remember."

"You said voices were calling you."

"I remember, Sheila. It wasn't something I would have chosen. It was something I had to do. I went back again, and a third time until I could no longer hear them calling."

"We are all in this with Joanie, Sumter. That's the way it's going to be."

"When I called Uncle Johnny," I started, "he assured me there would be no trouble. He knows a lot. He even knew the name of the boat in the river, the Osprey.

He is flying in tomorrow. He is bringing Marty Lupo to take some pictures. Marty is a nice guy. He often eats at our restaurant.

He is also bringing another guy, a Danny Bus Stop, who he says is the best surveillance guy in Cleveland.

Whatever is going on, Uncle Johnny knows more than anybody ever found out about Sister Marcetta."

"What can I say," breathed Sumter. "Last night I was holding hands and dreaming with you, Joanie. Now, you and your gumbahs, my good friends, are about to do something a lot of people would think of as crazy.

Remember that I've been around the block a bit. I'd like to meet your Johnny Seeds. You will all need help.

I'll talk to Frog. Frog and me will be with you.

Okay, Joanie?"

I could feel warm tears coming to my eyes. It was different than love. It was as if he were reaching out and offering us something, something he did not have to give.

We could all feel it.

"And, Sumter," added Bridie, "only Frog. Not a word about this to Alison. We all love Alison. But she is not as close lipped, as we all must be. You got it?"

"Alison is a southern lady," smiled Sumter. "A real southern lady. I know what you mean."

"What are we," asked Mary?

"You are more like guys," he chuckled.

"You are like the tillers of the field, the boys setting off in the early morn to go fishing in the river. You are like good old boys.

I don't believe I'm saying it, but you are like good old boys."

Sumter and I went walking on the beach as the sun was setting. The tide was out. The sea was settling for the night,

We took off our shoes and walked in the surf.

The sky was a mixture of azures, and the reds and golds of autumn leaves. It was luminescent and glistening, as if it was showing its brilliance to fight off the darkness of the night.

We were alone in each other's thoughts, alone in each other's hearts. We could feel each other's strength.

The island was so beautiful, so different. It was as if time and space had passed it by.

There were the thousand greens of the oaks and bush. There was the golden weave of the marsh. There were singular blooms amidst the sandy dunes.

"Ghosts," said Sumter. "The island has always been inhabited by ghosts. My daddy used to take me here. I came here with Frog when we were boys.

Fish in the surf. Fish in the creek. Light a fire when the sun would set. Everybody knew stories about ghosts.

The plantation owners would build cottages on the island to protect their families from the fever of the fields. The gray man walked the beach to warn of hurricane and storm. Kindhearted witches lived in the woods across the marsh.

Families vanished and fortunes were lost, wars were fought, but the ghosts are ever here."

"We all have ghosts," I whispered.

"I know, Joanie. We all have ghosts.

But the ghosts of Pawleys are kind spirits. They cling to the beach and the sea.

Sea captains and ships that have been lost forever, fishermen swept away by the surf, young maidens wandering, searching for love forever lost.

Sometimes you only get one chance at love."

"I know, Sumter. Sometimes we only get one chance."

Chapter 13

Are

Mike liked the fresh morning air. It took the kinks out of both his body and his mind.

He left his motel room, stretched back and forth a little, and walked across the parking lot to a small mound. His feet carried him across the dew laden grass to a putting green.

His eyes covered the green and peered down the fairway. He liked looking backwards over golf holes. It gave him a perspective of where he had been.

He stretched, looking at the clear blue of the Carolina sky. He looked at the long leafed pines outlining the fairway. He was alone in his world; soft shoes on the dew laden grass.

He and Jack had spent the previous afternoon outlining their thoughts on long legal pads. There was something there, but neither man could figure what it was.

Two careers on the concrete. Too many years to even remember, and they were sitting in a motel room, in the middle of nowhere, doing investigative primer 101.

"Morning exercise, Mike?"

The familiar raspy voice startled him.

He turned to see Johnny Seeds almost at his shoulder.

"Following me, Johnny? Here to play some golf? Taking a holiday?"

"Bus Stop made you last night, getting a coke in the lobby. I couldn't believe you were here.

You are in 106. Your gunsol is in 107."

"You guys aren't bad. I didn't see Bus Stop. Not that I'd be looking."

"Nobody ever sees him. He's the best that ever was. He knows everybody, where all the cars are parked."

"He don't play any golf," said Mike.

"Neither do I. Waste of time. No action! Bet fifteen cents on a hole and go pissing when you lose. It's a game for losers.

I shouldn't say that. A lot of the guys play the friggin game. But it's still for losers, if you get what I mean."

"Then what are you doing here, Seeds? There are maybe fifteen jukeboxes in all of South Carolina. Are you bastards trying to get everything?"

"The kettle calling the angels black," chuckled Johnny. "The question is, what are you and that stiff you are with, that Jack Foley, doing down here?"

"Bus Stop make him too?"

"No, yours truly. I asked the queen at the desk. She said you guys were checked in for three or four days. No tee times for golf. The stiff is from Chicago.

Want to know anything else? She would have given me the whole life history of everybody in the chateau if I had time to listen."

"Strange place. Strange birds. We should plant a girl like her on the Hill, we could save a lot of guys."

"If we ever had a broad like her around, she would have vanished yesterday."

"What are you doing here Johnny, you and Bus Stop? This isn't your kind of place."

"And you and the stiff, Mike? He's a long way from Chicago. You're a long way from your domain."

Mike could only smile as he looked down the fairway. The trip was taking some funny bounces.

"Lets talk this afternoon. Same place. We'll get some shade under the trees.

You owe me a big one. Remember, gumbah."

"I owe lotsa people lotsa things. We'll talk. I have to make some phone calls first. But we'll talk.

Bring Foley with you. I know you guys are asshole tight."

Jack Foley was waiting at the door of his room.

"Who was that ginzo?"

"John Loparo, Johnny Seeds."

"The Johnny Seeds," chuckled Jack. "We've spent a week in the boondocks talking to Black ministers and Irish nuns getting nowhere. Now, you're talking to the guy who is supposed to know everything.

What gives with him being here?"

"You know Seeds in Chicago?"

"They know him in Vegas. They know him in Miami. They know him everywhere. He is a legend, good buddy. And you pass him off as just Johnny Seeds."

"He's been a friend for a long time. He's not a made man. He's a hanger on, a soldier.

Makes a good living vending now. Used to run after hour joints, a little booking, a lot of loan sharking. Never no bimbos. Never no hits.

He always stayed on the edge. Never served time. Never even indicted for anything. He was an errand boy. Now he's a soldier. You know the story.

They say he saw a guy hit in a barbershop when he was maybe seventeen. He knew the batter. He knew the driver.

Never said a word.

They took care of him.

Got a nice family. Don't hang out all night. Runs a lot of errands. Never says a word.

Except to me once in a while. Not big things. Things that make our job easier. Things that someone wants to be said."

"Is he the guy you called about that Sister Marcetta thing," asked Jack?

"None other. Things that some of our guys want known, I call Johnny Seeds. Not big things. Not about guys we've brought over.

It's all about making things safer for both sides. Like keeping the ball in the court.

It's strange to meet him here. One of his guys made me in the lobby last night, their best eye in town. A guy named Bus Stop, Danny Moriarity. I was getting a coke.

If Seeds didn't want us to see him, he would have been gone, twenty-three skidoo.

He's got something he wants us to know. That's the way the game is played."

"Let's get some coffee and sit down with the pencil and paper again," said Jack. "We've got a lot of figuring ahead of us."

"Scrap all the bullshit," answered Mike. "Lets look back down the fairway, green to tee, starting with that message you guys picked up about Sister Marcetta.

That was a gift from somebody. Seeds knows who and why."

They each got a large cup of coffee from the motel restaurant. They set out the yellow legal pads on a round writing table.

"Message from Garcia," started Jack. "We pick up a message that a bunch of paisans are looking to hit whoever almost killed Sister Marcetta. They think the CIA is mixed up in the mess. Sounded reasonable to me.

That tap never really had any dirty stuff on it. It was always someone angling for a Vegas loan, or a payoff, or routine union gossip."

"You call me in Cleveland. Sister Marcetta was a local girl."

"First we sent the wire to Headquarters. Protocol!"

"What would Headquarters do with it?"

"It would be a Director's thing," answered Jack. "It was a pretty hot item. He would send it over to at least the second top man at the CIA."

"Then two tight assed guys from the agency show up in our Cleveland office asking questions about Sister Marcetta. You bet your badge it was hot."

"And you call Johnny Seeds."

"He says, 'thanks, I owe you one.'

You know, I called him off the cuff. She was one of their own. The SOBs came in and didn't give a good damn about her.

It was strange. He wasn't a bit surprised. It was like he expected a call. All he said was, 'thanks, I owe you one.'

He owes me about a thousand, but he only says that when it's something special."

"If you didn't call him, somebody else would have called one of their guys. That's the way the game is played."

"So we meet up with Johnny in some forlorn beach town in the middle of nowhere. He makes us, then comes forward like a Greek bearing gifts. Like he was glad we were here."

"He is still working on the Sister Marcetta thing, Mike. You can take that to the bank. That's the way they go. Everything's close to the vest. A whole lot of guys aren't involved in one project.

Somehow the ginzos shook the hens from the roost. If Seeds was in on it then, he is in on it now."

"He's got the best eye man around with him. Bus Stop is a trip."

"They fingered the CIA in the El Salvadorian thing," stated Jack. "You can bet your ass on that.

Why else would two of their agents come to Cleveland. Washington covered the whole mess up. Kaput!

Washington hears about the tap in Chicago. Two fools scurry to Cleveland. They got somebody's ear."

"This is the middle of nowhere," mused Mike.

"Look further back," said Jack with a twinkle,"after the war, the big one, when the mob no longer had prohibition and bootlegging to fill their coffers. They still had after hours and gambling in the big cities. But that wasn't enough.

They took the game to Las Vegas, the middle of nowhere, and put together the biggest scam of all. Financed, good brother, by the Teamsters and the Central States Pension fund.

They made their own rules. Great real estate. Coins of gold skimmed right off the top. Nobody knew what was going on.

They were in the middle of nowhere. And they hit the jackpot."

"Same thing here," whistled Mike. "Another secretive organization. They do a lot of stuff they can't do out of Washington. Cities can't keep secrets, especially that one.

Seeds is eyeballing something. And we are looking for Taggart."

"Two small for two scams down here," nodded Jack. "We're chasing thirty million dollars with only a telephone number and a name. This Mike Taggart and a phantom lumber company.

We've got another name in Alexandria, another ghost, this Bud Sweeney.

Do you suppose that the agency got in with the scam on the S&Ls? The Congress wouldn't give them any more money for the Contras. They knew it was Republican bullshit."

"So they scam the loot some other way," winked Jack. "They always have a way. Thirty million dollars off some fields of scrub. No condos. No golf courses.

Mike Taggart and Bud Sweeney. Two names that Johnny Seeds might have in his book, good buddy.

And he owes you a big one!"

Johnny Seeds was waiting for them in the afternoon. He had set up three chairs beneath the shade of the pines.

They looked like three golfers discussing their morning round. Only the birds could hear what they were saying.

"Jack Foley, John Loparo," said Mike introducing the men.

"From Chicago," asked Seeds?

"You got it. I've heard of you."

"Everybody has a rep," answered Seeds. "All this is quiet stuff. Everything under the hat."

"Depends on what it is," answered Mike.

"It's big. It's so big that we don't talk unless everybody has sealed lips."

"It may be big to you, Johnny," answered Mike, "but it may be nothing to the two of us. Nothing at all."

"I ain't going to Confession to no priest," answered Seeds. "I'm just talking to a couple of pricks, who may be interested in what I got to tell them.

Two guys who wouldn't be jerking around here under the trees unless they were interested in what I got to say. Two guys who got to tell me what they are doing, if I'm going to tell them what I got on my mind."

"You've got another guy, Danny Moriarity, with you," said Mike. "Let's begin with what he's doing."

"And I've got another guy, Marty Lupo, with me too."

"Who's he," asked Jack?

"He takes pictures," answered Mike. "Marty and Bus Stop are like private contractors. They use them when they need them. Hangers on."

"Marty takes good pictures," said Johnny with a smile. "He does all the pictures at our weddings and things. A good guy. We throw him things. He makes a good living.

He's got pictures of where Mike's guys park their cars when they go to work. Mike parks his car down by the stadium. An old Chevrolet. Pays fifty cents. Then walks up the hill to the Federal Building.

A cheap guy with an old Chevrolet."

"Morning exercise, Johnny. I'm not really cheap. But I'm not going to give three dollars to some Greek in a parking lot.

Okay, your guys are good, Johnny. But this isn't your city. This is nowhere."

"Nowhere," sniffed Seeds. "What are you stiffs doing here if this is nowhere?"

"We talk. You talk," said Jack.

"Straight," answered Seeds.

"We're looking at funny money," started Jack. "Maybe we're looking for ghosts. It's the S&L thing that has been all over the papers. It's white collar stuff.

Some guy named Taggart or maybe Sweeney has thirty million in loans that isn't worth shit. Your guys would be proud of the scam.

We've been all over South Carolina for a week. All over the God forsaken state. We have a telephone number for Taggart here at Pawleys. We have an address on a Bud Sweeney in Arlington, Virginia.

It's like chasing phantoms."

"Now, what are you doing, Johnny," asked Mike? "It's about Sister Marcetta, isn't it?"

"How did you guess," Seeds asked in surprise?

"We're not complete stiffs," answered Mike. "Both of us have a few whiskers."

"I was in on the tap in Chicago," said Jack. "Your guys never put any dirty stuff on that line. It was a message. We didn't figure it right away, but it was a message."

"You guys are smarter than I thought. Your new guys would have never figured it out. Too much accounting and business school.

You are right. It was a message. Some guys wanted to shake some apples from the trees. See where they would fall."

"Why," asked Mike. "You don't have any super religious guys in your outfit. You make money. You lose money. You are into unions, the vending, Vegas, almost everything.

Sure Sister Marcetta, an Italian nun gets hammered, almost killed, but your guys have seen a lot of this before. Why this Sister?"

"You ever hear about grudges," asked Seeds?

Our guys keep grudges. Sometimes the small ones are taken care of, forgotten. Time cures a lot of things.

Some are too big to be passed off. They simmer and fester and are remembered.

This is something like that. It goes back a long way. I'm only telling you guys this because I know Mike is solid, quiet."

"I can vouch for Jack," said Mike. "We went to the same school."

"It goes back to when Bobby Kennedy was chasing Hoffa," started Seeds. "Our guys could handle that. We had attorneys. We had Congressmen. We had Senators.

The Kennedy brothers screwed around. We knew that.

But when Jack Kennedy got hit, the fucking agency, the CIA, tried to put the rap on our guys.

Why would we hit him? He wasn't that bad a guy.

Jack Ruby, he came out of Chicago. A complete lonesome whore, and he shoots Oswald.

He was a nothing. He was a pimp.

And the CIA puts out the word that he was tied into our big guys in Chicago. No way! Ruby was a lonesome whore.

The CIA, they've got everybody. They have editors. They have columnists. They have guys writing bullshit in books.

They tried to tie our guys to trying to get Castro. If we wanted Castro, we could have got him. All bullshit!

You guys, the FBI, you chase us for what you think we've done. For what you think we might do. That's the game.

The other agency, the CIA, played us like sitting ducks. They went anyplace, whispered to anybody, anything that could take the heat off them. A complete bunch of bastards.

Totally protected. Totally American fucking patriotic.

They lied and chiseled in Vietnam. They lied and chiseled in El Salvador.

Our guys know what's going on. But they are so well hidden, so well protected, that nobody's got the balls to get near them.

They have spooks all over the place. They sell secrets to the Reds. They bring in a Red. The Russians get three of theirs.

But they are hidden. They have power. The bastards that write the papers, some know what's going on, but they bury it.

Total patriots! Total national security!

Well, Sister Marcetta gets almost killed. Our guys know they are in on it. They send out a message, knowing your guys would pass it on. A few ripe apples fall from the tree.

And here we are talking in the middle of nowhere."

"Quite a story," said Jack. "How many apples did you shake out?"

"Three. All with your unknowing help, my friends. We got three of them fingered, maybe four.

It's a funny life.

You know the one I owe you, Mike. I can maybe help you out with what you are doing.

But one other thing, guys. It's as quiet as, what do they say, church mouses. No calls to Chicago. No calls to Cleveland.

If what I think is right, almost feel is right, these SOBs will disappear so fast you won't even be able to smell their shoes."

"You got our word," answered Mike.

"One more thing, guys. I'm taking you out for a good meal tonight, down on the island.

I'll pick you up about eight, when it's getting dark. Dress casual, like tourists.

There are some people you have to meet."

I spent the afternoon in the kitchen. It was almost like I was running the restaurant, working off excess frustrations.

"What are you making, paisan," Sheila asked?

"Italian night, Sheila. Uncle Johnny and his guys are coming to dinner. It's just a little something. Some rigatoni. Some sausage and meatballs. A salad."

"Where can you get good Italian sausage down here," asked Bridie? "Good barbecue and hog maybe, but none of the good sausage."

"I use a lot of spice. Cover everything up like new paint on an old wall. I bought this country sausage. Soak it a while in a bit of vinegar and oil. Add a taste of garlic and oregano."

I was starting to feel back on top of my game.

"Clean the place up some, will you gang. We have a large crowd coming for dinner."

"It is clean," answered Mary. "Cleaner than all our houses ever are."

I scurried around shaking my head.

"Hair curlers, curling irons, nail polish, books all over the place. Get the vacuum. Straighten out the throw rugs."

They were astonished. Their kids had books and games all over the place. There were half written papers and sega wires everywhere.

"Jesus," said Peggy. "Who is coming, the Pope?"

"No," mocked Bridie. "Joanie has invited her waddeo buddy, the apple seed man."

"And the street car guy," laughed Peggy. "Danny Boy, Street Car."

"And don't forget the picture guy," added Sheila. "Marty, the picture guy. Don't any of Joanie's friends have regular names?"

"She knows the Frog guy," quipped Bridie. "Now that's a good Christian name."

They scurried about, picking up everything. Mary and Peggy even polished the coffee tables and the kitchen counters.

It gave the house the aroma of the freshest pine.

I could only smile as I stirred the sauce.

There was no doubt in the girl's minds. Joanie was their leader. She had always been out front. Now, as they approached mid life and grandchildren, she was still their leader.

"We'll have to serve buffet style," I said. "A lot of people."

"You want candles, paisan," chided Bridie. "A bunch of Italian friends and you want to make it like a restaurant on the Hill. Should we all wear peasant dresses with doilies on our heads?"

"Not a bad idea," I laughed. "But I could never pass my Irish friends off as Italian serving girls. Not enough oo-la-la. Too many freckles."

Sumter and Frog arrived first. The house permeated with the aromas of the rigatoni and the sauce.

"Italian cuisine," smiled Frog. "I love good Italian food. It smells like my favorite Italian restaurant in Charleston."

"You'll never get anything this good in Charleston," admonished Peggy. "Joanie's cooking is like nowhere in the south."

Johnny Seeds and two strangers arrived moments later.

Johnny gave me a big hug.

The two strangers stood back when they entered the beach house, as if surprised. They seemed uncomfortable.

"I thought you were bringing Marty Lupo," I said. "Is one of these guys Bus Stop?"

"No. No, Joanie. These are a few friends of mine; Jack Foley and Mike Blackwell.

Who are these other guys? You told me you had only your girl friends with you."

"Sumter Rutledge and Frog," I stammered. "They've been good friends from a long way back. I've told them what is happening."

"Well, we all have our surprises," said Johnny. "That's life.

Let's all sit down and eat some of what smells so good. Relax a little. Get to know each other a little.

Joanie and her father run 'Cipollas', the restaurant up on Mayfield, Mike."

"I've heard of her. You are the girl who is such a great friend of Sister Marcetta," said Mike. "I've heard you are a very good girl."

"A great girl," smiled Uncle Johnny, waving his hands. "You can take that to the bank. If Joanie says these two young men are straight, you can make book on that too.

We'll eat, relax, then we can all talk. Tell where we come from."

He was right. Good food and casual conversation relaxed everybody. We all had a chance to look each other over.

After we finished eating, we all went to the great room.

"All of us girls are from Cleveland," started Mary. "We are down here on vacation. We were here about twenty years ago, the year after we got out of high school. That's when we met Sumter and Frog."

"We are all working girls," Sheila chipped in. "I'm in computers out at TRW."

"I manage a doctor's office," said Peggy.

"The County Auditor's Office," smiled Bridie.

"I work with my husband," said Mary. "He is an accountant."

"You all have a lot of youngsters, kids," asked Jack kindly?

"A mess of them," answered Bridie.

The two men looked at each other as they sipped their coffee. It was as if they knew a little about us, but didn't know what to say about themselves.

Johnny Seeds could feel the tension as he leaned back in his chair.

"All the cards are on the table, Mike. These girls aren't going to hurt anybody. They are Joanie's friends, way back from school days."

"We are both with the FBI," said Mike. "Jack is from the Chicago office. I'm from Cleveland. That's where I know Johnny from."

They each pulled badges from their wallets, holding them up so we could see.

"Jesus," said Bridie. "I would have guessed you were pipe fitters. You look like my father and uncle."

"My father was on the buildings in Chicago," smiled Jack. "He's been gone a long while. I hadn't thought of him in a long time. Thanks, young lady, for reminding me. Sometimes we forget where we come from."

"How about these two other blokes, these Frog and Sumter guys," asked Mike? "Where do they fit in?"

"They are my friends," I answered. "I have told Sumter everything I know. He wanted us to go home to Cleveland.

Sumter was with me when I spotted the two men who visited me in the restaurant. The two men who came to 'Cipollas', asking about Sister Marcetta."

"Joanie made one of them on a boat anchored in Georgetown," interrupted Johnny. "That's when she called me."

"Those two guys might be here, but it's none of these girls business," said Jack.

"It's my business," I said. "The girls, my friends, know why."

"If it's Joanie's business, it's my business," shot back Sumter. "I don't know who all you guys are, but I know who Joanie and these girls are.

If you think Joanie and these girls can be involved, without me and Frog to look after them, you are pissing in the wind."

I had never seen Sumter like this. He was pacing and waving right in front of the two FBI agents. His voice was rising.

"Easy, son," said Jack in a soothing voice.

"We have heard good things about you. We have been around for a few days getting the lay of the land

Reverend Croffer, we met him at his church. He said some very good things about you and your father."

"Reverend Croffer is a good man," said Sumter as he eased back into his chair.

"But what business is this of yours," asked Mike? "Who are you, Sumter?"

"I'll tell you about Sumter," said Frog.

"No, Frog, I'll tell them. I'll tell them a lot of things that I don't speak to anybody about.

We are all here.

Maybe it's just the moon and the stars and the tides. It's like the fates and the muses. Some guys live, other guys buy it."

"Sumter was in Nam three times," interrupted Frog. "He has a box full of medals at my place. Never moved it since he put it there. The Medal of Honor is in that box."

I was standing in the door of the kitchen. I was frozen. I was ashen. My hand was gripping the counter.

"You don't owe these guys anything, Sumter," I half pleaded. "Your ghosts are your ghosts. We can let it all be. We can go somewhere else, just you and me."

Johnny Seeds looked quickly at me. He was shaken.

"Joanie, sweetheart, Joanie. I was wrong to get you all involved in this thing.

I was wrong. Old grudges aren't worth it.

Marty Lupo and Bus Stop are in this Georgetown, in a room over-looking the boat. Marty will take some pictures. Then we'll be gone.

I've told this Foley and Mike everything I know. This thing is bigger than I'll ever know.

All of you have lives to lead. We'll pack our bags, be gone tomorrow."

"No packing the bags," said Sumter. "Some things are fated to be.

I was in Nam three times. Three years I was there. The days are buried in my heart. Seventeen guys died in my arms."

"You don't have to go on," I pleaded. "You don't have to go on, dear Sumter. Let the dead bury the dead."

It was like the day we had first met him, so long ago, so many years ago, when he was just a boy. It was like the day we stood at the statue with him, asking why he had to go back.

Uncle Johnny was staring into nowhere. Jack and Mike looked straight into Sumter's unseeing eyes.

Mary came over to hold my hand.

"When I met Joanie, all these girls, so many years ago, I was broken.

I was recovering from a wound. It was more than that.

They gave me life. They gave me hope. They showed me a joy in life that I thought had vanished forever.

I didn't have to go back to Nam.

But voices were calling me. The voices of friends who had died. The voices of boys who weren't there yet. I knew I could help them, maybe not win a war, but maybe help keep some of them alive.

I knew the swamp. I knew the bush. I knew it better than most. I had grown up in it.

I knew where the devil crept. Could spot an enemy trail, knew where the danger lurked.

The guys on top, from the Defense Department and the CIA, saw it different. They traded bodies for bodies. They were carried away with themselves.

They fudged reports. They counted five hundred enemy dead, when there were maybe fifty. They said areas were safe, when they were full of Cong.

They didn't give a good southern damn about the corporals and the privates, the guys whose names are on the Wall.

Seventeen guys died in my arms, names on the Wall, guys whose only dream was to get home safely.

Other guys got home, but they were broken.

McNamara was cock sure of himself. The generals were cock sure of their strategy. It was all based on CIA bullshit.

So I've got some business with the guys you are hawking.

Joanie's friend almost gets killed in South America. Another jungle. Another poor people.

The CIA is involved. The CIA is always involved. It is always covering up something.

All you guys know it. I know it.

You know some of their guys are here, or you wouldn't be all here. We're all in this together."

"That's right, Uncle Johnny," I said moving closer to him. "Sumter is right. The CIA is down here.

You know. You told me things were going to happen before they happened. How did you shake the apples from the tree? Who are the apples? How did you know the boat was named the Osprey?"

"I can't tell you everything. You know me, Joanie. I got things I can't talk about."

"You said you owed me one," I said, moving even closer and kissing him on the cheek.

"I know it's hard for you old gumbahs to be open. That's the way you are. Frankie doesn't tell my mother everything. But he loves her.

You probably sang arias for these Mick FBI dudes. Why else would they be here with you. You guys are usually like cats and dogs."

Jack and Mike were smiling. They knew Johnny was cornered. The tension was easing from the room.

"This is all off the record, Joanie, sweetheart. All because I got all of you into this.

Like I told you, the guys in Chicago put out the word, through a telephone line they knew the FBI was tapping, that they were going to get even for Sister Marcetta.

They figure from the letters that the Sister had written to you, that the CIA was involved. An old friend in the convent told me about the letters.

The FBI sent word of the tap to Washington, where it was turned over to the CIA.

Two guys, the ones that visited you in the restaurant, came to see Mike in Cleveland. Me and Mike are tight for a long time. He calls me about the visit.

Marty Lupo is sitting in the restaurant when the two guys come to talk to you. He is on assignment. He snaps a perfect picture."

"So that's why Marty was always around," I had to laugh. "I thought he loved the food."

"He does. But he was also there on business.

I take the picture to a friend in Washington. It takes a long time. Sometimes these things take a long time. But he makes one of these guys. That leads to two others. Maybe another."

"Who are they," asked Jack? "This is about where you left us this afternoon."

"Who are they," I asked?

"Who are they, Uncle Johnny," pleaded Mary, edging forward in her chair.

"Out with it," said Bridie.

Uncle Johnny looked around. We were all staring at him. He waved his hands upward, as in defeat.

"The guy on the boat is named Edward Blythe, a professor at National University. He makes about 42 grand teaching. The boat is worth maybe half a mill.

We made a guy named William Lassiter. He is in international banking. He's in Switzerland, Prague, the Arab countries, Iran. He's all over like the weather.

We made a retired Navy Captain named Samuel Hasely. He works at the White House for the National Security Council. He's all over too. Spent some time with Lassiter in Paris and Prague."

"You guys are amazing," said Jack. "How did you do it?"

"They bought security systems for their houses when they thought they might be hit. We would never hit any of them they are too big.

When the rats are chased out of the woodwork, they are as scared as the smallest mouse."

"Amazing," said Jack.

"We almost made your guy too, Mike. This is the one I owe you. There was a Bud Sweeney in Alexandria who ordered the same security system about the same time. Then he canceled it.

A guy looked at his house, talked to a few neighbors, found out he spent a lot of time down here in South Carolina.

My guess is he knows this Taggart your chasing."

Chapter 14

Was

It was a long night. Jack Foley and Mike Blackwell were drinking coffee like new fathers in a hospital waiting room. Johnny and Frog polished off the rigatoni.

It was getting past midnight. We girls were tiring of the evening's events.

"What do you do, Frog," asked Mike.

"This isn't an inquisition," snapped Bridie. "We all know Frog. Why don't you guys wrap it up and we'll get some sleep?"

"I do a lot of things," answered the big man. "I catch a lot of fish. I rent out heavy equipment. I fix things."

"Frog does a little of everything," nodded Sumter. "Mention it to him, and he'll find a way to get it done. He's a mechanic. He's a river man.

If it's in the water, Frog can catch it. It's like the catfish jump on to his line. I can be sitting for an hour, talking and empty handed. Frog will have a line of cat."

"Don't like catfish," interrupted Johnny.

"If Frog simmers them, you'll eat them," answered Sumter.

"Can you put a bug on a boat, Frog," asked Johnny?

Jack and Mike were sitting silently, sipping their coffee slowly.

"I can put a cricket on a hook, if that's what you mean."

"A bug, a wire, a listening thing," answered Johnny, "Something that will snap on to the hull of the Osprey, maybe under a porthole. About as big as the tip of my finger."

"Does the moon come out at night?"

"Bus Stop has some things he's brought along for listening," explained Johnny. He was looking at the two FBI agents.

"He can't get near the boat, but he's close enough to tape a wire. We'll get it done tomorrow."

"Big time," nodded Jack Foley.

"We're all in this together," said Uncle Johnny. "Like what Woody Hayes used to tell the football team down at Ohio State. We know what we are doing. Nothing fancy.

The other team don't even know we are looking over their fence at the practice field. They don't even know we are around.

That's the way games are won on a Saturday afternoon."

"Yeah, team," yawned Mary, standing and stretching.

"I don't know about the rest of you, but I'm dead on my feet. I'm going to bed."

Eddie Blythe was getting tired of the wait. The Osprey had been anchored for five days. The threat of a hurricane had delayed the freighter from South America.

He had hoped to meet the freighter on Saturday night. Bud Sweeney had brought two passengers by boat in the afternoon. If the plan had gone well, he would be back in Virginia.

But the weather had set in delaying the plan. The two passengers were taken back to the safe house. Eddie could only wait, alone with his thoughts and his dreams.

He had always been a loner. That was his nature. Once he had thought it was because of his work for the agency, but other agents were happy family men.

Other times he philosophized that he couldn't bear to bring any one else into the mess. He couldn't bear to have a wife and children, not being able to share his life.

If he were only a professor he might share his books and knowledge. He might share the joys of the library. He might hold the children's hands, guiding them over the fields of Appomattox and Gettysburg. He might share his love of history, the American love of lore.

He had left his dreams behind a long time ago. He had chosen a fork in the road, maybe a fork not wholly of his own choosing, but a path that had become darker and more distressful to him.

On other trips he might have watched the shrimpers and fishermen of the bay. He might have walked over to the fish house in the evening. He might have found joy in the words and sonnets of the sea.

Eddie Blythe was in one of the funks that frequently visited him. They had come more frequently during the past year.

He hadn't enjoyed the trip to Cleveland to look into the Sister Marcetta thing. He hadn't enjoyed the pictures of the Sister the old FBI agent had thrust in his craw.

"That smug old SOB." Bud Sweeney had muttered as they left the FBI office. "That bastard was pulling our puds."

"Your jerks almost killed the nun," Eddie had grimaced.

"Our comrades," answered Bud Sweeney. "Our comrades.

Without them all of South America will be taken over by the Reds. Your comrades and mine, Eddie boy. They serve our purpose. Without them we'd have nothing."

"The will of the American people is against them," Eddie had answered.

"The American people are fools," Bud had answered.

Eddie dug an old book out of the pile in the Osprey's cabin. He read once more the conversation of two Waccamaw Neck planters during the days of the Civil War.

"Do you think the war can be won," asked one?

"The will of the majority of Americans is against slavery," answered the other. "The war is already lost."

"Like Ashley Wilkes," thought Eddie, "like Ashley speaking to Scarlet."

He was alone with his thoughts and his ancient ghosts. He had no eye for the happenings of the river. He had no eye for the large man in the rowboat who almost steered into the Osprey. He had no eye for the man's hand pushing off against the hull.

He was alone with the present and the past.

"We're going home next week, maybe Wednesday," Bridie told me.

They had talked it over in the morning. I was alone on the dock. I had been sitting on the dock since the sun first began to rise.

I couldn't sleep. Too much was happening too fast.

I had packed my toothbrush and a few overnight things when I had gone out with Sumter. They were still in my purse.

I was in love with Sumter. I longed for him to hold me ever so close. And then the dark tides came in.

"Jesus," I called, but he did not answer.

I saw the light come on in the kitchen. I could smell the aroma of fresh coffee.

I knew they were talking about everything.

I had to give them time and space.

"It's too crazy," said Mary. "We come on vacation to relax and let go. This is like a storm from nowhere."

"I agree," nodded Peggy. "I'm getting lonesome for home. A month is too long anyway.

Even if this didn't happen, we are all needed at home."

"Everybody's got a different angle on this thing," added Bridie. "Seeds has one. Foley and Blackwell have another.

Joanie has Sumter; her loyalty to Sister Marcetta."

"I'm so itchy," said Sheila. "I didn't sleep an hour."

"What about Joanie," asked Bridie? "We can't just leave her alone. She was almost paralyzed last night. She is so alone."

"She is our gumbah," said Peggy.

"She needs us," added Mary, "but not forever."

"I don't give a damn about the guys on the boat," bristled Bridie. "We all care about Joanie."

"So we're in a pickle too," said Peggy. "We can't leave her alone. And we can't stay here with all this going on."

I joined them in the house about ten.

"Been on the deck a long time," asked Bridie?

"Since dawn was breaking."

That's when Bridie told me they were going home in a week.

It didn't surprise me. I was relieved.

"We're not going to let you down, Joanie," said Mary softly

"You guys never do, never have."

"It's Wednesday," said Peggy. "We are all going in one week. It's been a long time away from the kids."

"That's what I was thinking," I answered. "Give you guys some time and space to decide what to do. I knew you would do the right thing.

There's really not much any of us can do. So much stuff is going on."

"Let's make the best of it," reasoned Sheila. "Try to put it all out of our mind.

Let's catch some shrimp. Joanie can make a salad, and we can all hang loose for a day or two."

"I'll go back with you next week," I offered halfheartedly. "It's the only way."

"What about Sumter," Bridie asked?

"Maybe it will all work itself out. If God wants it to be, it will be."

I was so afraid. But they had lifted their arms out to me. They had ever had.

Jack Foley and Mike Blackwell had their legal pads out, writing down notes, when Sumter rapped on their motel door. They weren't surprised to see him. After the events of the past day, few things could surprise them.

"There are a few things I have to get straight," Sumter greeted them. "A lot that was said last night went over my head."

"There were a few surprises for us too," answered Mike. "What's on your mind, Sumter?"

"Where do you guys fit in?

Why is the FBI working with this Johnny Seeds, who apparently isn't in the same line of work as you guys?

Joanie told me about Johnny Seeds, but she never mentioned you two."

The two agents looked at each other. There was more to Sumter than they had seen the previous night.

He was clean cut. He was sandy haired and bronzed by the seasons. His hands had the strength of a worker. He was as straight and lean as a pine. He was straightforward.

"Do you have something going on with Joanie Cipolla," asked Jack? "She's quite a girl."

Sumter ignored the question. He was direct and to the point.

"I'm here to ask what you guys have going with Johnny Seeds?"

"That's what we were figuring out," mused Mike.

"You ever hear of a developer named Mike Taggart," asked Jack?

"Everyone has. He was in the paper about a year ago. He has a development called Softwoods out by Kingstree. Never got it off the ground.

That's the way it is around here. Big hopes. A lot of disappointments."

"Ever meet him," asked Mike?

"Frog went out. Tried to get some work. Earth moving, digging ponds for the golf course. Talked to a contractor. Nothing really was going on.

He never met Taggart. I've never met Taggart."

"You and your daddy have a lot of land," stated Jack.

"Daddy and me, and the banker. How did you guys know?"

"Talked to Reverend Croffer along the road," answered Jack. "He said the Rutledges were good people."

"And Taggart," asked Sumter "what did he say about Taggart?"

"We didn't ask," smiled Mike. "We were getting the lay of the land."

"Why are you interested in Taggart?"

"What's the land worth, Softwoods," asked Mike?

"About $150 an acre. We wouldn't give a dime for it. It's a lot of wetland and bush.

St. Peter couldn't grow tobacco on it. But Taggart is a developer. He's in a different field than me and daddy.

We're farmers. I'm just a South Carolina farm boy."

"What would you say if I told you that a bank in Texas has loaned Taggart 10 million dollars on Softwoods," asked Jack?

"Jesus," Sumter answered in surprise!

"We were down here looking into this Taggart thing," continued Jack. "We have a telephone number for Taggart here at Pawleys.

That's when we ran into Johnny Seeds. We figured out who he was chasing, the Sister Marcetta thing."

"the Savings and Loans are going bust all over the country," explained Mike. "It isn't just Taggart.

When the Congress deregulated the banks every huckster in captivity crawled out of the woodwork. When the whole deck falls down, it will be quite a day."

"And you think Taggart is involved with the CIA," asked Sumter?

"Up to his elbows," said Jack.

"Why are you taking Seeds side? That's what I really came over here to find out.

Johnny Seeds is who knows what."

"Last night you said a lot of things, Sumter," started Jack. "We were listening.

We are just a couple of old dudes who have been around the block maybe too many times. We know black from white and a lot of the shades of gray.

Maybe its because we have been around the corner for so long. Maybe its because we know Seeds is right and the other side is wrong. Maybe its because we can get our pensions and get out. This is personal with the two of us.

Maybe its because we hear voices calling, like you heard voices. We're not as brave as you are, son.

No way! Bit it's the same world. It's the same country.

You understand?"

Sumter smiled as he looked at the men. They were one age with his daddy. Their faces were lined and furrowed by the seasons. Their eyes were clear and uncompromising.

"Same team," he said as he reached out his hand.

"And one other thing. This isn't just Johnny Seed's show. It isn't just your show. Me and Frog are in this thing with you.

If they have a boat on the water, we can catch them. That's the way it is. If you want more pictures and things, me and Frog will take care of it.

We know the rivers. We know the tides."

"It's not your job, Sumter," said Mike.

"Don't worry," answered the farm lad. "My days of blood and killing are behind me. I swore to it a long time ago. Nam was another place, in another world.

Me and Frog catch a lot of fish. They don't know they are going to be caught. Some are old and wise and have been swimming in the stream forever.

We catch them. Frog and me catch them. That's the way it is."

Marty Lupo and Bus Stop were perched in a small room overlooking the Sampit River. It had been used as a storeroom by the gift shop below.

The store owner was glad to rent it to Marty. The two hundred dollars was manna from heaven.

"Going to take some pictures of the river," Marty had explained. "Sunrises and sunsets. Fishing boats. Took some pictures in Savannah and Charleston. Going to go to Biloxi and Galveston.

Taking pictures for a writer who is doing a book on southern ports. Take three or four days, maybe a few more.

You know how writers are. They want the pictures just right.

Maybe get some storms coming in over the bay."

The room was hot. It was humid. Only a slight breeze coming through a half-opened window made it bearable.

They were only a little more than a hundred yards from the Osprey.

Nothing happened the first day.

Bus Stop sat back from the window looking at the boat. Marty wouldn't have had the patience.

"Don't you get tired, just looking," he asked his companion?

"Never. It's my job. Someone's in the cabin. He doesn't come out. You get some sleep or something."

"Does that electronic stuff work, Bus Stop?"

"When they are talking, it will be like you are back stage at the opera. You can hear them tune the fiddle. You will hear the butterfly's wings."

"The kid asked some good questions," said Jack.

"Real good. Sumter's nobody's fool. He was asking what we have been asking each other," answered Mike.

"It's all on the scorecard. Taggart; bank fraud, mail fraud, possible violation of the immigration laws, and God knows what else is going on."

"Central Intelligence," muttered Mike. "Central bullshit. We'll play it by ear, give it a few more days, then back to the real world."

"Our guys would bury a lot of this," mused Jack. "A courtesy from one agency to another. That's the way the game is played."

"we're not talking to our guys," said Mike. "Not now, anyway."

"And when the shit hits the fan," winked Jack.

"We'll wait and see," answered his partner.

"Another thing, Jack, what do you think of those young ladies from Cleveland? They have a lot of guts. They have a lot of class."

"Pick of the litter," smiled Jack.

"They made an impression," nodded Mike. "They are all loyal to Joanie Cipolla."

"They all pass muster," said Jack, "each and every one of them. They all pass muster with flying colors."

We went to Brookgreen in the afternoon. It was Bridie's idea.

"We can't sit around here and mope. We're getting like dweebs. Let's go up to Brookgreen, walk around the sculpture garden."

Brookgreen was unchanged. The great oaks of the avenue stood in silent grace. Statuary of Zeus, and Dionysus, Orpheus and Diana, gleamed under the ancient boughs. We walked the brick walled terrace where the old plantation house had been.

"Before the Revolutionary War, two hundred and fifty years ago, our people were here," I mused.

"You're still a teacher, Joanie girl," said Peggy.

"I remember when we first met," smiled Sheila. "Joanie would never tell a story on our front porch. My father, God rest his soul, said there was a star out there for Joanie.

He said someday 'little Joanie would tell a story.'

He loved the faith, but he believed a lot was written in the moon and the stars."

I had to smile when Sheila mentioned her father. Memories! They were a part of us, old tunes and memories.

"The rice planters had a house right here," I continued. "From this bluff they had rice fields stretching to the river."

We all looked over the former fields of grain. Time and nature had reclaimed the former fields of gold. Small streams and tributaries wound their way through acres of reed and bush.

We walked the winding paths of the sculpture garden, each of us alone in her thoughts.

We passed golden agers from tour buses. We skipped out of the way of racing children from school tours. We passed young couples holding hands. We came upon artists sketching the bronzed figures.

"Everyone comes for a different reason," said Mary. "It is so peaceful."

"The Gods of ancient Greece standing under the boughs," I said. "They are all here. The nymphs, the fates, and the muses."

We wandered the grounds seeming to go nowhere. We watched an alligator sunning himself on the edge of a simmering pond. We saw an eagle soaring overhead. We saw a thousand squirrels scampering in the trees.

As we rounded a turn in the path we came to the statue we had visited so many years before.

There was the Spirit of American Youth, his arm outstretched to the heavens.

Each of us had her own memory.

"The War Memorial at Normandy," said Mary.

"The baseball game with the sisters," said Peggy.

"President Kennedy," Sheila half whispered.

"Monsignor O'Donnell," smiled Bridie. "I'll never forget the police and the firemen. And the bagpipers playing Danny Boy."

I was silent. We each shared each other's thoughts.

The Youth stood motionless, bronzed and strong, rising from the wave.

"I visited the War Memorial Statue often," I started, "when I was Downtown with the other sisters. It was a ritual.

Oh, they had a faith. I have never seen a faith like I saw when I was in the convent. The sisters were so full of faith.

And love. The gospels call it charity. The sisters gave so much of themselves.

But Sister Catherine, you remember her. She told us of her brother Timmy in the cemetery at Normandy. I often visited the Memorial with Sister Catherine.

She told me the figure was a symbol of hope, the greatest of the Cardinal Virtues. The boy was rising form the wave, unblemished, looking to tomorrow.

Sister Catherine said that faith was great, and love was even greater, but when the storms do come, as the darkness comes to all of us, the light of tomorrow, the light of Hope, is where we find our nourishhment."

"Where is Sister Catherine," asked Sheila? "We have all lost track of the sisters."

"Knitting in the Mother House," I smiled. "The great war horses never left the convent."

"We were lucky," Sheila said. "It was the end of an era. We had sisters all the way through school. No offense, Joanie, but we were lucky."

"Boy, they could make you memorize," piped in Mary. "They had tables for everything. Multiplication and division were a bitch."

"The tables of seven will get you to heaven," rhymed Peggy.

"Sevens and nines were for the birds," laughed Bridie. "All the odd numbers were hard.

Now all the kids walk around with pocket calculators and can't add three rows of numbers."

"A long division problem would throw their butts," added Mary. "we used to go home with three pages of long division, and heaven help you if they weren't done the next morning."

"Remember how the boys would stop us under the railroad bridge, to snatch our book bags and copy the homework," chirped Peggy? "They cheated their way all the way through St. Phils."

"And remember how we said they could never remember the linking verbs," said Sheila. "We were so sure they could never remember. Do you guys remember?"

We held hands before the Spirit in the garden and recited them. We all recited them.

"Appear, become, continue, remain, feel seem, smell, sound, and taste."

"How about the one's from Benny in the tavern," added Peggy.

"Is am, be, are, was, were, been."

We couldn't help laughing. The great oaks and the sun's warmth had revived us. We were all who we were, and all the ams, and the seems, and the smells of the yesterdays.

We were linked by a lifetime of shared memories to each. We were linked like the verbs.

What brought joy to one, brought joy to all. When one needed solace, all were there to wheel the barrow.

Mary broke away from us. She did a soft shuffle around the spirit.

"What was that," asked Peggy?

And then we all knew.

We joined hands and shuffled to the right. Then we reversed ourselves and shuffled the other way across the needles of pine.

"Sixteen tons," we sang. "Sixteen tons and what do you get, another day older and deeper in debt."

Chapter 15

Were

Bus Stop had the patience of Job. Marty Lupo marveled at him.

"I ought to take your picture sitting by the window. It'd be like Whistler's grandfather."

"No picture of me, Marty," answered the pale figure sitting in the shadows. "Nobody got no pictures of me. It would spoil my game."

"Anybody ever take your picture?"

"Not since First Communion."

Marty laid in some bakery from a place across Front Street. He bought a few small packages of lunch meat. There was a small john in the hallway.

"All the comforts of home," he commented.

"Beats looking for a guy in a snowstorm."

After two days Bus Stop knew all the regulars; the guys who swept the boardwalk, the ladies in pastels and straw hats nibbling at pastry. The guy who walked his large dog in the morning and the evening, letting Fido expel himself on the potted plants.

He could tell a tour of immigrants, and knew the gracious ladies who guided them.

On Friday morning he spotted Eddie Blythe. It was just past seven-thirty when he emerged from the boat's cabin and leaned on the rail.

He woke Marty to get some pictures.

"Picture one and two," smiled Marty.

"Stay awake, paisan," smoothed Bus Stop. "He's looking around. This may be a busy day."

"I'll get some coffee and rolls from across the street," said Marty. "Maybe something will happen."

"Something always happens," coughed Bus Stop. "Sometimes you have to sit and wait. But this is like they say in baseball, a duck on the pond."

An hour later he watched a large boat come up the river. It docked farther down, near the fish houses.

A clean cut fortyish man alighted and tied up the boat.

"Get some snaps of that SOB," he snorted. "Him and the boat."

"Why him?"

"Too clean cut. He's out of place. Those fishermen down there wear yesterday's clothes. Not this guy."

Marty snapped about half a dozen pictures as the stranger walked to the Osprey and scurried up its plank.

"All the chickens come home to roost," commented Bus stop as he flicked on the tape recorder. "Now we'll listen to what they are cackling about."

"I'll take a walk around the front," said Marty. "Come up by the fishing boats. Get a close up of that other boat. Put the camera in a newspaper. Tell the boat to smile."

They both were major leaguers.

Marty blocked off the small window in the john when he returned. He took a small case of chemicals into the room.

"One hour developing," he laughed.

"Its going down tomorrow night," said the pale man. "No time to screw around."

"Tomorrow night?"

"These guys are real slicks," answered Bus Stop. "Who would have thought all this shit in a one horse town. Go to the pay phone across the street and call Seeds.

This is a crazy thing."

Johnny Seeds and the two FBI agents listened to the tape all afternoon.

"Bus Stop and Marty do beautiful work," said the dapper man.

"As good as they come," nodded Mike.

They had the pictures of Eddie Blythe and the stranger, and the two boats lying on the table in front of them.

"It's about time, Bud," said Eddie Blythe.

They could detect the irritation in his voice.

"Everybody's got problems," the voice answered. "It will be done tomorrow. Then you can go back to the teaching."

"This will be my last trip."

"You've been running the boat for too many years. There are always problems, delays.

You have the sweetest deal in the agency. This boat, travel, none of the responsibility of taking care of anything.

You should spend a few weeks with those dudes from the jungle. You never know what's on their mind."

"I don't like having them on the Osprey. This is it, Bud."

Mike hit the stop button.

"Bud Sweeney," nodded Jack, as he picked up a few pictures from the table.

"Small world," nodded Seeds.

"The same two guys who came asking about Sister Marcetta," chuckled Mike as he looked at the pictures.

He hit the play button.

"This isn't a quit easy job, Ed. This is top secret. You know that."

"At first I just sailed the Osprey," answered Eddie Blythe. "The big whigs from the agency would come down to Pawleys. Rest and recreation they'd call it.

They'd have a few cases of beer on the boat, sit back and tell war stories. It was like the President's yacht."

"We'd put them up for a week or so. Nice beach. Quiet. They'd play a little golf, relax. That was how it was when I got the job of managing the Taggart property."

Mike hit the stop button again.

"That SOB," he stammered, looking at Jack. "We are chasing all over God knows where, and Taggart is the guy who came to see me in Cleveland. Him and that other asshole on the boat."

"Slow down," muttered Seeds. "Everyone needs a little recreation. Our guys go to Vegas or Palm Springs. Get free suites, liquor, golf, whatever the want.

The CIA gets Pawleys. What do you guys at the Bureau get?"

"Nothing, so far," laughed Jack. "We don't even get free tickets to the Bears games."

"I'll take you two guys to Vegas," laughed Seeds. "Everything on the house."

Mike hit the play button.

"It was great duty," said Bud Sweeney. "Nothing was going on. Then Lassiter and Hasely went to the old man with all that Iranian shit."

"We shouldn't be talking about that," said Eddie. "Top secret!"

"That's why you can't get out. Neither can I. We're just two cards on the table. Cards that know too much."

"You can't, but I can. You ever hear about qualms of conscience? I haven't slept well for a year, ever since that trip to Cleveland. Maybe your conscience is dead, but mine is ticking."

"Go to Confession," mocked Bud. "It will do you good. Go to some Friar in a box.

Tell him you are a runner for the agency. Tell him you smuggle some Latin bastards in off the coast. Tell him they bring in a little cocaine. Tell him you sniff a little pot.

Tell him you make passes at your young female students. Tell him you have certain tendencies you can't control. Call it a congenital disorder.

Tell him you go hawking young girls. Tell him you've paid for three abortions for your students in the last six years."

"You bastard!"

"They've got a book on you, Eddie. The agency would be over to your campus in a hurry, drop a dime to the right ears. You'd be on your ass so fast; you wouldn't hear the bell ring.

The agency would be whistling Dixie."

"Nobody quits nothing," commented Johnny Seeds. "Everybody's got a book on somebody."

"So I'll be here tomorrow," continued Bud Sweeney. "I'll have the two gringos for you. Here is a map and the co-ordinates where you'll meet the Phillipe. It will be just inside the Gulf Stream about five in the afternoon.

That will give you plenty of time.

You'll pick up four guys and some small foot lockers of stuff. I'll meet you in the Bay about nine. Transfer two guys for Pawleys and a few of the boxes.

You take the other guys to meet the bus for Fort Bragg. We've done it many times, nothing to get upset about."

"You are a cold bastard," said Eddie Blythe.

"Save the world from the Reds. That's how you have to look at it, Eddie. Everybody's got problems. Nobody cares about yours. Nobody gives a shit about mine."

"You sleep at night?"

"It was great down here," continued Bud, "until Hasely got the ear of the old man. The SOB is a loose cannon. But he gets the old man's ear.

Him and Lassiter start selling arms to Iran. Free the prisoners. Fight Iraq. Use the booty to suppress the Contras. I'll bet they have more booty in Swiss Banks than China has rice."

Mike hit the stop button.

"Whew," whistled Jack.

"Bus Stop really hit em," said Seeds. "This is your guys game. It's more than our guys can cover."

Mike hit the play button again.

"Then those fuckers get the Taggart family involved in the real estate," continued Bud Sweeney.

"They had a perfect thing down here. They went to the old man and said they could raise some more money through the S&L deregulation scheme. And he bought their bullshit.

They couldn't get more money from Congress, so they raised the funds through the Congress stupid new laws.

You think you got troubles?"

"You are a true believer. A cold warrior," said Eddie.

"True believer, sure. In what we were, I was, the agency was. But they let Hasely go crazy, play tunes he couldn't or shouldn't play.

The old man ignored the guys at the desks, the guys who could evaluate things. He let Hasely and Lassiter fly by the seat of their pants.

The Taggart franchise is thirty million dollars in debt."

"How do you pay the piper," asked Eddie?

"Lassiter writes checks on an offshore bank. But Lassiter could disappear at any time. The thing could go belly up."

"Jesus," said Eddie.

"Everybody's got problems," answered Bud.

"Quite a story," commented Jack as the tape wrapped up.

"Everything's linked together. Nobody knows all this crap is going on."

"What do you do," asked Johnny Seeds, walking around the room? "Wait till our guys hear that tape. They make our guys look like a bunch of chintzes."

"Nobody hears the tape, Johnny," said Jack. "We are putting it in safe keeping, me and Mike."

"You gunsols are going to do, what," spat back Seeds. "I give you the guys you are looking for.

Are you all on the same side? They are tied up in every type of scam that God ever created. Now, you are going to bury the tape. Everybody covers for somebody.

You are all in the same messy bed."

"Easy, Johnny," answered Mike. "I've known you for a long time. You know me.

We are all in this together. You can take that to the bank.

We are going to keep the tape safe. It doesn't go back to Chicago. It doesn't go back to Cleveland.

It would be in Washington if word leaked out from your guys or from our guys.

Taggart or Sweeney, or whoever he is, would be gone."

"If we could catch the rascals," said Jack, "it would be like hitting a trifecta. They've got two boats, some illegal immigrants, and it sounds like a bunch of cocaine.

We could call the Coast Guard, but the game would be over. Same thing if we called Immigration right away. They could pick up Blythe and Taggart tomorrow when they meet.

They would have the illegal bastards. Blythe and Taggart would make bail and disappear. No dope! No CIA! No payoff!"

"But if you got them all together, you would hit the jackpot," smiled Seeds.

"Yeah," sniffed Mike.

"How, gumbahs," asked Johnny?

"How do we catch your guys," asked Jack?

"Not too well. Not often," chuckled Seeds.

Frog laid a map of the Carolina coast on the table at the beach house. We all gathered around.

There were Frog and Sumter, Johnny Seeds and Foley and Blackwell, and all of us. We knew something was going on when they all showed up late in the afternoon.

"This is Frog's show," explained Jack. "We found out a lot of interesting things this morning. Frog is going show all of us where everything is at."

"Us too," asked Bridie?

"Can you read a map," asked Frog?

"All you girls," said Mike. "You have all done yourself proud. You have a right to know what is going on as much as anybody. Without Joanie, and all of your loyalty to Joanie, we'd still be wandering off the beaten track."

"Amen," said Jack.

"I've got some crayons to make this easy to understand," said Frog.

He circled a large space in blue.

"This is Winyah Bay at Georgetown. This orange spot is where the Osprey is docked in the Sampit River. It's about fifteen miles from that spot to the ocean. Around this bend the Waccamaw River enters the Bay."

He drew a long blue line along the path of the river.

"The Waccamaw runs parallel with the ocean, past Pawleys, about three miles from the beach. The river is part of the Inland Waterway. Farther north a channel was cut past Myrtle Beach, to open the way from the Waccamaw to Little River near the North Carolina border.

That's the way the Osprey has to head north."

"Taggart has a boat, about a thirty foot Sting Ray, docked somewhere along the Waccamaw," interrupted Sumter. "He had it down by the Osprey this morning."

"Marty Lupo took these pictures," said Johnny, laying them on the table.

"Tomorrow, around noon, Taggart is going to meet the Osprey where it is docked," explained Jack. "Blythe is going to take the two Contras you saw out to a freighter in the ocean. He is going to bring back four more men.

He is going to meet Taggart in the Bay, transfer two men to his boat, and come up the Inland Waterway. Taggart is going to come back to Pawleys with two Contras."

"How do you know all this," asked Bridie?

"Bus Stop got it on tape," answered Johnny.

"The rivers are like a spider web," said Frog slowly. "When a fly gets caught in the web, it has no way to escape. It does not sense the danger. It is entranced by the frailty and beauty of the web."

"But you're not a spider," said Peggy.

"We have other help," said Mike. "When the boats are on the river, going up the Waccamaw, we can call in the Coast Guard. They have a station in Georgetown. We are also going to alert the Immigration Service in Charleston."

"In the meantime," said Sumter, "me and Frog are going to go on a pontoon boat and cruise along the Waccamaw. Find out where Taggart's boat is docked.

How would you girls like to go for a sunset cruise?"

We looked at each other. Sumter and Frog were so casual. They were up to their neck in the CIA, and the Contras, and the FBI, and who knows what else.

But Sumter knew the rivers and the streams. We had seen what Frog could do.

We were still the girls from East Cleveland, eager to take our penny loafers from the spindles and skip along the walk.

"Tomorrow will be a busy day," said Sumter. "The more we find out now, the better off we will be."

"You and Frog don't have to get involved," I said to Sumter.

"Nor do you and the girls," he answered.

"We are in it," said Mary.

We all looked at each other. We all knew what we were going to do.

Sumter drove us on a winding dirt road, through ancient oaks and scraggly bush, to the Waccamaw.

"A home boy named Teddy, he's got a shack by the river," said Frog. "Has an old pontoon boat for fishing. He's a mate on a fishing boat, never know when he's going to be around.

I've done some things for him. He's done some favors for me. That's the way things get done around here."

A fox ran across the road in front of the car. Squirrels hopped from bough to bough. Reeds stood tall in glistening ponds. Hounds could be heard barking,

"Spooky," said Peggy.

The four girls were squeezed in the back seat of the Fairlane. I was squished in the front, between Sumter and Frog.

"Why are the woods so wet," asked Mary? "There's water everywhere."

"Wetlands," answered Frog. "Half the Waccamaw Neck is almost a marsh. There's not much room between the ocean and the river. Dig a three foot hole and you're in the muck.

It's great for the otters and the beavers."

"Jesus," muttered Bridie. "It's almost a jungle. Are there any snakes, Frog?"

"There's everything," he laughed, "but if you don't bother them, they won't bother you."

The river was wide and beautiful. Fields of golden reeds stretched forever on the farthest shore. The hue of the setting sun sparkled on the shimmering stalks.

"The boat will be on this side of the river," said Sumter. "The other shore is all marsh, former rice fields. Great habitat for quail and wild geese. Small creeks are all over, but you couldn't get a large boat through there."

"On this bank there are deeper creeks," said Frog, "where the plantations had their docks. They would float the rice down the river on barges. The river was the lifeblood of the plantations.

We'll just cruise down the river on this side, look in the creeks."

It was so peaceful. The river was placid.

Sumter and I sat near the rail on the front of the boat. The girls sat near Frog as he guided the boat.

Frog guided the boat through creeks and small channels that only God knew existed. We passed small docks, and fine boats, and an alligator nesting in the reeds.

The fields were latticed with the rays of the setting sun. I had never seen anything so peaceful. It was as if the world had come to rest.

"Try the creek at Jericho," hollered Sumter. "Near the old fishing camp. It's hardly ever used."

"Jericho", said Peggy. "What a beautiful name."

"One of the great rice plantations," answered Frog. "Named after the walled city of the Bible. The creek is called Joshua.

They say the slaves named the creek. Named the stream after the great Biblical horn player. Hoped their chains would come tumbling off.

Most of the plantations had Scottish or English names, but Jericho was right out of the Bible."

We were rounding a bend in the creek when Sumter spotted the boat.

"Is that it," asked Sheila?

"It's the Sting Ray," answered Frog.

He guided the boat back to the middle of the river, moving it leisurely towards home.

Sumter seemed at peace on the river. It seemed an inner peace.

I took his hand.

"Will it be all right? Do you have faith in this plan, whatever it is?"

He looked me in the eye and winked. He squeezed my hand a little bit tighter.

I got the message. I made up my mind about a lot of things.

I looked at my friends, all gathered around Frog. Sumter's home boy and my forever gumbahs.

Oh, how I loved them all.

"What are you doing," asked Bridie?

"Thinking," the big man answered. "The evening is the most beautiful time on the river. When the sun sets and the birds flock through the reeds to their nests, it is the most peaceful time on the river."

"Like church used to be," said Mary.

"Never went to too many churches. But I spent a lot of Sundays on the water. That's the way I was brought up."

"We would have been killed if we missed church," said Peggy. "All of us."

"Different world," answered Frog. "You are a hell of a group of girls, I must say that, myself."

"And you are a hell of a good guy, Frog," said Bridie coyly, as she slid over to give him a kiss on the cheek.

We all looked to the front of the boat, at Joanie and Sumter, standing almost polarized beneath the setting sun.

She was a beautiful woman. She had been a pretty girl, but pretty girls sometimes stumble into the wilderness. Her olive skin contrasted with the golds of the far off reeds, only adding to their loveliness.

We looked at Sumter, the farm boy we had seemed to know forever. He was slender, and bronzed, and lithe. His arm was outstretched, pointing something out to Joanie.

Sheila thought back to that day so long ago, that day when she had watched Senator Kennedy from the window of Sacred Heart. He was tall, and bronzed, and lithe, as he reached out to wave goodbye.

For a moment she saw the lightning. Then she offered a silent prayer. She thought she saw all the Spirits, the boys rising from the waters. She could feel a chill.

Then Sumter reached over and put his strong arm around Joanie's shoulder. She could almost feel the strength they shared as they bonded to one another.

"What have you guys been talking about," I asked as Sumter and I wandered to the back of the boat?

"Church," answered Mary. "Frog was telling us the difference between church and the river."

"I guess this is my church," explained Frog. "Sumter knows that, Joanie. This is the Big Guys glory."

"You don't have to explain that to me, Frog," I smiled. "But you are going to have to come to church when me and Sumter are married. You are going to have to give this up for the day."

"What," stammered Frog?

"I don't know anything about it," said Sumter, looking at me.

My gumbahs seemed all floored.

"It's your show, paisan," said Bridie. "Go for it."

"I used to dream," I started, "when I was a little girl, that someday I would be asked by a handsome prince to marry him. I would be standing alone in a beautiful garden. He would be holding my hand."

I was looking into Sumter's eyes. I was looking deep into his soul.

"This is more than my beautiful garden. It is Sumter's. It is all that he has ever loved, the rolling waters, the silken reeds, and the sun setting overhead.

It is ours, Sumter."

"Well, Sumter boy," whistled Frog in his deep voice.

"I do. I will. I will, dear gumbah, I will."

Uncle Johnny, and Jack and Mike, were waiting for us when we returned to Two View.

"Getting worried," said Jack. "The sun was starting to go down."

"Stopped for a while on the river," said Frog.

"Find the boat," asked Mike?

"Joanie's getting married," squeaked Mary.

"Jesus," said Johnny Seeds!

"Joanie and Sumter are going to get married," answered Peggy excitedly.

"I told you so, Mike," said Jack Foley. "You owe me a sawbuck. I bet you a ten Sumter would propose to Joanie before we got out of here."

"You lose, Jack," piped in Bridie. "Joanie proposed to Sumter."

"That's right," I said.

"Fungula," said Uncle Johnny wiping his brow.

"We got the quietest thing going since the day Hoffa got lost. And my Joanie, sweetheart, has to get all involved with Sumter boy."

His smile was ear to ear as he walked over to me, squeezing me ever so tight. Then he turned to them.

"It's our Italian tradition that the father should kiss the daughter when the engagement is announced. Frankie isn't here, thank God. Almost everybody else is here.

So I'll be Frankie.

Take good care of her, Sumter. You have my blessing."

"You are amazing," Uncle Johnny," I said. "I love you so much."

"Thank you, Joanie," he almost whispered. "You make an old man feel so good."

Frog, and Jack and Mike, went out on the porch to talk. Johnny wandered out after them.

"Man talk," said Mary.

"Why only them," asked Bridie? "There are no secrets. We are almost up to our panty girdles with them in this whole thing."

"Aren't you going out with them, Sumter," asked Sheila?

He was sitting on the couch next to me. He was so at ease.

"Whatever Frog tells them I'll go along with," he answered.

"Frog," asked Mary?

"Frog is a Lowcountry river rat. He's the best on the water. You guys are city folks. Frog and me can do a lot of things that city folks would never dream of doing. We talked about a few things this afternoon."

"My proposal," I asked, pinching him on the arm.

"If you hadn't, I would have asked you sometime soon," he smiled. "But first we had to get this other thing out of the way.

There are a lot of ghosts that have to be buried. If Frog and me have our way they will all be buried tomorrow."

"No killing," I said softly.

"No killing, Joanie. Me and Frog catch fish. That's what the river is all about."

It seemed they were on the porch forever.

Jack spoke when they came in. He was as serious as we had ever seen him. They all had serious looks.

"Frog and Sumter are going to take Taggart and his two guys out of the game after they dock their boat tomorrow night.

We'll have some other guys, State Troopers or Immigration, take out Blythe and the Osprey. Frog laid out a plan we all agreed on.

We'll all get packed tomorrow and be on the road home early Sunday morning. This place will be crawling with guys from Washington by Monday."

"We'll all be gone, clean as a whistle," said Uncle Johnny.

"Sumter," I said pleadingly.

"You too, Joanie. You go back to Cleveland with the girls. I'll be up by the end of the week, meet your mom and dad."

"But gumbahs," added Frog, looking at us all. "When you pack leave out some old clothes for tomorrow. Blue jeans if you've got them, dark shirts, at least long trousers and an old pair of shoes.

Me and Sumter will probably need a little help."

Chapter 16

Been

None of us slept well that night. We were up at the crack of dawn.

"Coffee on the marsh," suggested Bridie. "In the office. Last day."

"Ugh," we all answered. We were as spent as yesterday's doughnuts.

"Come on guys," commanded Bridie. "No matter what happens, this is our last day."

An autumn chill had come over the marsh during the night. The reeds were laden with a soft fragile mist.

"You know," said Mary, "I thought of Smoky and the kids a lot last night. Remember the first day. We listed the things we had left behind.

Last night I was thinking how much those things mean to me. I am happy this vacation is being cut short."

"It's been a hell of a two weeks," said Bridie, "no matter what happens today."

"I wouldn't worry about today," said Peggy. "We've all had a lot of todays. I was thinking. I did a lot of thinking last night.

I was thinking about a long time ago. Sister Alphonse told us to wear old jeans and tennis shoes. Then, when we went to Sacred Heart, Sister Marcetta told us to wear jeans to steel wool the floors.

Last night Frog tells us the same thing.

It's like everything goes in circles. I don't know why. Frog reminded me of all the others.

But every time we put on old jeans and worked together, I don't know, something good happened. It's always happened like that."

"You've got a point, Peggy," said Bridie. "But God help me if I know what it is. But you are right."

We relaxed a bit as the morning sun slowly lifted the dew from the marsh. Sheila went in and brought out another pot of steaming coffee.

"We are what we left in Cleveland," said Mary slowly. "All the things we joked about; the kids, the husbands, work, the driving of the kids everywhere. That's what we have been. That's what we are."

"You are right," said Sheila, "but it's been nice to break away for a while. This trip was still a great idea.

The first week of relaxation did us all a lot of good. Pawleys is still a great place.

It was so different than a family vacation. Loaded station wagon, kids scuffling in the back seat."

"Pawleys in ten years," asked Bridie halfheartedly?

"Sure," we all answered.

"But only for one week," smiled Mary. "By that time my kids might have kids. Some of us will be grandmothers."

"Not all of us, paisan," I smiled.

"The way you are, Joanie," laughed Peggy; "you'll have a couple of red necked Italian girls scurrying around the kitchen with you, lost somewhere between crab cakes and ravioli."

"We'll all come back, for sure, to see that."

"You bet we will," said Bridie. "Jesus, Mary, and Joseph, you bet we will."

We spent the rest of the morning packing and changing into our old clothes.

Sumter and Frog came by about one.

"We saw the boats meet about an hour ago," said Sumter. "The Osprey headed for the ocean. Taggart took the Sting Ray out on the Bay, like he was going fishing."

"Saw Johnny Seeds early this morning," said Frog. "He's quite a guy. He was going to have some pictures taken of the boats meeting.

He's got pictures all over the place. He'll get Mike and Jack later this afternoon and meet us."

"Meet us where," I asked?

"Out by Jericho," answered Sumter. "There is only one old dirt road into there. It winds from the old plantation entrance to the creek where Taggart's boat was docked."

"We checked it out a while ago," explained Frog. "There is a station wagon parked back there. It has to come back along the dirt road.

I moved a front end loader back there just a while ago. Hid it down the road. Now me and Sumter are going back to do some work.

Set the possum trap."

"I've brought a couple of cans of insect repellent," said Sumter. "You'll have to spray yourselves all over before you come with us. Spray your clothes, your hands, your necks."

"You mean we are going in the woods," asked Peggy?

"The fox, the snakes," said Mary excitedly.

"Swamp Fox," chuckled Frog. "He's a legend around here. General Francis Marion, the Swamp Fox.

He was like a phantom to the Red Coats. He was all over them for three years and they never laid a hand on him. The snakes never bothered the Swamp Fox, Mary. And they won't bother us.

The Red Coats used the open roads. The Swamp Fox hid in the bush."

"Is that why the insect repellent, Frog," asked Mary? "Are we going in the bush?"

"You got it, girl. Not too deep though. We'll all be together."

"Jesus," said Bridie.

We could only look at Frog and Sumter. They were dressed in work clothes, old flannel shirts and field worn pants. They talked as casually as two paisans meeting on the street.

"We're only office girls," Sheila stammered.

"You are all more than that, Sheila," Frog answered. "I've been watching you all. You are all real ladies, with heart and spirit.

Sumter says you are like home boys. That's damn high praise from Sumter boy. He's a pretty good judge.

I'm going to dig a big hole in the old dirt road. That station wagon is going to fall into it, up to its axles."

"What are we going to do," I asked?

"You are going to help tie the net around the Red Coats, Joanie. We are going to catch all the old ghosts tonight, all the old ghosts. Then they'll be gone.

Sumter's ghosts! Your ghosts! All the old phantoms that have ever been. They are all going to be gone."

Frog and Sumter spent the afternoon on the road through Jericho. Frog chose a spot in the road about a quarter mile down from its curve, coming from the creek.

The road was lined with centuries old oaks. Bush and overgrowth surrounded their trunks.

Frog had old weathered 2x4s and old 4x8 sheets of plywood stacked by the front end loader.

"Old stuff I had laying out by my place. Never throw anything away. Everything comes in handy."

He had an old yard arm from a shrimp boat, its net tied loosely around the pole.

He spent a few hours digging a three foot deep trench the width of the road. He carried the sandy soil farther down the road and hid it in the brush.

Sumter built frames, hammering the sheets of plywood onto the old 2x4s.

"The more I see of this, the more I think it is going to work," yelled Frog as he guided his load of soil past Sumter. "The car will go plitz, right into the ditch."

Sumter could only smile as he hammered away. Frog made things look easy. He had always made things look easy. He was what someone might call ingenious.

The two friends laid the framed panels on the open ditch. They shoveled small tracks so that they would lay even with the road. They layered the panels with a covering of sandy soil and pine needles.

"Wow," said Frog. "You can't tell the difference, Sumter boy. I might even drive over that sucker myself."

"Where are you going to put the net," asked Sumter?

"Right here, leaning on this tree. When the car cracks through, I'll tip the arm right on top of it.

The fall through the boards will shock the hell out of those guys. The doors won't open because the sides of the panels will be flush against them.

I tip the yard arm and it cracks the top of the car, like a weight falling into the water. There are heavy ropes on all the corners of the net.

We all grab the ropes, wrap them around the trees. If all goes well, the twerps are caught."

"Frog, good buddy," smiled Sumter, "it's one hell of a contraption. But do you think it will work?"

"Can a squirrel climb a tree," answered the big man. "It'll be like catching catfish from the dock."

Jack Foley called the Immigration Office in Charleston in the morning. He did not identify himself.

"I've got a hot one for you," he said to the agent. "There are four illegals with a large cache of cocaine from South America up on the Waccamaw Neck."

"Who are you?"

"Doesn't matter. What I am telling you is what matters."

"Shoot," said the agent.

"Can you get any help. This has to be real quiet."

"State Police at Georgetown."

"This is real big. You get your guys to Georgetown. Give me the number where you will be. I'll call you about seven tonight."

"Can't do that on a whim and a prayer. You'll have to tell me a little about yourself. You sound like a straight arrow."

"Between you and me," asked Jack.

"I got you."

"I'm with the FBI out of Chicago. Can't give a name. Undercover."

"Tell me three things about Chicago."

"Central States Pension Fund, Michael Jordan is from North Carolina, and all our immigrants are legal."

"I got you," said the agent.

"We need your guys, buddy. Don't stiff me."

"I'll give you a number," answered the voice. "We'll be there before seven. Need anything else?"

"Can you get the Coast Guard? They might come in handy. But don't call them until I call you."

"Really undercover."

"I'm counting on you," said Jack. "After this goes down, you'll be glad you trusted me."

"Tough nut to crack," smiled Mike from the other side of the room?

"They are all tough. Unless they see the badge and the gun, everybody is a non believer.

What would you do? A beautiful Saturday. All the guys are running around doing everything. Some old asshole calls you on the phone and says all hell is going to break loose. What would you do?"

"The same thing he's doing. Signal the alert. Bring everybody in, all you can find. Listen to the cussing.

Hope the old asshole was right or be ready to crawl in a hole. I've been there on both sides.

It's one heck of a job. Wrong three quarters of the time, but we're paid for the other twenty-five percent."

"Hope we're not wrong about Frog," said Jack. "That SOB has as nutty a scheme as we ever heard and we go for it."

"No choice," answered Mike. "I like Frog and Sumter. This is their world. It's Joanie Cipolla's world. It's all those girls world.

They are all hanging tough, hanging on by the seat of their pants.

I've seen, you've seen, a lot of guys who would walk the other way. Not go in the front door. Not go in the back door.

Stand wavering on the walk."

"Us," winced Jack. "We've all done it. It's the way of the world. Send the word upstairs. Let some other asshole decide."

"That's the game," answered Mike. "Never right! Never wrong!

So here we two old blokes are, in the middle of nowhere, in the sunset of our careers, ready to step to the plate.

I had almost lost the feeling."

"Me too. It's like Ernie Banks with the Cubs. Great career. Mister Cub. Mister Chicago right to the end. Never lost his dignity."

"We all lose something along the way," smiled Mike. "Even the legends grow old.

These young lasses have given us a breath of fresh air. They are full of trust in all the tomorrows. They have knocked the cynic out of us."

"So we walk the garden path with them," mused Jack. "Rekindle our faith in the sunset."

"Take our pieces. We take our pieces just in case something goes wrong," said Mike.

"And hope Frog is right," said Jack softly. "I remember when I was still a boy in knickers, an old nun used to tell us that Hope was the greatest of the virtues."

It was a beautiful day on the ocean. Eddie Blythe had the Osprey on full throttle, gliding smoothly through the soft rolling water. His passengers were hidden below.

"Much of my life is hidden," he thought to himself. But he was going to get out. Bud Sweeney didn't know everything. Sweeney was a bluffer. Eddie Blythe had heart.

He had hope. He could look to his tomorrows. He would press the agency to let him go. Say he no longer had the stomach for the job.

Too much anguish, mental pressure. The agency had more heart than Bud Sweeney gave them credit for. They had a staff of psychologists to evaluate their employees.

Eddie Blythe knew how to play the game. He would see his own private psychologists for a few months, get treatment. Tell him he could not sleep. Tell him he was depressed. Tell him he was feeling suicidal. Then he would approach the agency.

It was subterfuge. It was hope. It was his doorway to tomorrow. It would bury what he had been.

The Salvadorian freighter was waiting for him. Four locker boxes were lowered to the Osprey. Two passengers climbed up, four came down.

Eddie was at peace with himself as he motored back to Winyah Bay. The transfer had been as easy as pie.

Twelve more hours and his guests and the foot lockers would be gone. He would be on his way through North Carolina toward home.

It would be his last trip on the Osprey, the boat he loved so much. He had a plan to set himself free.

Johnny Seeds was eager to get back to Cleveland. He should have been gone yesterday. All that he had sought to accomplish had been accomplished.

Marty Lupo had taken great pictures. Bus Stop had done his job, even wired the boat, made a great tape.

He wasn't worried that Jack Foley had requisitioned it. He knew the score. That was Foley's job. Everyone had a job.

The plane was waiting for him at the airport. Marty and Bus Stop were already on the plane.

He had never figured on Joanie Cipolla and Sumter.

"Love," he half whispered to himself. "Who can figure it out?"

He knew he had to play the game out. He owed it to Joanie. He owed it to Frankie. He owed it to all of Joanie's friends.

"Tough little Mick girls," he whispered admiringly. "Whipper snappers, street wise, salt of the earth. What the hell is a half boiled old man like me doing with them? I owe them all one."

It was his way of life, getting a favor, giving one back.

He had no fear of the evening's work. Frog had laid it all out like he was planning an everyday hit. He was as sure of himself as an old man in a darkened room.

A heck of a plan, but the big farm boy was sure of himself. Foley and Blackwell had bought it. Who was he to say no? He didn't have a voice in the parlay.

Johnny Seeds wasn't worried. But just in case he took a small revolver from his suitcase and put it in his jacket pocket.

"Love," he whispered. "Who can figure it out?"

We waited anxiously it seemed forever. We had our bags packed and piled by the door.

Mary got some old tapes and played Lean on Me and Autumn Leaves, My Special Angel and Who's Sorry Now.

They eased us through the afternoon.

"Scared," I asked?

"Everybody's a bit scared," Sheila answered.

"No we aren't gumbahs," said Bridie. "We don't know what's going to happen. That's all. But we all know Sumter. We all know Frog.

They wouldn't let anything bad happen."

"And Johnny Seeds, and the FBI guys," said Peggy. "They wouldn't let anything happen either."

"These old tunes remind me of the restaurant," I interrupted in a lighter tone. "Frankie thought I was nuts for putting them in. I would be in the kitchen, whipping up this or that. I could hear him cussing.

I'm going to give him a great big hug when I get back. He's quite a guy."

"We're all going to hug somebody," quipped Mary. "Smoky is going to get one good working over."

"Slow down, girl," laughed Bridie. "You'll put poor Joanie into therapy."

We played Slow Boat to China and Rag Mop. We were playing Will You Love Me Tomorrow when Sumter walked through the door.

He had a dark cap pulled over his hair. He had on an old pair of army boots. Around his neck hung a great bronze medal on a ribbon of purest blue.

We were struck by the sight.

"Sumter," I said!

"One day I knew I'd get it out." He answered in a serious tone. "Me and Frog figured this would be the night. All the ghosts are going to be buried tonight. Banished beneath the limbs of the ancient oaks.

This is for a lot of guys I've never forgotten. For a lot of friends. For a lot of names on the Wall. And for you and me, Joanie.

After tonight we can get on with our lives."

Chapter 17

Sh-Boom

There was a rusted gate leaning between two brick pillars at the entrance to Jericho.

We were huddled in the back of Frog's work van. It had rusted nets, and grimy toolboxes, and who knows what all over everywhere.

There were no back windows. A bit of light filtered in from the front. It creaked and clanked from all the tin, and metal, and tools.

We had sprayed ourselves from head to toe with the insect repellent. We smelled like yesterday's chorus girls. Our buckets cringed at every bump. We had to hold on to each other to keep from toppling to the floor. We rode for a few minutes down the dirt road, then Frog veered off and took us over some of the biggest bumps of the trip.

"Shit," yelled Bridie as she bounced to the floor.

"We're almost there, sweetheart," Frog yelled back as he took us over two more fanny splatters.

A wide grin creased his face as he let us out the back door.

"Not as smooth as Sumter's old Fairlane, huh girls, but this old van will take me anywhere."

"This is hell," grimaced Bridie as we looked around.

Johnny Seeds, and Jack and Mike, were waiting for us. They looked like three old farmers, with chewing tobacco hats pulled closely over their eyes.

In the rising light of the autumn moon we could see their years. They were three old men; men whose best years, their vigorous years, were behind them. Yet, here they were, amidst the bush and the bough, ready to walk the walk.

We followed Frog along a path until we could see the outline of the road.

"Everything's set on our end, Frog," said Jack. "I called the Immigration guys at the State Police like I told you. They are going to be waiting for the Osprey at the Socastee swing bridge. Won't open the bridge.

The Coast Guard is going to help. They have boats, drug sniffing dogs, everything but grandma's drawers.

I told them to hang loose. We'd give them another call later. They are going to have a hell of a busy night."

"I haven't told you guys," answered Frog. "You guys are all right. Straight as a rod. You two, and Mister Seeds.

I'm just a Lowcountry farm boy. We usually stick to our own. We take our pleasures from each other, like me and Sumter do.

But you guys pitch in and do like everybody down here. And that Bus Stop and Marty are good guys too. I've learned something this week. Peoples people."

"Thanks Frog, big guy," said Mike. "We all think a lot of you. Now, you show us what to do. What you have laid out. We'll all try to do our part."

It was strange. It was mysterious. But as they talked, all sense of foreboding seemed to vanish from us girls.

It was starting to get dark. A few darts from the moon shone through the trees. Brush and bush scraped against our legs. We trod on crumbling leaves and stepped on mushy soil.

Frog took us to a spot in the road where the trap had been set. He showed us the yardarm and the dangling net. He let us feel the heavy ropes.

He assigned each of us in pairs to a rope. He showed us which tree to pull it to, how many times to loop it around, and how to tie the knot.

"We've got maybe forty-five minutes, an hour," he said. "It's going to get a lot darker."

"Everybody up to it," asked Sumter? He was a shadow in the bush. We could hardly see him.

"Sure," we all answered. It was the only thing we could say.

We all went to our assigned spot. Peggy and Jack had one corner. Bridie and me had the next. Johnny Seeds and Mary came next, then Sheila and Mike on the last.

"I'll stay on this side of the road to tip the net and help with the tying," said Frog. "Sumter will be on the other side of the road. We'll all have to be real quiet now. Are there any questions?"

It was dead quiet. There wasn't a sound in the air.

"What happens if the boards don't break," squealed Mary?

"Don't worry, Miss Mary," said the deep voice in the darkness. "The whole mess is made out of scrap that I should have thrown away long ago. If it don't break, my name's not Frog."

"Crazy," I thought as I crouched next to Bridie. I was with people I belonged to. I no longer felt alone. And all I could think of was pulling and tying the rope.

"Pull it tight," I whispered to Bridie.

"Are you crazy," she whispered. "I was worried about you. We'll pull that sucker so tight, that it will be whistling for help."

We crouched and we waited. It seemed like an eternity.

"What happens if they don't come," I whispered? "What happens if the boat doesn't come?"

"The SOB is going to come," answered Bridie. "I'm willing it to come. I'm praying for its headlights. Then, me and you, Joanie, are going to pull this rope and tie that sucker to the tree."

Neither of us had a watch. We couldn't see it if we had. We held each other's hands tightly. We gave strength to each other.

`I could picture the Sting Ray coming up the river. I could picture it swinging into Joshua Creek. I could picture the three men loading the chests into the station wagon and starting up the dirt road. I looked for the headlights, but all I could see were shadows and darkness.

We were almost shocked when we saw the headlights.

Bridie punched me in the arm.

"Ready gumbah," she whispered.

"You bet."

It took no more than a minute.

The car was lumbering along the road, its headlights bouncing from the ruts.

Then there was a roar, a racing of the motor, as it cracked into the pit.

There was dust all over.

"Here it comes," yelled Frog.

There was a thundering bang and a few quick shudders as the metal arm clanged onto the car's roof.

"Ropes," yelled Frog.

It took us a few seconds to find our rope.

Bridie and I pulled it in the darkness, stumbling over bush and root, and looped it two times around the tree. We tied it as tight as we could.

A light came on in the car.

Jack ran to the road. "Turn off that fucking light," he yelled.

His hand roared three times as he shot out the headlights and splattered the radiator.

The light in the car went off.

"Jesus, Mary, and Joseph," gasped Bridie.

Eddie Blythe guided the Osprey easily through the moonlit night. His thoughts were of tomorrow.

The men in the galley didn't bother him. The cocaine didn't disturb him. His light hand on the wheel was in consonance with the tides. The stars sparkled on the water.

He guided the Osprey easily past the plantations of the Waccamaw. The ghosts from Hagley, Caledonia, and The Oaks were asleep and at peace.

"Follow your dreams," he thought to himself.

The Waccamaw was a beautiful river. It was most beautiful under the stars. Its banks were shadowed by the bends of the boughs and the waving of the reeds.

He guided the Osprey into the man made Waterway.

He approached the Socastee Bridge slowly, giving a soft toot of his horn. The bridge did not move. He thought the tender must be asleep in his shanty.

He gave a couple of shriller toots. There was no traffic on the road, nothing to hold back the turn of the bridge.

The Osprey moved a little closer as Eddie hit the horn again

The Osprey was still in the water when searchlights, and red and blue flashers, hit him from every side.

A floodlight from a Coast Guard Cutter hit him in the stern.

"Coast Guard to the Osprey," came a voice from a bullhorn. "Coast Guard to the Osprey, stand by to be boarded."

He had no time to react. He had no time for fear.

The Cutter was at his side within seconds.

"Name," asked the officer, as he and two seamen clamored onto the deck?

"Edward Blythe. I'm a history professor at National University."

"Papers?"

"In the cabin. I'll get them for you."

"We'll get them," answered the officer courteously. "My men will get them, Mr. Blythe."

Then Eddie noticed the dog. It was a large German Shepherd. It stood as still as a statue at the knee of one of the seamen.

"Is anyone else on board?"

"Two hands that sail with me."

The dog started yapping as the seamen entered the cabin door.

The two Salvadorians were startled as the large Shepherd plunged its nose into their dreams.

An excited stream of Spanish spewed forth from the cabin.

"Bring whoever is down there up on deck," the officer yelled. "Pat everybody down. We don't want any surprises."

"What's this? What's going on," asked Eddie?

"Does your crew speak English?"

"No."

"Tell them to turn around," commanded the officer.

Eddie circled with his hands.

"They have no identification. They have no papers," said a seaman.

"Cuff them," said the officer. "Cuff Mr. Blythe too."

Then, turning to Eddie he spoke again.

"You are under arrest, Mr. Blythe. Your crew is under arrest.

We are going to detain you until we can fully investigate this matter."

"Where will I stay?"

"In the Georgetown County Jail with your crew. I am placing you all in custody.

You do not have to make a statement. You have the right to call a lawyer.

Neither myself nor my men speak Spanish. When you remember your Spanish, Mr. Blythe, you can inform your crew that they have the same rights."

We were down the road in a flash, ten shadows shaking in the night.

"Ropes on my side as snug as a bug," said Frog.

"Other side is the same," said Sumter.

"Had to do it," stammered Jack. "Put out the lights and put the fear of God into them."

"Shook me," said Sheila.

"All of us," I said.

We stopped down the road and looked back. It looked like a large square platform in the road. There was no sound. There was no movement.

"Got to call our guy at the State Police," said Jack. "Get their cans out here."

"I'll stay here," said Mike. "Keep my eye on the car."

"What's that," asked Johnny in surprise?

"Everybody's got to scam," said Jack. "Just like we planned. It all went down according to the sheet.

Frog laid the whole thing out. Me and Mike can never thank Frog and all of you for what you did tonight.

You did it all, God bless you.

But the lock up is part of me and Mike's job. That's what we do. The lock up and charges.

We've got two pages of charges against these SOBs. Without us, Immigration and the State Troopers will be whistling in the dark.

We have to let them know a part of the story."

"A part of the story," questioned Johnny?

"Yeah, a part of the story, Johnny," said Mike. "The part we picked up in our investigation.

You are not in it. Sumter and Frog are not in it. The girls are not in it.

We tell them about our wholesome, straightforward, FBI type of shoe work. That's all we tell them. That's all they need to know."

"The tape," said Johnny.

"Never heard of it," answered Jack. "But I've got the song of the mockingbird in this envelope. I'm giving it back to you. It's yours."

"Thanks," said Johnny. "I owe you one."

"Nobody owes anyone anything," said Mike. "We all pulled this off together. We were all in it together."

We stood in the middle of the road and embraced. It was that kind of night.

We rode back to the cottage in the back of Frog's van. Nobody said a word. Nobody felt a bump.

Frog took the two pink rockers from the porch and put them in the van.

"Can't forget these," he smiled.

"Nor, will we ever," sad Mary.

Sumter and I said goodbye on the corner of the porch.

All of us girls were spent. We had no heart to stay the night.

We changed into fresh clothes and threw our old clothes into a few plastic bags.

We packed our duffels into the station wagon.

We were going home.

We opened the windows to catch the evening breeze.

Mary caught some tunes on the radio, but each of us was alone in her thoughts and her dreams.

Chapter 18

Sixteen Tons

It was late Sunday afternoon when Sheila dropped me off at Frankie's house.

Frankie was asleep in his easy chair as I dragged my luggage through the front door. The aroma of the Sunday meal was still in the air.

"Lasagna," I said. "If I knew you were baking lasagna I would have been home earlier."

"You're two weeks early," he looked up in surprise. "I've been busting my buns in the restaurant, so your mother cooked the meal."

I gave her a squeeze as she came out of the kitchen.

I had to tell them. I was bursting.

"Good vacation, Joanie," she asked?

"Very good."

"So now you can save your old man," said Frankie. "You can carry the load."

"Mama, Frankie, I'm going to get married in the spring."

I could see their surprise.

"I met a wonderful young man twenty years ago when I vacationed with my friends. His name is Sumter Rutledge. He was a soldier then.

He never married. I never married.

Now, we are going to get married."

"Jesus," said Frankie leaning forward in his chair.

"Jesus, Joanie, you surprise me every time you come home from this Pawleys Island.

Do you love him?"

"With all my heart," I answered.

By Monday morning Sheila was back in her mother mode. There were kids to get off to school. There was a quick cup of coffee with Tommy. The basement was loaded with washing. Shopping to be done. House to be cleaned. Beds to be changed.

She was still on vacation from work. She had a sixty hour week in front of her. It invigorated her.

There was no way of knowing what was going on at Pawleys. She had too much work to give it much thought.

Sheila made a Mick classic for supper. The complete works. A pot roast. Mashed potatoes and carrots and peas. Thick gravy, the way her mother used to make it.

"What's this," clamored Brian? "It's not Sunday."

"Mom has guilt feelings," spiked Kristen. She had always been a smart aleck.

"She was off with her old friends, a vacation without us. Now she's making it up."

"She came back early," quipped Tommy. "Didn't think we could get along without her. Tell your mom how we did."

"Pizza Hut and Burger King," smiled Kristen. "Brian stayed home from school three days and played Sega. Dad says I can get my nose pierced if I clean my room."

"Tommy," Sheila crowed.

"We are just teasing you," he smiled. "No nose job. But we did spend a lot of time at Burger King. It's great to have you home."

"I second the motion," said Brian. "But we had you, mom. We had you in the trick bag."

Monday afternoon, an attorney from the Justice Department was waiting in Charleston for Jack Foley and Mike Blackwell.

"You can't indict Mike Taggart or Edward Blythe for anything," he explained.

"Why not," asked Jack.

"They were undercover. Work for us. It's an affair of national security. It's a top secret project only their agency knew about."

"Smuggling cocaine," asked Jack?

"Illegal entry," said Mike.

"It looks bad to you two," answered the attorney. "You were undercover. They were undercover.

You happened to run into their operation."

"Eighty pounds of coke," commented Jack wryly.

"They were going to confiscate it. It never would have made the street."

"The South American guys," said Mike. "Where are they from? What country? What happens to them?"

"They will be deported. It will send a message back to their bosses. Controlling all this stuff is a dirty business. You understand that."

"Sure," Mike nodded.

"We've checked with your home offices in Chicago and Cleveland. You were in South Carolina on a S&L investigation."

"Right," answered Jack. "It's all in the investigative report. We were looking into the thirty million that the Taggart Corporation had borrowed on three pieces of land.

It stood out like a hen in a cockfight.

We followed Taggart all over the state. He was like a phantom. The land looked like shit. It appeared to be a real scam.

I suppose you guys at Justice knew all about that."

The attorney didn't answer.

"We got a telephone number in the Pawleys area," continued Jack. "We talked to this guy and that guy, you know how investigations go.

That's how we found Taggart and Blythe were bringing in the powder. And about the foreign lads."

"It's all in the report," said Mike. "But one thing I'd like to know, as a point of personal interest. I'd seen those two guys before. They were in my office in Cleveland together.

They were asking about a Sister Marcetta, an Ursuline nun who almost got killed in El Salvador. They were from the CIA.

We didn't see them before they were busted the other night. Had no idea what they looked like.

Surprised the hell out of this old man when I recognized their kissers in the slammer.

What I'd like to know, and maybe you can't answer me, is what all this has to do with national security?"

"Just remember that it does, Mister Blackwell," answered the attorney stonily. "You too, Mister Foley.

No indictment. Nothing happened."

A Monsignor from the Cleveland Diocese called the religious editor at the Plain Dealer on Monday afternoon. He asked her to come to the Cathedral office as soon as possible.

"I have a story for you, Celia," he said.

He let her listen to a copy of the tape.

"Who are these men," she asked after she had listened for about an hour?

"I was told they are with the Central Intelligence Agency," answered the Monsignor.

"What happened to the boats," she asked?

"I was told they were stopped by Immigration officials from Charleston, South, Carolina on Saturday night," he answered.

"How can I confirm it?"

"I am giving you the name and telephone number of an old man on Murray Hill," answered the Monsignor. "He is expecting to hear from you."

"This is an unusual source," she smiled as she looked at the name. "He doesn't often meet with representatives of the press."

"This is an unusual story, Celia," said the Monsignor. "But we must remember, that the Good Lord works in mysterious ways."

Sammy Castiglione, a Vice President of the Teamsters Union, made an appointment to see Senator Basil Meade on Wednesday morning.

Senator Meade was his favorite contact on the Hill. He was from the old school. He was as ramrod straight as a Puritan walking stick.

He had been an infantry officer, wounded at Salerno during World War II. He had unsparingly sided with Labor during his almost thirty years in Congress.

He could laugh at a good story and tell a better one in return

"Samuel," he smiled as the Teamster official was ushered into his office.

"You sounded disturbed when you called. I hope everything is well with you and the family. I haven't seen you in a long time."

"Everything is fine with everybody, Senator," said Sammy. "Thank you for seeing me. Thank you for setting aside the time. I know how busy you are.

This is some very important business. Real quiet for now."

"Trucking regulations," asked the Senator?

"Nothing like that. That's simple stuff," answered Sammy. "Something is going to break in the next few days. Something is going to break in the papers on the CIA, and the Contras, and the nun who almost got killed in El Salvador, Sister Marcetta."

"Is she okay," asked the Senator? "I remember it distinctly. Nothing could be uncovered. There was a blanket thrown over the whole ugly business."

"The quilt is going to come off the bed," said Sammy quietly. "We got names, places, guys in the CIA and the National Security Council, guys that never figured they would be ever made.

Something is going to come out in the papers. The big guy says we need your help."

"Tell him I'm always here, Sammy, but what is it?"

"I'm only a spear carrier," Senator Meade. "That's who I am. Two CIA guys got busted with some cocaine down off the South Carolina coast. The CIA is working its ass off to cover it up.

One of our guys was there, but that is only for your ears.

There is more than I know. When the story comes out, you ask for hearings, Congressional Hearings. Take the bastards down."

"Is it that big," asked the Senator?

"It is that big," nodded Sammy.

Bud Sweeney and Eddie Blythe met their controller in a safe house in Chevy Chase. It was in an old building that the agency had owned forever.

Both were uncomfortable.

"What the fuck went wrong," asked Sam Hasely?

They could feel the enmity in the room. Hasely's normally placid face was drawn. He bounced around like a chimpanzee.

"It was perfect until I got to the turn bridge," said Eddie. "Then all hell broke loose."

"You were instructed to blow the boat," shot back Hasely. "Blow the fucking boat and dive overboard."

"There were two men in the galley," shot back Eddie.

Hasely only stared at him. He had a consummate arrogance. He was a man of action.

"Lose you nerve," he asked?

Then he turned to Bud Sweeney.

"Same thing," answered Bud. "I was on an old dirt road coming from the river. Someone dug a wide ditch in the road, covered it with boards and dirt like it was the road. The car busted through, almost broke my back.

Then a voice yells from nowhere. Some SOB shoots out the headlights.

I tried to get out the door, but the doors wouldn't open. I tried a window later. There was a moldy old fish net over the whole fucking car, strung as tight as a cat's ass.

The two assholes in the back were chattering like two old whores. I was in a pickle."

"Who blew your cover," roared Hasely.

He had talked to the attorney at Justice. He knew that Foley and Blackwell had stated that they had been checking out the Taggart real estate dealings.

It had been checked out with FBI Headquarters.

"Did you ask them who dug the pit," Sam Hasely had asked the attorney. "Who dropped the net?"

"I didn't have the balls," answered the man. "They were as cordial as they could be. Their investigative report was as clear and concise as I'd ever seen.

I could follow them from Kingstree to Camden, from the land to the Post Office Box. It all made sense.

Then it was preachers and nuns, and this guy along the road and that."

"The fuckers," said Hasely

"I didn't have the nerve to ask them," repeated the attorney.

Celia Baxter wasn't at ease when she met the old man.

It was in the kitchen of a bakery on Murray Hill. He was wearing a faded sweater and chewing a half lit cigar.

"Doughnut," he asked? "They're free."

"No thank you," she smiled.

"Do you know who I am?"

"Everybody knows who you are."

"I am meeting with you," he started, "because I wanted you to know that this is not idle chatter. I want you to feel that it is most important. You heard the tape?"

"I heard it."

"You believe it, what the Monsignor told you?"

"I would have to verify it."

"I am not a source," he smiled.

"I could call you a reliable source," answered Celia. "I could call you a reliable source if I could verify the tape in other ways."

The old man took a wrinkled racing form from his back pocket. He handed a few pieces of paper and some pictures that had been cradled between the sheets.

"The complete story is on those papers," he said. "There are pictures with names, and places, and times on the back. I don't know how you do your work, but if I was looking for the story I would be making a lot of telephone calls to South Carolina.

There are some places and numbers on the papers."

"You would have made a great reporter," said Celia.

"Maybe I shoulda been," he chuckled.

Celia Baxter called the Immigration Office in Charleston. They had never heard of Michael Taggart or Edward Blythe. Nothing had happened on Saturday night.

She called the FBI Office in Charleston and got the same results.

She called the State Police in Georgetown and got the same reply.

She called the County Jail in Georgetown and got a new office girl.

"May I speak to Michael Taggart," Celia asked?

"He was released on Monday."

"May I speak to Edward Blythe, then?

"He was released the same time as Mister Taggart."

"They are friends of mine," said Celia.

"It was a heck of a night, Miss. Mister Taggart was all banged up. Some foreign men hi-jacked his car and drove it in a ditch.

Their buddies boarded Mister Blythe's yacht and were sailing it up the Waterway."

"Is there any way I can contact one of them," asked Celia? "Do you have a telephone number?"

"Sorry, Miss, I can't give out that information.

You might try the Winyah Bay Marina. Mister Blythe's yacht is still tied up there.

Sorry I couldn't help you more. But if they were here and you could talk to them, they would still be behind bars.

Since they're gone, and you can't talk to them, they are better off."

"Thank you. I understand," said Celia.

Samuel Hasely was holding court in the agency office. His peers were gathered around a conference table.

"Sweeney and Blythe screwed up."

"And you didn't," asked an older man?

Hasely gave him a scathing look.

"They ran it a dozen times and never had a bit of trouble," continued the older man.

He was an old cold warrior. He didn't bow to Sam Hasely's brashness. He had counseled the Director against many of Hasely's ideas.

"The real estate thing. You got us into it. There was never a hint of a problem at Pawleys until you got us into real estate. It's in the FBI report we received from Justice.

Those two dudes were following the real estate thing. Somehow they came across all the other stuff.

No real estate, no FBI, no trouble!"

"They'll be quiet," Sam Hasely said scornfully. "We were in a bigger thing. I've met with the old man. The program is too important to shut down.

The old man said, 'hunker down.' That's what he said, 'hunker down.'"

"Bud Sweeney and Blythe, what happens to them," asked another man. "They are both good guys."

"Good guys don't win wars," answered Samuel Hasely.

The Plain Dealer ran the story on Sunday morning. Six reporters had worked on it, giving background information on Sister Marcetta, the Contras in El Salvador, and the S&L scandals.

A photographer had flown to South Carolina with Celia to take pictures of the Osprey and the road into Jericho. Celia had interviewed a man at the marina and two felons who had spent the weekend in jail with Taggart and Blythe and the Contras.

Banner headlines heralded the story:

CIA LINKED TO COCAINE SMUGGLING
NETTED WITH ILLEGAL ALIENS

Last Saturday night, in quiet Georgetown County on the South Carolina coast, two CIA operatives were netted with 80 pounds of cocaine. Four illegal aliens, who have not been identified, were captured with them

They were captured in a joint operation between the FBI, The Immigration Department, the Coast Guard, and the South Carolina Highway Patrol. None of the agencies will issue a statement on the operation.

A reliable source has linked the CIA operatives to having knowledge of the 1984 beating of Sister Marcetta, a local Ursuline nun, in El Salvador____.

The text ran two full pages. There was another half page of photographs.

The story ran in the New York Times, the Washington Post, and the Chicago Tribune the next morning. All the national papers picked it up.

Jack Foley walked into the Bureau Office about ten on Monday morning. He was worn and rumpled. He looked as if he had been riding three days on the el.

He was greeted by a huge round of applause. Every agent in the office stood and applauded. He could only smile.

Senator Basil Meade called a news conference late Monday afternoon. He was accompanied by a group of thirty Senators and Congressmen.

They issued a joint statement, calling for Congressional Hearings.

An old man pulled a racing form out his pocket up on the Hill. He fumbled for a few matches to relight his cigar.

"Got the sons of bitches," he muttered to himself.

Chapter 19

Love is a Many Splendored Thing

We were married on a beautiful Saturday in May. We were married at St Phils.

"St. Phils," grimaced Frankie. "You belong to St. Paschals."

"Old tunes and memories," I smiled.

"And moving to South Carolina," said Frankie!

"That's where Sumter belongs, Frankie. That's where I belong."

He could only chuckle.

"I like your Sumter. He is a quiet guy.

My father was a farmer in Italy, sort of like Sumter. He never did much. A quiet life in the old country. He showed me everything.

But you Joanie, sweetheart! Never pay no attention to your father.

I say St Paschals.

You say St. Phils.

I say Puccini and Caruso and the classics.

You say rock and roll and the Twist.

Jesus!"

He was my Frankie. I loved him so.

"I've got three cases of wine ready for the wedding. Made it in the basement."

He was my Frankie. I could only smile.

Sheila was sitting in the back yard with Tommy the night before the wedding. It was a clear night. She could see the stars and the ways.

"Life is sometimes governed by the moon and the stars," she said.

"Joanie met a guy in South Carolina," Tommy answered. "She is going to marry him. We don't see many stars here.

We see them tonight because the wind is blowing off the smog. I can count the nights when the stars are out."

Tommy was a good man. He was a kind man. I squeezed his hand.

"And the fates and the muses," I said.

Tommy looked at me.

"You're getting crazy, Sheila. Remember when we got married.

It wasn't the stars and the muses. It was more like the necking and the hugging."

The lawn in front of the church was wall to wall. There was a gaggle of Ursuline nuns. Sister Marcetta was there.

All of the girl's families were there.

Uncle Johnny was there. There were so many Italians that it looked like the Feast on the Hill.

Jack Foley and his wife had come in from Chicago. Mike Blackwell and his wife were there.

Marty Lupo was strolling around taking pictures.

Sumter and Frog and Alison arrived in the 57 Fairlane of teal and cream.

"Wow," said Smoky. "I used to have a Plymouth that sparkled like that."

"Sure," said the twins.

I arrived in a long limousine with Frankie and my mother. I was a little nervous.

I looked at my gumbahs as I walked up the stairs to the church. Then I glanced across the street.

There was a lone man standing by the bus stop. He was leaning on the pole. He had on a casual wind breaker and an Indians cap.

He was looking me straight in the eye.

He lifted his arm and gave me the thumbs up.

And I knew.

I was at peace with the world.

"I would have bet on it," said Jack. "I felt it the first night I met them at the beach."

We were all gathered in a corner of the lawn. Mary and Peggy, me and Bridie, Mike and Jack, and Johnny Seeds.

It was the first time we had all been together since the road at Jericho.

"Bet on what," asked Bridie?

"Joanie and Sumter, the fates and the muses," he said with a big Irish grin.

"Always bet on love," said Johnny. "It's like a Catholic horse on Friday. It's chalk."

"Speaking of horses," said Jack. "Today is Derby Day. If I was in Chicago I could lay a bet."

"Look around," said Mike. "Half the guys in front of this church can book it for you. You can give it to Seeds."

Jack handed Johnny Seeds a twenty.

"There's a filly going today. It's a long time since a filly won the Derby. Name is Winning Colors.

The name reminded me of these girls."

"I got you," answered the Seed man. "All five of them are winners. I'm getting on that horse, myself."

It was like it was written in the book of long ago.

Held forever in the stars and the ways.

9 780595 001705